Paperback IBSN: 9798991535823

Editing by Cynthia A. Rodriguez

Proofreading by Alexa at The Fiction Fix + Andrea Halland

Cover art, Typography and Internal Images by Lilith B. @lilitherie__

Interior Formatting by Evelyn Leigh

1st edition 2025

shadowed obsession

A Dark Romantic Comedy

evelyn leigh

a note from evelyn leigh

Welcome to the darker side of the universe you've come to know so well!

Please review the content warnings on the following page before reading.

I am writing this a few weeks shy of my thirty-first birthday and life has changed drastically since the author's note I sat down to write this time last year. If someone told me 5 years ago that I'd be a romance author, I would've asked for your plug's number. I am so grateful to be here and waking up every day to write about love has done wonders for me.

This era was a rough one mentally and creatively, but I'm proud I fought for this story all the way to the last word. I am the most unserious individual who can find humor in anything, so, it was impossible for me to write something dark without comedy. I can proudly say that while I'm running on E, I wrote this off the strength of pure spite, excessive amounts of caffeine and UGK.

Rest in peace, Pimp C.

I was pulled to write something very different from what I'm known for writing, but the story needed to be told, and in order to do it, I went back to my roots, Dark Fiction. My writing journey began with writing screenplays and you'll soon meet a character in this story that started it all for me, 15 years ago. They're finally being set free from the depths of my mind and I hope you love them as much as I have. Bonus points if you can guess who it is.

It was important for me to tell a story about a Black woman determined to overcome generational trauma while laying down roots for future generations to come and I am so proud to have done that within the dark romance genre, where characters like Deirdre Klarke are needed.

I ask that you enter this story with an open heart and empathy for both Deirdre and César. As the internal and external battles they face are far too common and while some are cultural, some are not. Thank you for picking up another love story from me. I hope you enjoy this time with Deirdre and César as much as I have.

Deirdre is a Black woman living with anxiety, PMDD and PCOS, and while that is within my lived experience, I treasured working with my team of advisors, both in the medical field and fellow "cysters" and those living with anxiety and PMDD. I am so grateful for my advisors and sensitivity readers for sharing their experiences/expertise to ensure I portrayed Deirdre in a way that captures her how I intended.

César is a second-generation Puerto Rican and Dominican man whose parents hail from San Juan, Puerto Rico. I had the best time researching and learning more about Puerto Rican and Dominican cultures while working on this story. I am so thankful for my amazing sensitivity readers for taking the time to speak with me about their culture and experiences. You made this story shine and truly helped me bring César to life.

I recognized the importance of sharing a story about a Latino man in the romance genre and handled César with the utmost care. While he is a fictional character, I understand how crucial it was for him to be accurately represented. With this being said, I have not altered his or Deirdre's experiences to make them more appealing to the masses.

content warnings

There are mentions of *addiction (mentioned), anxiety, attempted murder, blackmail, blood, body worship, bratting, breath play, breeding, car accident (mentioned), chronic illness, death, death of a grandparent & death of a partner (off page), fatphobia (mentioned), forced marriage (mentioned), gore, grief, gun play, gun violence, home invasion, infertility (mentioned), kidnapping, manipulation, mental distress, microaggressions, murder, organized crime, panic attacks, physical assault, religious trauma, stalking, substance use, therapy, trauma, violence, voyeurism, wrongful accusation of a crime (mentioned)*

As far as spice goes, this is my spiciest book yet, so let me list what you're getting yourself into: *aftercare, barebacking, begging, degradation, domination, edging, exhibitionism, fingering, guided masturbation, impact play, marking, mask play, masochism, oral, praise, primal play, rimming, role play, rough sex, spanking, submission.*

This is an open door romance for readers 18+ that features a generous amount of consensual sex. If that isn't your cup of tea, this book may not be for you. I would also recommend reviewing the Dick-tionary on the following page to know what chapters to avoid if you would still like to enjoy this story without the sexually explicit scenes.

For a detailed list of events, please feel free to visit the

'Content Warning' tab on my website authorevelynleigh.com, contact the author via Instagram DMs @evelynleighauthor or email at contact@authorevelynleigh.com with any specific questions you may have about the contents of this book.

Shadowed Obsession is a dark romantic comedy that contains heavy topics that may be triggering to some. Please do not hesitate to reach out if you would like to inquire about specific chapters to avoid or avoid reading this novel entirely. Your mental health is far more important.

dick-tionary

If you'd like to jump straight into the spice, know how far ahead the fun times are, or if you'd like to skip the spice entirely. *Chapters with an asterisk * are partial scenes.*

Chapter 16 | Chapter 18*
Chapter 26 | Chapter 27*
Chapter 28 | Chapter 35*
Chapter 36 | Chapter 37*
Chapter 38* | Chapter 51*

To my 16 year old self, who wanted to see Black women in gangster flicks so badly that I wrote them.

&

Whether you're the eldest child or hyper independent, prepare to feel seen and cared for. Cèsar is here.

playlist

Harlem's Nocturne - Alicia Keys
Too Sweet - Hozier
Pick Up Your Feelings - Jazmine Sullivan
You Don't Know My Name - Alicia Keys
Dreams - J. Cole, Brandon Hines
Southern Hospitality - Ludacris & Pharrell Williams
Alligator Tears - Beyoncé
You Know I'm No Good (Remix) - Amy Winehouse
It Will Come Back - Hozier
Clan In Da Front - Wu-Tang Clan
Country Shit (Remix) - Big K.R.I.T., Ludacris & Bun B
THIQUE - Beyoncé
WTF I Want - Megan Thee Stallion
Dangerous Woman - Ariana Grande
Good Times - Styles P
Movement - Hozier
Crown Royal - Jill Scott
Daddy Lessons - Beyoncè
Thong Song - Sisqo
Sittin' Sideways - Paul Wall & Big Pokey
Stay The Night - Mariah Carey
Oops (Oh My) - Tweet & Missy Elliot
NFWMB - Hozier
Homewrecker - Travis Garland
Bones - Melanie Fiona
Movies - Ashanti
Still Tippin' - Mike Jones, Paul Wall & Slim Thug
Party - Bad Bunny & Rauw Alejandro
Front, Back & Side to Side - UGK
I Wanna Be Yours - Arctic Monkeys

A Tale Of Two Cities - J. Cole
Fergalicious - Fergie & will.i.am
HYFR (Hell Ya Fuckin' Right) - Drake & Lil' Wayne
Diary - Alicia Keys & Tony! Toni! Tone!
On It - Jazmine Sullivan & Ari Lennox
Desert Eagle - Beyoncé
Masterpiece (Mona Lisa) - Jazmine Sullivan
No Angel - Beyoncé
Forever Don't Last - Jazmine Sullivan
Samsonite Man - Alicia Keys
I'd Rather Go Blind - Etta James
I Say A Little Prayer - Aretha Franklin
Think - Aretha Franklin
Ain't No Sunshine By Bill Withers
Volví - Aventura & Bad Bunny
Monaco - Bad Bunny
#HoodLove - Jazmine Sullivan
Shirt - SZA
Crazy In Love (Remix) - Beyoncé
Mercy On Me - Christina Aguilera

APPLE
MUSIC

prologue

Deirdre

6:08 p.m. | 42 hours before 'the incident'

Drafting a script for what may be my last words turned out to be more taxing than I had anticipated. I don't plan on harming myself, but one could argue that's exactly what I'm doing by engaging in this dance with death. This is how I could be remembered, and after all I'm currently known for, an opportunity to redeem myself. Only to those who truly matter, though. Everyone else can go fuck themselves.

My trembling hands clutch the weighted note like a lifeline as I attempt to not wrinkle it any further. I fumble around for the tiny remote, and my coffin-shaped acrylics make it difficult to press the record button after a few attempts. With an unsteady grip, I try until a beep resounds, followed by a red blinking light indicating the recording has started.

"My name is Deirdre Klarke, and I'd like to document my recent…experiences. Unfortunately, if you are watching this video, that means I didn't survive."

My eyes drop to the page, following along.

"I'd like to explain the events that have led me to carry a gun on my person at all times. Even as I sleep," I add, pausing to swallow.

"Let this serve as a documentation of my efforts, so should you assassinate my character with your whole chest again, you'll at least have your facts straight. *Whoever* finds this first.

"No one asked for this, but as the family *fuckup*, I'm admitting I didn't ask for your help and was willing to die in order to prove a point. I can handle myself and take pride in the fact that I stood my ground.

"This video should be used as evidence in the instance I am kidnapped or murdered. If anything happens to me, I'd like for this video to be shared with my parents, Elgin and Dorothea Klarke. I ask that you do *not* show this to Darius Klarke or Regina Delvecchio and do *not* involve the police."

The page crinkles as my hands continue to shake, but I take a breath and power on.

"I felt I was being watched for the past few weeks and tried to convince myself it wasn't true until I found a microphone planted inside my home. I can't say what has made me a target, but I suspect it's either an enemy of my family or my late ex-boyfriend. *That* I'd also like to address.

"I did *not* kill Lawrence Wiley, and if killing me is your plan to avenge him, you've made a fucking mistake. If this is regarding my family, they'll find you, and I hope you're prepared for it," I state, and the uneasiness in my voice subsides as I share my truth.

"When I returned from a trip earlier this month, a scent lingered throughout the house. Citrus, wood, and smoke. Two weeks later, it still remains. I then noticed my spare house key was missing, and I've been on high alert since.

"A few days later, I was greeted by the scent again as I settled into my SUV, where I discovered a full gas tank, knowing I hadn't left it that way. It was on my to-do list, and when I checked to make sure that I wasn't losing my mind, it had been marked as completed.

"This person has been in my home since, and while I haven't

had the *pleasure* of confronting them, I promise to make my family proud when I do.

"Earlier this week, my camera notified me of movement detected in the backyard. This stranger had the audacity to sit on the edge of the pool with their feet in the water, dressed in black, their face covered, legs exposed. They're large in stature, like a linebacker, and with deep-brown skin. I can only assume this person was a man.

"I spoke to him through the microphone in the app and was ignored. He didn't react to my voice and continued to relax. Shortly after, he left and my cameras failed to capture views of him beyond that angle," I continue, my voice laced with anger and regret.

"I've never had many enemies, but I can assure that I will continue to document my experiences up until this threat is eradicated. Should I fail and disappoint you once again, mom and dad, I am terribly sorry. You instilled so much in me and—" I pause, my voice quivering under intense emotions I had yet to fully acknowledge until this moment. "I hope I'm not your biggest regret. Maybe grandma was one of a kind and her bravery couldn't be duplicated." My eyes sparkle with unshed tears in the viewfinder as I clear my throat, pushing the emotions down as best I can.

"Please tell Darius that I'm sorry I didn't ask for help. He would never let me suffer, but I needed to do this on my own. Tell Regina that I'm still angry, but I forgive her. To my parents, I love you and always dreamt of being a mother so I could love my children as much as you love us," I say, taking a deep breath to collect myself.

"I love you all. Goodbye," I finish as I scramble to end the recording before my face crumples.

Tears stain my lap, my hands swiping to remove them as quickly as they came. What should be a private moment isn't, now that I have an audience. I left a few things out of that script intentionally, because it would only prove them all right. Danger follows me and I've been too distracted to acknowledge it… until now.

The man who walks in my shadow both frightens and excites me. It's a delicate dance between the two emotions, one that causes me pause when I think about ending his life in order to survive this. The guilt would be all-encompassing, but there *is* a certain thrill to his chase.

Two dings interrupt this moment, and I brace myself as I reach for my phone. Two messages from the man I've come to know as Scar. I don't know his real name, but I am aware that he's become a constant presence in my periphery. I'm certain he just heard everything and has some critiques about my performance. I swipe to open our thread.

SCAR

That was a bit dramatic, Doe.

You like being watched.

A chill spreads through me, and I stare at the message for a moment, unsure of how to respond.

What gave you that impression?

SCAR

The bedroom curtains you leave open every night.

I can't explain why I'm addicted to pushing the limits here, or why I simultaneously hope luring him in will make ending this easier for me. In fact, I don't mind his sense of humor and will miss our humorous exchanges when he's gone. But he can't be the *only* funny man to exist, so life will go on.

Just not his.

Fuck you, Scar.

SCAR

On your command. 😉

Is that a threat?

SCAR

A promise.

I'm a man of my word. You'll see.

A thought crosses my mind that I shut down the moment it arrives. I am not entertaining him beyond this little song and dance. This ruse is just so he lets his guard down enough for me to find out who sent him. That's what I tell myself when I feel like I'm going too far.

It's been a while since I've been with a partner, and I will not sleep with this man before I kill him. That would prove disastrous to my cause, and I'd rather die than prove my family right.

1 / incite

Deirdre

12:42 a.m. | 'the incident'

A loud crash jolts me from my slumber, and I sit up as my heart nearly thumps out of my chest. I search for the gun hidden in my pillowcase, and as soon as the cool metal is in my grasp, I switch off the safety. My bare feet pad toward my bedroom door, and with bated breath I listen closely. When I'm met with silence, my trembling hands turn the knob to investigate. Faint clatters sound below me as I exit the room, keeping my back flush to the wall as I toe toward the stairs.

When I reach the mezzanine balcony, I lower into a squat and will myself to remain silent despite the deafening thump in my chest. Heavy footsteps travel the ground floor, followed by the sound of running water. They're not in a hurry to leave, and I'm growing more impatient by the minute.

Wiping my sweaty palms on my pajamas, I strengthen my grip on the handgun.

Catching my first body—or "first blood" as we Klarkes like to call it—is uncharted territory for me, and I'm ill-equipped. Obviously not with weapons, but mentally I'm out of my depth. I imagine the real thing is *never* like what you practice. Far messier too.

Shit. I'll need a clean-up crew, and I don't even know the protocol.

My thoughts cease as the footsteps grow closer and closer until a pair of arms come into view, holding a broom and dustpan in each hand. The rest of their body comes into view with their back to me, and what I assume is a balaclava is on their head. Their movements are intoxicating, and that's when I realize, this isn't just anybody. *It's him.*

This is it. The moment I've anticipated and dreaded. Curiosity has led me here, staring down the man who's remained a mystery while invading my every thought. The chaos in my mind has silenced, replacing itself with *him*. If I keep waiting, I'll be too late.

Take the shot. Now.

"I can do it," I whisper softly for only me to hear.

I fire two shots off into the darkness. Bullets whiz past his large bicep as he finally angles himself toward me. My couch explodes with feathers as it absorbs the blows. I fire twice more, mere inches in front of him as he remains still, rooted to the spot. Duck feathers litter the air from my bloodlust.

My poor sofa didn't deserve this.

His gaze travels up the staircase before locking on me. The gunshots echo in my ringing ears as we face off.

I drink him in with bated breath, unsure of his next move. He's tall and broad, would surely overpower me if given the chance, and I just wasted four bullets. His eyes pierce me, and his head tilts slightly as he stretches his arms to the sides and releases the broom and dustpan.

Clattering sounds flood the space between us, and the broom smacks the floor. My breath hitches as his feet pull him slowly toward the bottom of the stairs. His hands raise in surrender, his focus on me. At this moment, I consider why I didn't just lock myself in my room, but it's too late for that.

"Who do you work for?" I bellow.

His lack of response unnerves me.

My trembling hands remain on the weapon, nervous to fire again, but I will if he approaches me. Unable to enjoy awkward silence, an inner thought tumbles from my lips, betraying my stance.

"Do you plan to kill me?"

One of my grandmother's many mantras rings true as my index hovers the trigger on standby.

Klarke's don't hide from danger, they incite it.

2 / a new assignment

César

45 days before 'the incident'

Overwhelmed with the silence, I tap my fingers rhythmically on the arms of the leather chair. I glance at my watch to see how much time has passed when I hear hushed voices outside the door.

"I don't know about this," I hear a woman's voice whisper-shout.

"Bloody hell. You've got to toughen up," another voice counters, and the knob turns.

I whip my head forward as the door clicks and heels clack along the hardwood. Glancing up, I see Dara Hale with her brother, Dax, holding a thick manilla envelope likely containing the details of my next assignment.

Should I be taking on more work at this time? Absolutely not. But here I am.

Hale Whiskey has outsourced me for years. They're a European-based whiskey manufacturer currently expanding their American distilleries.

I'm often hired for surveilling and blackmail cases, usually for members of their board or to get intel on competitors. Blackmail is strongly discouraged in my line of work as a private investigator, but I tend to bend the law often and the pay is *always* worth the trouble.

When their uncle Theo launched their Austin headquarters, he was determined to make an impact, hiring me for any and everything necessary to solidify their brand in the States.

I respected him greatly as a businessman, and we developed a good working relationship. That is the *only* reason I was open to maintaining my contract after he retired. His nephew and niece took over recently, not skipping a beat with assignments.

Unfortunately, some things simply can't be taught.

Dara speaks first. "Glad you could make it," she welcomes with a nervous smile, extending her free hand to me.

I quickly shake and release it.

Dax crosses over to repeat that motion, greeting me as well. "Good to see you again, Cesar," he says.

Fucking gringos.

"César. Repeat after me: seh-sar," I correct, maintaining eye contact.

Mi abuela *always says, "If you want respect, never let anyone mispronounce your name. Correct them every time."*

I keep my eyes locked on him as he shifts uncomfortably and clears his throat. "My sincerest apologies, César," he corrects himself slowly as he sits at his desk facing me.

His sister comes around to stand beside him, clutching that envelope like she's afraid to hand it over. There's tension in the air, and I don't usually feel on edge around them, but there's something's off about these two today.

After twenty or so odd jobs for this family over the years, I've gathered they're ridiculously wealthy and peculiar. They're also British and can't be in a room together for more than ten minutes without bickering.

That part I can actually relate to.

The oldest Hale, Dean, I've had the pleasure of meeting a few times. He's a levelheaded guy and a good businessman, but he resides back in London, overseeing their headquarters.

Unfortunately, I am stuck with *this* one and his very quiet sister, who's nice but acts like she's nervous around a big brown man.

I'd much rather do business with Dean than these two, but we don't always get what we want, do we?

Straightening my spine and rubbing my hands together, I ask, "What've you got for me this time? The usual?" *Following one of their execs around? Or a potential investor? Blackmailing a contractor?*

He shares a look with Dara before focusing on me. "Uhh—sort of, but there's a challenge with this one."

"Okayyy..." I trail off with a raised brow.

Dara interjects, her tone uncharacteristically serious. "This job has the potential to be dangerous, and I'd like you to be aware of that before agreeing to anything," she warns, glaring at her brother.

"They all have the potential to be dangerous when backed—" I start.

"Not like this one," Dax interrupts with a shake of his head.

"Stop talking in circles and give it to me straight. I don't have time for this," I snap, my tone laced with irritation. I eye my watch. "You were late, and now you're bullshitting me. Tell me now, or I'm out."

"Of course, my apologies once more," he replies.

Dara sets the envelope on the desk, pushing it toward me, but I don't retrieve it.

Dax starts, "There's a property we're interested in, and this fellow bidder is making things difficult for us. We need you to look into their master distiller so we can get them to back out. Name is Klarke. This family is rather notorious for doing *anything* to get their way. We want to avoid any bloodshed, so you'd have to get in and out quickly. Make sure they never see your face."

Bloodshed? Ay bendito.

"We'd like you to run surveillance and let us know what you

find so we can blackmail them into backing out of the deal," he summarizes.

"And if blackmail doesn't work? What's your plan B?" I ask, already curious about these Klarke people.

"Force," Dara blurts out. "But it shouldn't have to come to that. Not with our best PI on the case. I-if you still want it, that is."

"Nobody is as skilled as you are. I'm sure we can avoid anything unsavory," her brother adds, his words rushed.

They've warned me of dangers, possibly putting my career and life on the line, but still haven't mentioned compensation. I don't like this shit. My family relies on me financially, and I need to know if this payout will be worth the risks.

I shouldn't even be considering a new assignment. Not now. Abuela *has stage four kidney failure and doesn't have much time left. She wants to be back in Puerto Rico when she passes, and it wouldn't be wise, especially if I get myself killed in the meantime. And Mariana will never forgive me if I die before she graduates college.*

Yanking me from my thoughts, Dax states, "I understand your hesitation, so we're offering half a million."

An incredulous laugh escapes me. "Shouldn't you be using that money to outbid them? What exactly are you asking me to do? And for *that* much, it sounds like you expect more than blackmail."

He shakes his head. "These aren't the sort of people you outbid. Think about it and call me tomorrow with your decision."

The fuck does that mean? And just a night to think it over?

"Alright. Expect a call from me soon," I assure them as I stand to leave, tucking the envelope under my arm.

"Thank you for your time, César," he says, coming around the desk to shake my hand once again.

"Appreciate the opportunity, Dax." Meeting his handshake with the force of my own, I tilt my head to peer at his sister. "And Dara, it was nice seeing you."

"Take care," she croaks.

I see myself out and settle into my SUV to find some music to drown out my thoughts. I'm hoping to somehow release the energy of this meeting when an alarm blares from my phone, reminding me of *Abuela's* upcoming dialysis appointment.

It also serves as a reminder that this assignment is a bad idea. She needs me. Taking a deep breath, I pull off the lot to head toward her house. Like second nature, I twist the knob to raise the volume, getting lost in the music.

* * *

MY FEET SHUFFLE into the house, and I'm greeted by darkness as I feel around for the light switch. With a flick, my living room is illuminated, revealing a near sterile home. I step inside the kitchen where the stove light was already on and release an exhale that feels like it's pushing the stress of the day out of my body. Resting the manila envelope on the kitchen island to scour my fridge for dinner, I decide on *pollo guisado y arroz* leftovers. My decision window is hours away from closing, so I'll need to review this file soon.

I warm up dinner, staring down the envelope as if it's going to tell me what to do while I wait for the microwave to beep. I recount this morning's strange meeting and the warnings that *didn't* set off alarms in my head the way they should've.

I've taken many assignments with dangerous subjects, and not once have I been deterred. Always doing the job and accepting my check, nothing more, nothing less. But half a million could help *a lot*. It could cover expenses for *Abuela*.

Flying back and forth to Puerto Rico to get everything settled for her hospice care hasn't been cheap, nor will it be when she eventually passes. She insists on being home when that happens, and work has served as a nice distraction from the inevitable. Outside of work, I spend as much time with her as I can, trying to make her laugh. I can hear her now, calling me *fresco*.

Then there's my sister and her tuition. While these high-profile cases have their challenges that often involve bending the law, they've also helped to put her through school, and I don't regret it. Crime pays far better than doing the right thing, and I set my own boundaries. As far as I'm concerned, anything that benefits my family *is* honest work.

I eat in silence as curiosity fills me about what I'll find in that folder. Anticipation builds as I fill the dishwasher, and I'm practically buzzing with excitement once the envelope is in my hands as I head to my bedroom.

After changing into sweats, I climb in bed and lean against my headboard. I retrieve the stack of papers from the envelope that detail all the things I need on the subject, or in this case… subjects. Elgin Klarke moonlights as the chairman of Divin Distilleries, specializing in whiskey and more recently cognac. Impressive and all while maintaining as the head of the Klarke crime family, a role he assumed when his mother, Celosia "Cici" Klarke, passed away in 2014.

Elgin married Dorothea Gardner thirty-three years ago, and they have a set of twins, Darius and Deirdre. They reside in Brooklyn and operate mostly in the tristate area, but this new venture has brought their chief operating officer, Deirdre, to Austin.

I scan several clippings of articles about Elgin and his family's impressively grim history making a name for themselves in white-dominated fields.

Another article I come across links Elgin as a known associate of Angelo Biavati Sr. and Regina Delvecchio (née Biavati). Angelo, the head of the Biavati crime family, happens to be his brother-in-law. Regina, his niece, is the newly appointed head of the Delvecchio crime family upon her husband's recent disappearance. I remember hearing about this on the news, and can now understand the Hales' reservations about this assignment.

My eyes catch on a grainy family photo featuring multiple generations of Klarkes surrounded by whiskey barrels. A magazine spread shows a more recent image of Elgin and Divin's CEO, Darius.

Then a smaller envelope falls from the stack of papers, containing more photos. As I riffle through them, I come across several shots of a woman who's seemingly unaware she's being photographed. She must be the disruptor and my "dangerous" subject.

A chill dances across my body as I take her in. This must be Deirdre, who is…fuck, she is breathtaking. She steals your attention with those dark doe eyes and media-trained smile. Her wrinkled forehead and slumped shoulders clearly indicate she's far from comfortable at this event, and I wonder where it is she would rather be.

She sports a unique piece in every photo that compliments her shapely figure and deep-brown skin, carrying herself as someone who doesn't wish to blend in. Someone you can't help but to admire. Assuming she uses that to her advantage, the Hales hired me to cut her off at the knees.

"Deirdre Klarke," I say out loud, savoring her name on my tongue. Laced with sugar, and I bet she's anything but.

Dulce.

A buzzing sound snaps me out of my trance. Tanya's name lights up my phone screen with a text. She's informing me she has a layover for the night, something we'd typically take advantage of. While we usually hook up whenever she's in town, it's never been serious.

I could blow off some steam tonight, but for once, I'm not interested. And technically I *am* working.

I thumb through the stack, and a photo of Deirdre stops me in my tracks. Her hourglass figure stuns in a backless formal gown, hair pulled back into an updo revealing her big brown eyes, and I relish the idea of those eyes looking up at me.

What a pretty, deadly little thing you are, Ms. Klarke.

Beautiful, troubling, and spoiled.

I'm familiar with her type and can imagine by how flashy she seems, that this'll be an open and shut case. One week *max*, maybe two, depending on how clean her dealings are.

Not much about this job reads differently from the others, mafia affiliated or not. Surveil, gather intel, deliver the blow to the Hales, and don't get burned. Same shit, *different case*. But a part of me is curious as to what's so terrifying about this family, specifically her.

All signs point to my decision being a firm no.

Still, I impulsively pick up the phone and dial Dax.

I have until the morning, but I'll do this now. The line picks up, and he clears his throat.

"I didn't expect to hear from you so soon."

"I'll do it, but not for five hundred k," I grit, leaving no room for argument.

"I'm listening," he responds calmly.

"One mil. Half upfront, half upon completion. I won't put my life on the line for less."

Silence takes over the line, and I'm anticipating him to tell me to fuck off. Never have I requested *that* much for a job. Maybe I've grown too comfortable with these people and their audacity has rubbed off on me.

But audacity is what got them to where they are now.

So I won't back down. One million, or I'll pass.

He breaks the silence with a chuckle. "You have got a deal, mate. You're worth it. Start tomorrow. I'll wire the payment in the morning. Thanks."

"Don't thank me yet," I grunt, ending the call.

My eyes drop to her photos splayed across my bed.

What have I signed up for?

3 / you don't know my name

César

31 days before 'the incident'

I spend two weeks following her routine only to find that my dangerous subject is a philanthropic, considerate, and seemingly kind woman. Nothing about the way Deirdre carries herself publicly or privately screams criminal or murderer. Unfortunately, this extends my time on her case, because the Hales are determined to find *something*. If only she'd let the mask fall enough for me to wrap this shit up, I'd be outta here and everything would go back to normal. Well, as normal as things could be for me.

Deirdre Klarke may be the most fascinating subject of my career. It amazes me how she moves as a woman in the mob while presenting herself as an upstanding citizen. A pretty girl with a bright smile can easily fool everyone around her.

But not me.

The most challenging part of this case isn't her attractiveness, it's that I haven't actually witnessed her doing anything worth reporting. When you keep eyes on someone long enough, they'll grow comfortable and eventually reveal themselves as if someone isn't watching.

I'll admit the complexity of this case has taken my mind off of worrying about my *abuela* every second of the day. She's been sick for a while and doesn't have a lot of time left. So I'm sure to spend every free moment I have with her, like I am right now.

I always accompany her to her dialysis appointments, and we make the best of it. Before Deirdre, I'd find myself bored whenever *Abuela* fell asleep, exhausted from the treatments. Since I hacked into her office cameras, I now have a source of entertainment as I monitor her working through her webcam from an app on my phone.

Her life is structured, often relying on reminders and alarms to hold herself accountable. She leaves little room for error and panics whenever something doesn't go according to plan. Hardly says no and struggles to enforce boundaries in her professional life.

For some reason, she's reliant on little white lies to assure those around her. If she was a talking doll, her voice box would say, "don't worry, I'm fine," "everything's okay," and, "no worries, I'll take care of it."

All the while, she is one hiccup away from bursting into tears, which usually ensue after interactions with her family and friends. I've witnessed the outbursts firsthand, and they're uncomfortable to watch. That still doesn't explain what it is that weighs on her.

She's a puzzle that keeps my mind sharp; her scattered pieces only make things more interesting. She's mindful and behaves like someone who suspects they're being watched, but I'll credit that to her upbringing. Or a bad case of anxiety, maybe even guilt.

However, no one in her family has been convicted of anything. Even when she was named as a person of interest in the death of Lawrence Wiley, it was brief and the local police issued a statement to clear her name.

It's no secret what her family does, but they're too thorough and well respected within their communities to be placed under fire. They haven't even gone to war with a rival family in nearly thirty years.

On paper, the Klarkes are clean as a whistle compared to their colleagues, but they wouldn't have the reputation they do if that were the truth.

And once I discover who Ms. Klarke is whenever she slips—well, I'm on the edge of my seat, because this reveal may surprise even me.

Is that so wrong that I'm tempted to see just what lies beneath the character she plays? Will she be afraid, angry, or intrigued by my interference? Only one way to find out, and the thought has my heart racing.

Provoking her could either be life-threatening, turn me on, or both. And if it does, I vow to attend therapy more than twice a month. I'll admit I should've scheduled a session once I felt compelled to install cameras in her home, but I can't explain that without setting off alarms.

Also, my therapist is a woman, so the last thing I want is to make her uncomfortable around me or say anything she'll need to report. Safe territory topics will have to suffice for me to maintain some semblance of control over my mental health.

I've learned how to navigate therapy, and censoring myself is key since I'd prefer to avoid grippy socks and handcuffs. Unless I consent to using them, of course.

A few ideas cycle through my mind as to how I could disrupt Deirdre's routine in an unthreatening way. I'll give her a choice to engage or not, and see if she takes the bait.

* * *

I FIND myself tossing and turning tonight. I'm not as tired as I should be, and I'm fighting the urge to check on her, curious if she's awake. I reach for my remote, flip on the TV, and pull up the app for her camera feed.

I press the arrow button to change the channel until I find her in bed reading with a book light hanging around her neck. How does she get anything done when she hardly sleeps? And how does she manage to still look incredible even when she's exhausted?

She's reading a romance novel, and to my surprise, stalking is a main subject of the story. At least she's familiar with the idea.

This could possibly unveil some fantasies she wouldn't dare express out loud. Her dedication to being the "good" Klarke is admirable, but I get the sense that something darker exists within her. And I plan to uncover it.

Only because I'm very good at my job. That's all.

Her lush curves are hidden by a hoodie that's about six sizes too big, but she's comfortable and that's what matters. Whatever makes Deirdre feel safe enough to remove the mask and be herself without judgment.

I've noticed how her shoulders drop whenever she crosses the threshold of her home. A literal fortress shielding her from the outside world.

I'm aware I shouldn't invade her privacy the way I have, so I don't have cameras everywhere, only in her frequent spots. Though I could argue that she could stand to have better security to protect this fortress of hers.

Something about her calmness entices me to disturb it a little, but with good intentions. A thought crosses my mind that the voice of reason in my head is advising against, but I'd like to nudge her. Something to make her feel seen without compromising myself.

I'll come to regret moving this needle with her, but I must. One time is enough. For a conversation starter, I browse Kiwi Music on my burner phone for an album she can't resist appreciating, even with a stranger.

I settle on *The Diary of Alicia Keys*, entering her number to open a thread and hovering my thumb over the send button. There's still time to turn back, but I don't. I hold my breath, unable to hear anything but my heart thumping in anticipation as I tap the send button and wait for a response.

Unsure of what to do with myself, I glance at the feed, and her phone chimes. She tilts her head, placing a bookmark to save her spot and setting aside her book. Her brows scrunch as she stares intently at the open thread. I'm certain she'll ignore it and keep reading. After all, it's one in the morning and she doesn't have to respond.

But her finger taps the screen, and a chime fills my room as her response awaits me. She reacted to the link with a heart, but hasn't returned to her book yet. I fire off an apologetic response, curious of what it may coax out of her and wait, assessing her reaction through my screen.

¡Coño! I meant to send this to a friend. Realized I have the wrong number, sorry to bother you.

DK

No worries! I don't know who you are, but your taste in music has me curious.

👀

She follows her last text with an eye emoji. Three bubbles dance around as she types another message.

DK

Tell me, what's got you listening to this album in the middle of the night. Heartbreak or nostalgia? Hopefully the latter. :)

Nostalgia. My mom loves this album and had to replace it a few times from playing it so damn much.

DK

Our moms have good taste. I was reading, but I had to stop and listen. This album was a staple in my household.

You didn't have to stop reading for me.

DK

How presumptuous of you to assume. I needed a break. What are you doing?

Being presumptuous is sort of my thing. lol

DK

This is how you admit you're a man. I'll allow it. What's your favorite song on the album?

Lol was it that obvious? Now you know that's unfair when there's no skips on that album.

DK

Very obvious. Since ladies come first, I'll go. 😂 Samsonite Man.

She follows that with a crying laughing and shrug emoji.

Doesn't take herself too seriously. Her mask is slipping, and I'm here for it.

Well, alright then. 😂 I'd have to say You Don't Know My Name.

DK

Shy one, aren't you? Fine. Let's not spoil this with names.

So, what do you suggest?

DK

Code names, of course. Let's see...fave childhood movie?

Mine is Bambi.

Easy. The Lion King. What about Doe?

DK

I like that. 😌 Least favorite character?

Scar, obviously.

DK

That's what I'll call you then 😂

It's nice to meet you, Scar. I'm Doe.

Damn. It's like that? 🤣 I'll allow it.

It's nice to meet you too. Would you mind if I texted you on purpose next time?

DK

Why else would we be picking code names?

Fair enough. Figured you may just be slap happy. You are texting a stranger after all. 👀

DK

It's possible, but so are you. Maybe I'm having a fever dream.

Is your head warm? I could teach you how to make a mean sancocho.

DK

My head feels fine. Puerto Rican, huh?

You know it. 😉 Dominican too, from my dad. You?

DK

Just good ole Black from both parents. 😂

I heart react to her message. This is going better than I anticipated. She's quick-witted; everything I toss her way is served back, and I can't help but feel as if I'm no longer the one in control here.

I could see myself becoming addicted to her conversation and humor. My observation of her needing to feel in control before acting on something was accurate, though I threw out a line with a baited hook, and she found a way to reel me in instead.

I already spend my days monitoring her, but this is who she

is when she's alone. Something you can't view through a lens, but by invitation. If I'm not careful, I could stay up all night learning the ways her mind works, but I shouldn't. I type and delete several responses before settling on one.

We should probably get some rest. Thanks for talking to me tonight.

DK

No, thank YOU. Goodnight, Scar. 😌

ME

Sweet Dreams, Doe. 😊

4 / uninvited guests

Deirdre

19 days before 'the incident'

Nothing irritates me more than uninvited guests, and sure enough that's what I was faced with when I stepped into my meeting today. I prefer to be notified before I have visitors, but my family tends to show up unexpectedly, giving me no time to mentally prepare myself and my staff for their arrival. While I should be used to their random pop-ups, I'm not, and it only adds to my anxiety.

My brother and cousin flew in without so much as a phone call. They then viewed the property we're bidding on without me before deciding to grace us with their presence at the debriefing with my staff this afternoon.

Darius was on time and would typically be focused, but he's being fidgety and skirting around every question I ask.

Regina arrives late, sucking the energy from the room once the door shuts behind her. She chooses an empty seat beside Pilar, my head of marketing, who stiffens. Of course there are rumors about my cousin, but none that can be proven.

Regina notices Pilar's reaction, greeting her with a smile as she settles in. She removes the gun tucked in her waistband, setting it on the boardroom table with a soft thud, and everyone stifles their reaction as Pilar's eyes widen. Regina whips her head around with a smirk, and I narrow my eyes at her.

"What? It was digging into my side," she responds innocently with a shrug. Even though the rumors can't be proven, she does her damndest to make sure people have reason to believe them.

My nostrils flare at her behavior, but I proceed.

Thankfully, she sits poised throughout the hour, reacting accordingly, while Darius continues to glance out the window whenever his eyes aren't glued to his phone.

I reach for my Hydro Flask, asking if there are any questions before we conclude, and heads shake in unison around the table.

A weighted silence settles in the boardroom, and the energy is palpable. My staff remains seated, avoiding eye contact and clutching their belongings as they wait impatiently to be dismissed. They aren't usually this quiet, and it has everything to do with my cousin.

It's no secret who Regina Delvecchio is, and by the looks on everyone's faces, they're aware. She has made quite the name for herself over the years and is proud of it. It reminds me of what it was like growing up with my father, a man everyone loved and feared. I'll admit him showing up would've been worse. I dismiss everyone but Regina and Darius. Brian, my assistant, stays back to gather all the meeting notes.

Regina stares daggers at my brother as his unsuspecting ass doesn't even look up from his phone. He danced around my questions the entire meeting, delivering short responses and clenching his jaw as if I was bothering him.

He gets on my fucking nerves. It irritates me how much he acts like Dad, completely disinterested in anything that isn't *his* way. He knows how important this project is to me and couldn't care less. You'd think my own twin would have my back, but at the end of the day, it's our parents' approval he seeks, and I can't say that I blame him.

I have my father to thank for their impromptu visit since he doesn't trust me to handle this deal on my own after what happened last time. So he sent babysitters in his place to "check" on me. I'm just as capable of running this business as they are, and I'll prove it without getting anyone else's blood on my hands. There's gotta be a better way than the Klarke way, and I plan to find it.

Our family owns whiskey and cognac distilleries, several stateside and one in France. I oversee multiple plants but recently moved from Brooklyn to spearhead our Austin location with plans of expanding. So when my realtor mentioned a vacant distillery nearby, I made a bid.

While I'm hopeful, one of our biggest competitors caught wind and we're now in a bidding war, making what should've been a relatively easy deal an absolute nightmare. These fucking trust fund babies have more than enough money to set up shop anywhere else, but for some reason, they just had to come here and fuck with me. I have too much riding on this to back down without a fight, and I'll be damned if my family swoops in to save the day. *This will be my win.*

I'm confident but would be lying if I said I didn't have any concerns doing business here as a Black woman. While Texas is diverse, it's *still* the south, and it's been a culture shock. But my eye remains on the prize.

Darius is handling a merger back home with a company that's been a challenge to work with, all while overseeing our marijuana farms in the tristate area. While it's mostly legal in the United States, our business dealings aren't entirely ethical.

We as a family are far from ethical, but I digress.

I'm focused on our liquor and spirits company in an effort to change this, making us more legitimate than ever. The problem is, not everyone in our family supports this dream, Darius included.

Thankfully, Regina became an integral part of this when she proposed a deal offering our liquors exclusively in her casinos, which she'd taken over recently in her husband's absence. I'm usually paid dust whenever I talk about going legit, but I appreciate her help. While she has absolutely no interest in life outside of crime, she is an excellent businesswoman as long as you stay in her good graces.

I sip my water, eyeing my absent-minded brother until I feel Regina staring at me. She steals my gaze, tilting her head toward my assistant Brian. He's typing away on his laptop, keys clicking rhythmically with the pounding in my chest. I nod in understanding and tap his shoulder.

We don't discuss the family business around civilians.

"Could you give us a moment?" I ask with a smile, and he obliges, gathering his belongings and seeing himself out.

Once the door clicks behind him, my eyes narrow on Darius and I whisper-shout, "Why did you even come if you were just going to waste my time? What does Dad need to know that he couldn't just ask me?"

I know he thinks I won't pull this off or that I'll fuck everything up like last time. If there's one thing about this family, they don't sweep a damn thing under the rug or forget.

My relationship with Gina is strained, but she's the only one who doesn't blame me for the sins of my ex-boyfriend, even though he stole from our family. Still, her kindness isn't lost on me, especially after the year she's had.

I turn my focus back to my brother, who refuses to answer me. So I try a different angle.

"What's wrong? Why are you acting so weird?" I prod.

"Nothing is wrong," he finally says, still avoiding eye contact.

Darius and I haven't been like this with each other since we were teenagers. Something is bothering him. I peer under the table to check if he's bouncing his foot, and sure enough, he is. A surefire tell when he's nervous.

"Darius? Please tell us what's going on," I say, softening my tone.

With a deep exhale, he sets his phone face down on the table, granting us his full attention for the first time since his arrival.

"It's the farm in Jersey. We've encountered some setbacks," he mutters.

"What kind of setbacks?" Regina asks, sitting up in her chair. Nobody fucks with our money.

I chime in, "Let me guess, there's a problem with us being Black and acquiring land in their town."

He nods. "Something like that."

My stomach drops at his confirmation.

"And you didn't want to mention it because—" I start, before Regina cuts me off.

"You don't like my process of elimination. Nobody does, but it's far more effective than asking nicely," she reminds us, twisting a pen between her fingers.

That's what we're calling murder now? A process of elimination?

He sighs, shaking his head. "Unfortunately, that's not all. I think I'm being followed. But don't trip, I got it handled."

That doesn't make me feel any better.

"You're sure this isn't one of your little girlfriends again?" I ask teasingly, grasping for a different possibility to distract the churning of my stomach.

He shakes his head before saying, "I have no reason to believe it's any of my girls."

"Did they follow you to Austin?" Regina asks with concern. But I recognize the calculation in her eyes. If anyone followed him here, they're as good as dead.

"I don't think so," he states, sitting up straighter. "I was careful. Swapped flights and cars. Tariq can confirm."

My eyes bounce between the two of them as Regina clicks her ballpoint pen in irritation. When provoked, she will destroy anyone who stands in her way or ours. Her unwavering loyalty is both admirable and terrifying.

She sucks her teeth, leaning forward, her tone laced with indignation. "If you thought you could handle it, we'd be digging graves right now. Give me a description, make, and model of their car. I'll have this little setback gone by next week. What threatens *you*, threatens us all," she finishes, leaning back in her chair.

A chill dances over me, and I suck in a breath and hold it in. Now isn't the time to have a panic attack. This isn't new to me. It's *our* normal, and I didn't always have this reaction when they'd talk business. A department that I choose not to be a part of: clean up and removal.

Thinking of what cleaning up entails causes bile to rise in my throat, and I swallow. I scramble for grounding techniques I learned in therapy to hold it together until they leave.

"I actually have a license plate, too," he adds, picking up his phone. His thumbs swiftly dance across the screen. "Texting you now."

As a ding fills the room, she holds up her phone. "I'll take care of it. I gotta get to the airport. I miss my kids," she says with a frown as she stands, pushing in her chair before sticking her gun back in her waistband. We round the table to embrace her in a hug, and she steps back to place kisses on both of our cheeks.

"I love you. It's just—I don't take kindly to threats after..." she trails off, eyes welling with tears.

"I know," we say in unison.

"Better to be safe than sorry." Her voice wavers. "I know what it's like to be terribly sorry."

Fuck.

My stomach sinks, and I nod in understanding before grabbing a nearby box of tissues to offer her one. She sniffs, reaching for a tissue to pat under her eyes.

"I'll meet you at the car, Gi," Darius says.

She nods, exiting the boardroom with a final wave, and takes off down the hallway with her bodyguard, Mr. Price, in tow. As if the trigger-happy woman needs one.

Darius exhales deeply, rubbing his hands over his face. "Dee? I'm sorry."

"It's okay," I tell him, even though it's not.

"It's really not, though." That damn twin energy.

"You're right. Don't keep shit like that from me. It's weird not living in New York, and it's a lot harder to protect you from a distance."

He lets out a chuckle. "Regina's got me covered. It's not like you're willing to catch a body. I don't take it personally that you're not a killer. I know Pops gives you a hard time over it, but at least one of us sleeps at night."

My brow raises. "Who said I sleep?"

"Well, then maybe you are one deep down," he says, patting my shoulder. "Everything is gonna be fine. I'll call you when I land."

"Please do."

He leans in for an embrace, and it feels like home. "I'll call before we drop in next time. We were just following orders, but that wasn't fair to you."

"I appreciate that. If you don't piss me off next time, I'll take you to dinner."

"Now, that I can't promise," he tells me with a smug smile.

"Of course not. Have a safe flight."

"Thanks. Love you, Dee."

"I love you, too, Dare. See you soon," I say, and he closes the door behind him.

"Never a dull moment with the Klarkes," I think out loud, taking a moment to embrace the stillness of the empty boardroom. I'm desperately in need of a field to scream in after the day I've had that's far from over. Thankfully, no one stops me as I stride down the hall. A relieved sigh escapes my lips as I enter my office.

I lock my door and proceed to riffle through my purse for my anxiety meds. With a tablet on my tongue, I take a swig of water and swallow before I focus on my breathing. I hold my breath as I count to four and repeat the action as I exhale. Eventually feeling at ease, I tackle the pile of paperwork on my desk, opting for a spicy audiobook to tune out the world.

Later, a text comes in from the man I dubbed Scar, serving as a pleasant distraction that I don't mind indulging in.

SCAR

How's it going?

I'm surviving. How about you?

SCAR

That's too bad. I'm thriving over here.

I've never been jealous of a man before and won't start now. Lol

SCAR

Ooh. She bites in the daytime. I can't say I mind it.

Of course you don't. Lions like the chase.

SCAR

And deer meat is delicious, so I've heard.

Wowwww. Enjoy time out with the hyenas. Take thirty and try again.

SCAR

Damn! Alright then.

I'll have a better attitude.

I'll believe it when I see it.

5 / rough day

Deirdre

19 days before 'the incident'

Never have I been more grateful for five o'clock. Usually I stay late and find something else to focus on, but after today, I am out this bitch.

The ride home calms me, R&B crooning from my car's sounds system. A glass of wine and curling up with a book is about as much as I have energy for this evening.

Between the impromptu pop up and hearing about Darius being followed, I've had enough to think about today. Had it been me, I wouldn't leave my house until the issue was eradicated. A climb in power creates more enemies than friends, and if I can't handle people wanting me dead, maybe I'm not as brave as I thought.

The music quiets, interrupting my thoughts, followed by my Bluetooth announcing an incoming call.

"Call from Dad. Answer it?"

I huff, "Answer it." The call connects a moment later. "Hey, Daddy," I say as cheerfully as I can, all while rolling my eyes.

"Hey, Dee," he greets me. "Are you still at the office?"

"I'm heading home." I pause, wondering how I should

handle my frustration. And then I just go for it. "What did your spies say about me?"

An exasperated sigh sounds from the other end. "Don't get emotional about me checking in on our investments, Deirdre. You're my daughter and I love you—"

"But you don't trust me," I interject flatly. "Because of Lawrence. Like it's *my* fault that he turned out to be a thief. I'm working my ass off to prove myself, and you send them to fucking spy instead of trusting me. How do you think that feels?" By the time I've finished my spiel, my voice is raised to a level I never use with my father.

"You want me to forgive you for bringing a thief into the fold? Fine, you're forgiven. But if your discernment weren't called into question, I wouldn't have to send them to make sure everything is okay," he tells me, his voice low and his words slow. "If you won't include me in daily operations, I'll find out what I need to know for myself."

His words punctuate the lack of trust in me and my abilities, and it's like a blow to the gut. Because even though I should be used to it, I always hope for a different response.

Silly me.

"Why did you have to send Gina, though? She scared the shit out of my team," I seethe, hating how lax he sounds about the situation while I'm constantly on edge.

He chuckles, further annoying me. "Regina scares everybody, but she's family. You two need to work your shit out. *That's* why I sent her."

"There's nothing for us to work out after what she did," I warn, hating that even after everything, his ghost haunts me.

"Accidents happen all the time. Lawrence was a grown man and knew better than to drive drunk. Didn't know better when it came to you, though, but he fucking learned, didn't he?"

Cracking jokes about taking a man's life?

"Dad. Please don't," I choke out.

"You're gonna listen to me now, Dee. We took him in. Treated him with respect, and *that's* how he thanked us? Fuck him." He spits the words out, like they're poison.

The click of my blinker fills the space as I turn onto my street. I couldn't be more grateful to see my home.

"Deirdre? You better not be crying over that sorry motherfucker," he warns, like I would be so stupid. It's not about *him*, it's about the lack of humanity when it comes to others. We are not gods.

No matter what Elgin Klarke thinks.

"I'm not crying over him. It's just...been a rough day," I say with a sniffle.

He sighs. "You know I'm not good with tears. Listen..." he trails off, and I wait for him to continue, hoping he's going to offer kind words. "I just want you safe. I love you, Dee."

"I love you, too, Daddy. I just made it home."

"Alright. Well, I hope you have a better night."

"Thanks," I say, disconnecting the call.

Of course, my dad doesn't trust me to lead. Between running an empire, dealing with my mental and physical health, and finding time for myself, I'm at my wit's end.

Darius was born for this and carries himself as such, leaving Dad with far less to worry about. Then there's me, the thirty-year-old fuckup, spearheading this project because I'm paying for the sins of someone else's wrongdoings. All while trying to restore the family name to something greater than the bodies it was built on. My brother has our parents' trust, makes them proud, and as a result he oversees both organizations—and well, I might add. Fortunately for me, we're both unmarried and childless, so at least the scale is even in one respect.

While we're twins, I'm still the oldest and reminded of it by how much stricter Dad's always been with me. If he could have it his way, I'd be exactly like my grandmother, acting more like Regina and less like...me. But if I inherited anything from Cici, it's how dedicated I am to proving others wrong.

I travel up the driveway before stopping midway and taking a moment to appreciate the place of refuge that's become my home. I shut my eyes, quietly affirming myself that I'm doing the right thing no matter how many odds are stacked against me, and I will prevail. Releasing a deep breath, I proceed into the garage and park. I adjust the leather tote on my shoulder as I exit the car. With ease, I input the security code and enter my house.

I head to the kitchen for a much-needed glass of wine, setting my bag on the island before turning toward my fridge. I notice the grocery list I tacked up and filled out this morning now has lines drawn through each item. I send a quick text thanking my housekeeper, Flora.

Hey! Thanks for placing a grocery order for me. I would've done it eventually, but I appreciate you so much!

Bubbles flash across the screen moments later with a response I didn't expect.

FLORA

Hi! I didn't order groceries today. The fridge was full when I arrived.

What? Scrambling for a quick lie to avoid suspicion, I apologize as the earlier panic attack I worked to subside rears its ugly head.

Oh. My family was in town today, so one of them probably took care of it.

Sorry to bother you. Enjoy your night!

Neither of them would've handled my groceries, nor do they have a key to my house. So, someone was definitely in my house today before her shift started.

Okay. *Um.*

I exhale, reminding myself to breathe. When my phone chirps with an incoming message, I slap my hand over my now racing heart.

FLORA

You're not a bother, Ms. Klarke. Have a good night!

Quickly shoving my phone into my back pocket, I proceed to the fridge and tug on the door. It's exactly *not* how I left it this morning, with everything I once needed staring back at me. Including a fresh milk carton that has a note attached. I angle it toward me to get a closer look:

SORRY YOU HAD A ROUGH DAY.
GROCERIES ARE ON ME.
P.S. I GOT CHERRIES. ;)
– YOUR SECRET ADMIRER

What. The. Fuck?

My heart pounds loudly in my chest at the realization that someone was in my home. I'm unsure of who it would be, until my mind shifts back to Darius. Could this be who's been following him? He assured he was careful so they wouldn't trail him to Austin, but what if they did?

And why the fuck would they be running errands for me?

I reach for my phone to call him, but reasons why I shouldn't flood my mind. I tuck my phone back into my pocket as I charge up the stairs to retrieve my gun. Relieved to find it untouched, I nervously assess my home, room by room, and find no one else here. But my anxiety levels are fucked.

As a Klarke, I have no interest in calling the police, even the ones on our payroll. I consider Regina to be worth a call. But I'm unsure of how I would even explain this to anyone, so I sink to the floor and consider what she would do instead.

I suppose she wouldn't sleep without her gun. But that's *if* I manage to sleep at all tonight. Eventually I trot back downstairs, managing to heat up some leftovers and ignoring the nausea settling in my gut. I force myself to eat at least half of it, before I toss it down the garbage disposal.

Yanking the fridge open, I scour it again looking for clues. That's when I notice a jar toward the back of the top shelf that appears to be something homemade, labeled "*sofrito*," with another note attached.

SOFRITO – IT'S A COOKING BASE.
INGREDIENTS: ONIONS, GARLIC, BELL PEPPERS, TOMATO, CILANTRO + CULANTRO.
START WITH 2 TBSP AND ADD AS NEEDED.

I rip off this note and the one taped to the milk carton, clutching them as I nervously charge upstairs to analyze. Today was shitty, but I don't remember telling anyone that. The comment about the cherries has me questioning if I know this person. I sift through every text thread from today to see if I'm just trippin', but I come up empty.

In my thread with Scar today, I mentioned I was surviving, causing me to comb over our entire conversation since he first reached out "accidentally," a few days back. I find no mention of cherries in our previous conversations.

Somehow I manage to get ready for bed, only to climb in with no intention of sleeping. After fighting off another panic attack from not seeing any footage on my cameras of this person, I begin searching for anything out of place and discover that the spare house key I keep in my home office is missing. And when I look up Scar's number, it's linked to an online phone service. So, that's a dead end.

This stranger I've been kind to may be stalking me, could have broken into my home, and I can't tell my family because I can't afford to make another mistake. Not again and especially not now. As much as I argue that I can defend myself, I need to prove that now and clean up this mess. The thought makes my stomach churn, but if and when he comes back, I'll be ready for him.

6 / southern hospitality

César

12:43 a.m. | 1 minute after 'the incident'

"Who do you work for?" she asks in a stern tone, her pistol aimed at my chest as she nervously chews her bottom lip.

Good evening to you, too, Ms. Klarke.

A weighted silence surrounds us after the gunfire that greeted me moments ago. I gotta say, she's an entertaining hostess. Never seen a party trick like that one. Must be a New York thing.

She toes down the stairs hesitantly, closing the distance between us while maintaining eye contact, and stops a few feet in front of me. This is the closest we've ever physically been, and she holds the power to end it all at point-blank. She's rattled, and the trembling hands on the trigger have my heart pounding in my ears. I've been in life-threatening situations before, but none like this.

She parts her full lips to speak, but nothing comes out. Still, I anticipate her next words. The deadly weapon creates a barrier between us as I take her in. She lives up to her nickname, her body quaking as she zeroes in with a gaze full of ire.

I wonder if she knows that her eyes can ruin a man's resolve.

If death looks this fucking beautiful, I may reconsider.

Usually, I wouldn't mind saying that out loud, but this barrel I'm currently staring down is an incentive to bite my tongue for once. There's no excuse that would suffice for why I'm standing in her home in the middle of the night or why I've been following her. Anything I say that's truthful will get me killed.

I understand that now, shaking my head in disappointment because I cannot say I don't know better.

Protocol is once I am seen, I must remove myself from the case and pass it over, but I don't like the thought of anyone else watching her but me.

Six weeks I've gathered intel and surveilled her, only for someone else to come in take my fucking payday? Fuck that. What my clients don't know won't hurt them.

Why am I even doing this shit? My life is currently in the hands of an unpredictable woman who has every right to drop me where I stand.

Guns aren't something I fear, though having one pointed directly at me is an unfamiliar experience. Haven't been one to plead for mercy and won't start now. I'm man enough to accept whatever consequences I'm entitled to, but my heart hurts for my family, should I not make it out of here alive.

"Do you plan to kill me?" She squeaks her question like she's trying to gauge whether she has to kill me or not.

This is not how I expected our first conversation to go, and I've blown it if that's what she thinks of me. A murderer? Absolutely not. Now, her on the other hand? The jury is still out on that one. My head tilts as I eye her from head to toe.

"I wouldn't dream of it. You have a weapon pointed at *me,* but have the audacity to ask if I'm going to hurt *you*."

She stammers, "I—I'm defending my home from a *threat*."

Me? A threat?

My eyebrows lift in shock, and before I know it I'm speaking. Biting my tongue wasn't going to last very long. It's impulsive around her, and she *always* has a comeback.

"Lions love the chase, isn't that what you said?" I ask, and she backs up, careful not to trip. "Look, I'm an intentional man. If I wanted to harm you, I would have." My feet drag me closer, entering her orbit, and she surprisingly lowers the weapon to her side, a silent invitation that my foolish ass accepts. Her tart cherry scent fills my nose, and I crave more of it. "And if you wanted to kill me, *you* would've done it. Instead, you destroyed your couch over there," I tease, pointing my thumb toward the wreckage in her living room.

She grimaces, and it's kinda cute.

"You think you know me?" she huffs.

Duh.

"I know plenty, but you still manage to keep me on my toes," I tell her, wagging my index finger in her direction. "I know about your upbringing, passcodes, how you like your eggs, and that you have a tattoo inside your lip, Doe," I taunt, reaching to touch her chin. She understandably swats my hand away. Though I don't miss how her breath hitches at my proximity.

Too soon for niceties. Understood.

Backing away to resume my spot, I place enough distance between us and continue. "Now, it's my turn to ask questions. First, can we have a civilized conversation without weapons?"

"You tell me. You're the one who broke into *my* fucking house."

"I did not break in. I have a *key*. If anything, I'm a guest here. Is this how you treat houseguests, Deirdre?" I stupidly add, lifting the balaclava up to rest on my nose.

It's fucking hot in this thing, but I can't let her see my whole face.

"The hell you are," she barks, her free hand balling into a fist.

My jaw drops, and I rub my chest as if she wounded me. This is the first time her mask has slipped, revealing the anger that boils beneath the surface.

"What happened to southern hospitality?"

"I ain't fucking southern," she quips, adjusting her grip on her gun.

"Fair enough. Maybe I'll leave *if* you ask nicely," I challenge, stifling a laugh as I await her response.

She tucks the semi-automatic pistol into her waistband with a devious grin. "I'll show you fucking nice. Get the fuck out of my house, Scar," she spits, emphasizing her nickname for me and pointing at the deep scar on my top lip. "I bet you earned that from running your fucking mouth."

Well damn.

The guffaw that escapes me startles her. I throw my head back as my body shakes with laughter.

"I did, actually. That wasn't a question, but I figured I should tell you something about me since I know so much about you. I came prepared and brought an overnight bag, in case you'd like to get to know me some more," I say, tilting my head toward the backpack resting by the front door.

She rolls her eyes, crossing her arms over her chest, pressing those full breasts together. I lick my lips and drag my eyes up quickly, hoping she didn't notice.

"That's cute and all, but you ain't fucking staying here," she states.

"The hell I'm not," I argue, amusement in my tone, mocking her voice as she glares at me. I'm not staying here, but she doesn't need to know that.

She's cute when she's angry.

"Alright, alright. You were supposed to find it tomorrow, but since I ruined the surprise, I'll give it to you now," I tell her, backing up carefully to retrieve the backpack.

My moves are timed and deliberate as I make a show of unzipping the bag slowly, and when I catch her hands rushing toward her waistband, I tut. "Hey, trigger fingers, I came bearing gifts. Keep it up and I'll take this thing back."

Her brows furrow as I hold out a gift box, her hands wrapping around it reluctantly as her focus remains on me. With a nod, I urge her to open it and see for herself.

Eventually, she removes the lid, sifting through the tissue

wrap, revealing a wooden mortar and pestle. Her mouth parts, and I observe as her fingers trace along the engraving. Rivera, my mother's maiden name. I clear my throat to push down the emotion, and her eyes meet mine, kinder than before.

An explanation is needed, so I muster one up quickly.

"We call it a *pilón*. I know you love to cook with fresh ingredients and noticed you didn't have one…" I trail off, glancing at my feet. "It's already seasoned and everything."

A twinge in my right arm grabs my attention, and I instinctively graze the area. My fingers dampen at the contact. My body stills at the realization, and she stares at me expectantly.

She fucking shot me.

I'll deal with that once I get out of here. In an attempt to savor the moment, words tumble out of my mouth, and I hope they make sense.

"It belonged to my *abuelita*. She won't be needing it anymore," I say softly.

"Thank you, I appreciate it. I'll be using this next time I barbecue."

My lips shift into a relieved smile, knowing I couldn't bear to hold on to it. Too many memories to hold on to, mingled with the notion that she'll soon be making her own with it.

"I knew you'd use it. It's in good hands now," I say, slipping my backpack over my shoulders, careful to avoid my wounded arm as I turn to exit. A sigh escapes me, and I drag my balaclava over my mouth, shifting back into the invisible man I'm supposed to be.

"I'll save you a plate next time," she says softly, stopping me in my tracks.

"Looks like you've got southern charm after all," I joke, and for the first time tonight, she fights a smile, and it's a sight to see. "I overstayed my welcome, and I apologize."

With an incredulous stare, she assesses me. "You realize you helped yourself, right?" she asks with a chuckle.

My hand cradles my wounded arm, and her eyes travel me, landing on my bicep.

"Right. Sorry about that," is all I manage.

"You're bleeding," she says in a hushed tone.

"You clipped me, but no need to worry. Like you said, I earned it," I admit, and her eyes widen in response.

She looks concerned. She better watch it, or I'll think she likes me.

"I should get checked out. I'll say I came home late, scared *mi beba,* and you greeted me with a gun like a good girl," I add with a wink, but she isn't amused. "It's Texas. This shit happens all the time. *Buenas noches,* Deirdre Klarke," I bid her adieu, tugging the front door shut behind me.

Not the meeting I imagined, but I survived.

7 / deer crossing

César

12:57 a.m. | 15 minutes after 'the incident'

The drive home is the most agonizing thirty minutes of my life, and it has nothing to do with the gunshot wound in my arm. I've assessed the damage and thankfully I can avoid a hospital visit. The last thing I need is to go there and run into my sister, who is doing her PA clinicals in the emergency room in the nearby hospital.

I wouldn't know where to begin explaining this unique relationship with Deirdre, and I'd rather not try. It doesn't help that I don't even understand what it is *I* am doing anymore. What happened tonight could've been avoided, had I *actually* been doing my job.

What I did instead was reckless and extremely unprofessional. *Estupido.* I'll admit a lot of my recent actions have been unprofessional and invasive, but I can't explain it. I can't tell anyone either, because it feels so wrong and so right all at the same time.

I have this aching need to know everything there is to know about her; things I shouldn't be allowed to know and aren't my business. Like why can't she sleep at night? What makes her so anxious and why are her eyes full of sadness? *None* of that is my business, yet I can't shake it.

Deirdre Klarke isn't someone who hides from danger. She embodies it, and you cannot fear what you are. However, I'm to blame for the fear in her eyes tonight. My stomach churns at the thought of this unfortunate first impression.

I came straight home from the airport, itching to check her camera feed, and decided to keep myself busy with tasks around the house instead. Once I completed them, I showered and climbed into bed, hoping sleep would take me. But I was wrong.

I couldn't sleep in Puerto Rico while surrounded by photos and memories in my *abuela's* home. The realization became more apparent as I prepared the space for her to spend her final days in hospice care.

Eventually, I gave in and checked Deirdre's cameras, relieved to find her sleeping soundly in bed. As I paced my home, I stared down *Abuela's pilón* that no one else wanted. The thought crossed my mind, and before I knew it, my keys were in hand, and I was heading for her house at two in the morning.

It was bold of me to stride inside as if I lived there, but at least I wasn't empty handed. I'd been quiet enough, and have done this countless times without disturbing her. Except the layout was different; she'd moved her vast collection of plants from the kitchen, nearly filling her spacious living room. I toed around, thinking I'd been being careful, but my size often complicates things.

I'm not usually a clumsy guy. But I was, and at the wrong time tonight, I stubbed my toe on a planter *hard*. Then I jumped back and knocked over *another* huge planter with a loud crash. If the crash didn't wake her, cursing to myself did. It made a huge mess with soil and shattered ceramic all over the floor.

Thinking quickly, I rushed to toss the shards, not wanting her to get hurt, attempting to clean it herself, and the hunt for a broom is how she spotted me. The least I could do was clean up after myself, and I would've taken care of it if she hadn't shot me.

The fact that she lives alone, has an arsenal of weapons, and doesn't go anywhere without a gun, would make a wise man wait for a vacant home before breaking and entering. Except I never said I was wise.

I'll admit I hadn't considered that she'd really shoot me until she actually did. Silly me for thinking all of our inside jokes meant she changed her mind. Let that be a lesson: you can't laugh yourself out of a death sentence.

At the time, it felt like a grand gesture and so necessary, but instead I earned a reality check *and* a gunshot wound.

I'm ripped from my thoughts when a white-tailed deer darts out in front of me. My feet slam on the brakes in time to avoid a collision, and she stops in her tracks to pin me with a stare. The familiarity of this standoff sends a chill over me, and my gaze doesn't waiver as I wait anxiously for her to either pass or lunge toward my truck. The latter seems impossible, but the Doe in my life *did* just shoot me. So maybe I ought to have more respect for quarry.

I roll down my window slightly, clicking my teeth to encourage her to move along. She breaks our gaze, staring into the woods as if she's waiting for someone. Moments later, a fawn emerges from the rustling brush to join her. She glances at me once more before they retreat across the road.

"What a fucking night," I say, taking a deep breath as I resume my drive.

* * *

THANKFULLY, I had everything I needed at home to clean my wound and wrap it. I lean over the sink as I swallow some acetaminophen for the pain and remove my blood-soaked hoodie, tossing it aside.

I examine the graze wound before rinsing it with saline and

cleansing. It looks like shit, but at least I'll have another cool scar. I'm turning off the water when I hear my front door open followed by a familiar voice calling out. My sister's timing couldn't be better.

¡Maldita sea!

My eyes dart around at the bloody towels surrounding me, and I glare at the ceiling, mouthing, *you think this shit is funny, huh?*

A lie isn't going to convince her once she walks in to see all the blood-soaked towels. The floorboards creak as her footsteps grow closer, but I remain silent as I frantically scramble to clean up. Of course, she finds me…as I'm shoving bloody towels under the sink. What do I even say? My girlf—*subject* shot me?

How did I end up here?

"What the fuck happened, César?" she exclaims, and before I can respond, she's at my side assessing me.

"I'm fine. I just got caught on something," I lie.

"I know what a gunshot wound looks like. I'm in medical school, *estupido!* Or did you forget since you're DIY-ing my job? Does *Mami* even know you're back?" she asks, fishing her phone from the tote bag on her arm.

"Please don't tell her. She doesn't need this right now," I beg.

"Start talking, Chuki. Now," she demands, crossing her arms and sucking her teeth. She stares at the wound, shaking her head as it starts to bleed again.

"Okay. I'm seeing someone. It's new." Her eyebrows jump up, and before she can start asking more questions, I continue. "I was hoping to surprise her when I got back from Puerto Rico. You know I was getting the house set up for *Abuelita*."

"Yeah, and?" she urges, waving her hand for me to hurry.

I sigh. "Well, I scared her and she…shot me. I promise I'm okay. Just grazed me."

Her face scrunches in disbelief, and she asks, "If you're dating…and you came over to see her, why would she shoot you?"

"She—uh, scares easily."

That's a fucking lie.

"She would *never* intentionally hurt me. It was an accident, and she's pretty shaken up, and I'd like to get back to her. You know, more women should carry weapons," I suggest with a shrug, ignoring the pain. "So, are you going to keep interrogating me or will you help wrap this up since you barged into *my* house?" I say, pointing at the gauze on the counter.

Now, I understand how she felt about uninvited guests.

"Uh—sure." She crosses over to my sink, washing her hands before applying gauze to my bicep. "You know, for a dummy, you did a good job cleaning this wound."

I snort. "Thanks. You can learn anything on the internet."

"You could've called me," she reminds me in a soft tone, focused on the task at hand.

"You mean to tell me I'm paying for you to learn shit like this when it's online for *free*?"

She rolls her eyes, stifling a laugh. "You're an idiot. So, when can I = meet the woman who shot my brother? Maybe she could give me some pointers," she adds with a cackle.

I mock her laugh. "I'm not ready for her to meet everyone yet. The last thing I want to do is scare her off. And *don't* tell *Mami*."

"Fine. You're all set. I'll get out of here," she tells me as she pats the now covered wound, making me hiss out my exhale.

"Please. It's late, and I know you love the guest bed. Go on," I assure, tilting my head toward the hallway.

She stands on her tiptoes to kiss my cheek. "Goodnight. Be safe.

Maybe *call* before you drop by this time," she teases as she proceeds down the hall.

"Says *you*," I chime after her, and she blows a raspberry before shutting the bedroom door.

The drive back to Doe's is calm and free of deer. I stand outside her bedroom window at a respectful distance to find her peeking out the curtain as if she's been expecting me. Her eyes widen when she realizes I've returned, and I greet her with a text.

> I live to piss you off another day. Go to bed, Doe. 😉

She picks up her phone and smirks. I give her a wave as I head back to my truck. I shake the curiosity of what it would be like to sleep beside her. *That ain't happening,* I tell myself when my engine roars to life.

I know *exactly* what makes her so dangerous, yet I'll be back tomorrow and the next day. She ain't getting rid of me that easily.

8 / viola the monstera

Deirdre

7:42 a.m. | 5 hours after 'the incident'

My eyes blink open to the sun illuminating the space. It's a bright reminder that I haven't been closing my curtains before bed. I suppose my plan to lure him in was successful, unless I dreamed up the events of last night. Which would be a great explanation for the man who broke into my house and looked at me like he belonged here.

It's possible that in that state of unreality, an opportunity presented itself that would've allowed me to prove my worth as a Klarke. One might've considered it divine intervention. Except that for people like us, God oscillates between screening our calls or declining them. Sure, we've earned that treatment fair and square, but foolish me holds out for miracles every once in a while. Even the damned gotta believe in something.

Except last night wasn't a dream. I got *exactly* what I asked for, and they came bearing gifts. Not exactly what I'd expected from my secret admirer, but at least he was raised right. A man should never enter a woman's home empty-handed, so it was a kind gesture.

But even pigs are well-fed before being led to slaughter.

For weeks, I psyched myself up to finally face him, and it was *nothing* like I'd imagined. I was ready, like I promised, but all of that practice left me ill-prepared for the audacious target whose presence both frightened and aroused me. While I didn't finish the job, I'd kept my word to an extent, surprising myself by pulling the trigger.

But then my stomach sank when I noticed he was wounded.

This heart of gold *will* get me killed on day, but until then, fuck it, we ball.

That encounter left me sitting on the stairs thinking of all the times my dad compared me to Regina. Growing up, she always fought my battles for me, and he couldn't stand it, telling me to have thicker skin, to be less sensitive and defend myself more. He's done it so many times that it's second nature at this point, and only adds to my resentment toward her. I understand his comments aren't her fault, but the blood on her hands *is*.

Why can't he accept that I'm not like Gina? I could never find joy in senseless killing, and if that means he won't let me take on more with Divin, then so be it. I'd like to be allowed to choose my own path while still feeling like a member of this family I didn't choose to be a part of.

Whiskey and cognac distilling is another lane paved by the Klarke name, though I feel valued at this company in a way I've never been at home. My voice is heard, my ideas are appreciated, and they gave me a chance to gain their trust. I did have the advantage of signing their paychecks, but I still bust my ass to be the best boss I can be. In turn, the amount of faith these strangers have in me is baffling when I consider how little faith my family has in my abilities.

I stretch my arms above my head and kick off the covers, sliding my house shoes on as I glance around the room. My eyes catch on the *pilón* I brought upstairs after he left. I examined it for a hidden camera and came up short, but I couldn't stop staring at it whenever I wasn't peeking out the window.

After a few frantic texts went unanswered, I unsent them and waited around for some indication he'd be okay. I can't explain why, but I suppose I needed to know if I was even capable of hurting someone. At least if I was accused of murder again, this time I would be guilty. Even if it were self-defense, it'd be another mess my family would get stuck cleaning up. And my father would never let me forget it.

This is by far the weirdest situation I've ever been in. The idiot survived, and a rush of relief washed over me once I noticed him, quieting my anxious thoughts enough to finally get some sleep.

The more we interact, Scar slowly chips away at my guard, and I hate it. He isn't the *most* insufferable man, but his audacity aggravates the fuck out of me. Then again, so does *every man,* including my father. The small part of me that doesn't fear Scar can appreciate how he helps around the house, fills my tank and replaces my groceries. Selflessness goes a long way with me.

It might be why I let him live last night.

The man is a stalker, I have to remind myself. Stalking is not something sane people do. Unfortunately for me, I attract crazy. It's not shocking that another one has found something he liked in me. With past partners, there's always been some dark secret they're hiding that ends up being an absolute dealbreaker. It's possible that Scar's obsessive personality *is* his dark secret. Either way, something is fucking off with him.

For starters, I shot him and he came back. Any other man would've had my place surrounded with red and blue lights, caution tape outlining the scene of the crime as I leave my house in a body bag. I shot him, and he still sent a text, wishing me goodnight. It's safe to say the dark romance novels I've been reading have fucked with my logical thinking. *Either that or the bar is in hell.*

It's definitely in hell.

A stalker who sends consistent morning and nightly texts. That's the bare minimum I'd expect when being courted. I shouldn't be impressed, but if he were fictional, I'd let him take me to dinner. He appears to have a job, since he doesn't lurk around my place *all* the time. Which is good, because I'm not a cheap date. A horn honking outside distracts me, followed by my phone lighting up with an incoming call from Scar.

I can't help my sigh as I lift my phone to accept the call. "Why are you calling me?"

"To see if you'd answer. Good morning, Doe," he says with a deep chuckle. "I didn't want you to be late for work. Grabbed your coffee order and donuts for breakfast."

"You cannot be serious," I deadpan.

"I'm *very* serious. Devil's food cake, your favorite," he sings, and I stifle a laugh at his lighthearted silliness in spite of the fact that he's nursing a gunshot wound that I inflicted.

I nearly ask how he knows that, but of course, he does. Mindlessly, I pace around my room, debating on whether to take this exchange further, when a question rushes out of my mouth.

"What do you do that gives you so much free time to bother me?"

"Is this your way of asking about my career?"

"Oh, he's got himself a *career*," I say in a mocking tone.

"Funny. I wouldn't expect a nepo baby to know what that word means."

My jaw drops at his response, and I'm not even mad. *He got me with that one.*

"Oooohhh. He bites in the daytime," I respond with a chuckle, flipping on the light switch in my en suite bathroom to assess myself in the mirror. *I could look much worse.* A nap during my lunch hour will do wonders.

"I'm always up for a bite, Doe. I'm a grown-ass man," he assures in that cocky tone of his. "Matter of fact, I'd like to talk for the rest of my commute. If that's all right?"

"Only if you answer my questions," I negotiate, exiting my room.

"It's my job to know things. I'll answer two more, so choose wisely."

"What kind of *things*?"

"Whatever is asked of me."

I trudge down the stairs, considering my last question. But I get distracted by the clean floor beneath me that was left in disarray the night before. The scatter of feathers, shattered ceramic, and soil gone.

What the hell?

I continue the journey through the foyer, entering the kitchen to find the source of the commotion last night. My favorite plant rests on the tile unpotted. I'm at a loss for words.

My monstera? He knocked over my fucking monstera plant!

Her name is Viola, she's twenty years old and belonged to my late grandmother, Cici. It was one of the things she wanted me to have when she passed, and I've taken pride in caring for it. If I'd known *this* was what he damaged, he wouldn't have made it out of here alive.

His gruff voice snags my attention. "You still there? Did you get the donuts yet? I left them on the counter," he informs me, like it's completely normal.

"What do I need to do to keep you from breaking into my house?" I finally ask, realizing this motherfucker might insist I clear out a drawer for him instead.

He snorts before saying, "Simple. Either aim for the head or invite me in."

Before I can respond, a beep sounds, notifying me of a call on the other line. I pull the phone away to glance at it and see Regina's name flashing on the screen.

What impeccable timing she has. As much as I'm enjoying this conversation, I suppose I should see what she wants. Ignoring her is childish of me, but I'm not the best at expressing myself because I'm not usually heard.

"Um, I gotta go, Scar. Work is calling," I rush out.

"Go ahead, boss. Have a good day."

"You, too. Thanks for breakfast," I say, noticing the box of donuts and coffee cup resting on my kitchen island. I waste no time clicking the other line to answer.

"What's going on, Gi?"

"Are you doing okay?" she asks, her voice heavy with concern.

"Yeah, why do you ask?" Mindlessly, I open the box of donuts, smiling when I see it is, indeed, filled with my favorites.

"I'm surprised you actually picked up. I have an update about Darius's problem."

"How's that going?" I ask, even though I'd rather not know.

"The situation has been taken care of, and it won't come back on either of you," she answers in that resolute tone of hers.

It still amazes me how casually she talks about killing, as if she's discussing the weather. It brings me back to the night I got a similar message from her, but it was *me* she was protecting.

You don't have to worry about him again. The debt is paid.

A life was taken, and that was it. I was left to sit with those words. *The debt is paid.*

"Dee, do you hear me? What's going on?" Gina asks, pulling me from my thoughts.

"Um—sorry. I'm all right. Was just thinking about Cici," I say, which isn't a complete lie.

"Oh. I just left her gravesite," she murmurs, the weight of grief slowing her down. "Brought fresh flowers—"

"Because it's Thursday," we say in unison and share a chuckle.

"Well, I'll let you go. I love you," she tells me, and I know it to be true.

"I love you too, Gi," I respond before disconnecting the call.

Memories of my grandparents flood me as I stare at the beloved plant splayed across my kitchen floor. They weren't fans of being called grandma and grandpa, which was odd growing up, but we knew better than to argue with them. So, he was our Ace, and she was our Cici, named after celosia flowers. They were her favorite.

Our grandpa always had a bouquet of celosias delivered to her every Thursday. It was even in his will to continue the tradition. Long after she passed, we all took turns replacing her flowers every Thursday, no matter what. It pained me to have to stop that tradition when I left the city. I can only hope to be loved as deeply as she was someday.

Half an hour and one failed attempt of lifting *and* repotting the plant later, I've officially given up.

I'm so sorry, Cici. I'll fix this. Or better yet, he *will.*

I fire off a text to Scar. Since he wants to be in my damn house, he can make himself useful.

Since you can't watch your big ass feet, YOU can repot this damn plant.

It's been in the family for 20 YEARS.

Watch your step OR I won't miss next time.

SCAR

It was an accident and I promise I'll make it right.

Sure you will.

It better be back to normal by the time I get home.

SCAR

You have my word.

Who did I piss off enough to send this man here? It's the only rationale I have for why he's stalking me. Especially when I factor in the "family business." I'm on the cusp of such a big opportunity that I can't help but feel like he's meant to be a distraction to divert my attention. Someone wants me to fuck up this deal.

My stomach turns as a thought crosses my mind. My dad is so insistent on sending family members to report on me, it's possible that he hired someone to do it round the clock instead.

If that is true, killing him could be another one of my fuckups to add to the running list. It's not like I can just call him up and ask about this man who's been stalking me. Because if I'm wrong and someone else hired him, history will repeat itself, and I can't have that on my conscience.

Either way, Scar's blood will be on my hands, and it won't matter if I pull a trigger because we're both fucked.

9 / the stalkee

César

8:30 a.m. | 4 days after 'the incident'

It doesn't matter what time I fall asleep, I'm a morning person and have to stick to my daily routine. As much as Ms. Klarke has shaken up my regimen, having me repot that big-ass plant before she got home from work yesterday, I refuse to slack on the tasks that help me maintain my sanity.

I wake up at 5:30 in the morning and meditate before my early gym session. I work out for an hour, come home to shower, have breakfast, and journal before I hit the road.

I'm ready to head out when I hear a car door slam shut outside followed by keys jingling in the doorknob. Judging by the time, Mariana just finished her shift and was too tired for the drive home. She enters my apartment with her shoulders hunched and her eyes already at half-mast. I ignore the blood on her scrubs and reach for her.

"You know I would've picked you up," I remind her, wrapping my arms around her in a hug.

She yawns before saying, "I know, but you have a life."

When I release her, she trudges down the hallway for the guest room.

"All I do is work, Mari. I'll pick you up next time you work a double," I call after her.

"Fine. I'm going to go—" she attempts to say over her shoulder, another yawn cutting off her sentence.

I smile to myself with a shake of my head.

"Get some sleep. I love you. Let me know if you need anything." With my keys in my hand, I open my front door to head out.

"Be safe. Love you, too," she mumbles just before I shut the door behind me.

I'm headed to meet with another client about a new assignment. Fingers crossed it's an open and shut case, because I am desperate for something normal lately.

Speaking of normal, it's not normal for me to have Doe's camera feed playing as entertainment on the road, but I am curious what music or audiobook she's starting her day off with.

Today's selection is a Kiwi Music playlist of New York hip-hop classics. The best part is her shouting out the lyrics to "Clan In Da Front" by Wu-Tang Clan while applying her makeup in her bedroom. For someone who doesn't know she's currently being watched, she sure puts on a show.

She spritzes her face and removes the pins from her hair before she starts looking around. She's likely searching for her phone. She loses it several times a day, and it's never more than six feet away from her every time. After retracing her steps, she finds it hiding on her bed beneath her dressing robe and begins typing a message. To my surprise, my phone lights up with her name.

1 unread message from Doe.

DOE

No good morning text today?

You're slacking on your job.

Well, good morning to you too.

Kissing your ass isn't my job btw.

Sleep well?

DOE

I didn't, but when do I ever?

Good thing it isn't your job. You'd suck at it.

Wanna bet? 😏

No. I have a question though.

I might have an answer.

DOE

Do you have cameras in my house?

The question gives me pause as I weigh the options between being honest or not. Because I see no benefits to being honest, I say what I must.

No.

DOE

So, it's only the bug mics?

I'll only confirm that because you found one of them.

DOE

So there's multiple? Ha!

¡Maldita sea! Smart cookie. It's one of the things I find so attractive about her.

Anyways, you said "a question," not plural.

DOE

As the stalkee, I think it's fair that I know something about you.

A stalkee? Did you just make that up?

And I am NOT a stalker. 😮

That part is true. I'm not a stalker, I'm a licensed professional. If anything, I am *legally* allowed to stalk for a purpose. But I'll admit everything about the way I surveil *her* is far from legal. Between the in-house mics and cameras, breaking and entering, and corresponding with her, it's all *very* illegal.

DOE

No, it's a real word for a victim of stalking.

Are you the victim or am I?

Don't remember you getting shot. 😉

DOE

Get the fuck outta here. That was self-defense!

And I am NOT stalking you.

I think you would if you could. 😏

I chuckle as I wait for her reply. The bubbles appear and disappear as she thinks of her response. Getting a rise out of her is becoming a favorite pastime.

DOE

Are you an FBI agent, spy, or a peeping Tom?

I never thought I'd see the day you'd call me another man's name.

And I am none of those, actually.

DOE

Shut up. I don't even know your real name.

What color panties am I wearing?

Coño. That's a way to change the subject. *Red.* I stop myself before my fingers begin typing. She's wearing a red lacy thong, but I only know this because she lays her outfits out the night before like a grade schooler.

Of all the strange things I've witnessed this woman do, *that* is definitely in the top ten. I know the truth is that I don't watch her change, but she wouldn't believe me, so I lie instead.

Orange.

DOE

I know you're bullshitting me and I'm insulted that you'd even suggest I'd wear orange panties.

I'm gonna find these cameras.

Have a good day now, Sir.

What are you going to do, Deirdre?

DOE

I can show you better than I can tell you.

Bye, bye now! 👋

You aren't going to find anything.

DOE

Lie again.

I said good day!

🖕

🤣

There is never a dull moment with this woman, I swear. I really am going to miss her antics once this case is closed. And I try not to think about that too much.

10 / mediating with muppets

César

11:23 a.m. | 4 days after 'the incident'

My phone buzzes in my pocket while I'm conducting tech surveillance on a subject. My client has reason to believe their senior partner has been embezzling funds, and I have news for them.

This man is guilty, your honor.

I hope that buzz indicates Deirdre has actually left the house and isn't running late again. She is the boss, but lateness is a pet peeve of mine. If you have no consideration for anyone else's time, you can't expect to build solid business relationships.

My clients are mostly CEOs, attorneys, and high-profile leaders that tend to provide me with *unique* cases and subjects. Even being outsourced for the Cartel keeps things interesting, but there are more dull days on the job than fun ones.

I fish my phone from my pocket to see a screen capture from my camera's motion sensor that Deirdre has left the house. She's on a call with her friend Alora and is on track to actually be on time for work today. That's more like it.

She often admits to being homesick when talking with friends. Which makes me suspect the sad eyes have something to do with the distance from her loved ones or possibly the late boyfriend. Though I can't imagine he was anyone worth missing, judging from his rap sheet and how quickly she relocated to Austin.

Her phone taps are entertaining, to say the least. For someone who works so hard, she rewards herself in unique ways. Often unwinding with romance audiobooks and something called audio erotica, where people provide pleasure using only their voices.

I haven't had the honor of witnessing her pleasure herself, because I was raised right and give her the privacy she's entitled to.

As for conversations, she rarely discusses business over the phone. Most of her friends are scattered all over Texas and back in New York. From my understanding, they vacation together regularly.

They communicate with mostly voice messages, FaceTime, or group texts that consist of catching up, sending memes back and forth, and links to songs on Kiwi Music. I'll admit, her music taste is attractive, and her most listened to song this month is "Pick Up Your Feelings" by Jazmine Sullivan.

I also couldn't have predicted her having an interest in chopped and screwed music, which automatically makes her even finer to me.

A New Yorker with an appreciation for both east coast and southern hip-hop? As well as 2000s R&B, Neo soul, and Motown? If circumstances were different, it would be foolish to sleep on a woman like Deirdre.

This is yet another finding that affects my ability to view her as simply a subject. The intel I gather doesn't reveal things I'd otherwise learn from getting to know her as a person, like her all-time favorite songs, favorite food, or favorite color. These are all interests that I shouldn't be concerned with, but I can't help myself.

I want to know her.

* * *

ONCE AGAIN, the Hales are late for our meeting. Their voices travel up the hall, bickering like children, calling each other "bellends," whatever the fuck that means. I'm not sure what they're upset about today, and I don't care. It's a debriefing that should be over quickly since Ms. Klarke still leaves *a lot* to the imagination, despite the fact that I've surveilled her for the past six weeks.

On paper, Deirdre reads unbelievably clean for a mafia princess, but my instincts believe otherwise. Her family's name holds entirely too much weight for her to be in this role without dirtying her hands.

Except intuition doesn't solve cases, evidence does. And the lack of it isn't helping me get any closer to wrapping this shit up. As frustrating as that is, the thought of sticking around a bit longer isn't the worst thing.

Mi abuela has thankfully been less stubborn lately, listening to my sister and I about her diet. Her doctor has been pleased and assured us at this rate, it's possible that we could have a bit more time with her.

That news makes me feel less guilty for taking this assignment and somewhat enjoying it. After all, Deirdre has become a part of my routine, and I pride myself on being disciplined.

I've found more about her relatives, which could be the leverage I need to blackmail her, giving my clients exactly what they need to win this bid. And while I've gone against protocol egregiously, crossing many lines for reasons I'm unsure of, I still intend to do my job. My family comes first.

She surprised me as a worthy opponent in this game of cat and mouse. Or lion and deer, in our case. A folktale with two possible endings, and the lion gets the raw end of the deal in both. If I'm not careful, the deer will outsmart me. I can't allow that to happen.

Deirdre will be fine and can continue to do whatever the fuck it is she does. After I close this case, she'll move on and find someone more acclimated to her lifestyle. I'll pay off my sister's tuition, and if we're lucky, *Abuela* will be able to see her graduate.

And when the time comes, I'll be able to honor her with the proper memorial in San Juan she's asked for. I know better than to let my moral compass stand in the way of what's best for those I love *and* provide for.

I stand to greet them when the door swings open. Dara leads with determined steps across the carpet to shake my hand, followed by Dax, who addresses me by name with correct pronunciation. They sit opposite each other at the conference table and stare expectantly at me.

"What've you got for us, mate?" Dax asks, rubbing his hands together in anticipation.

"Well, she had some interesting dealings in Brooklyn and was a person of interest in her boyfriend's death last year."

"Bloody hell. Even she doesn't seem capable of murder," Dax says, mussing his hair.

I agree, I think. Vowing to keep my opinions out of this, stating facts only.

My eyes catch on Dara's hands, absentmindedly tearing at her cuticles as I speak.

And I thought Deirdre was an anxious girl.

"Her name was cleared quickly, and the cause of death revealed no foul play. She had an airtight alibi. Wasn't even in the same state when the death occurred," I clarify, looking directly at Dara so she'll stop picking at herself.

She lets out a relieved sigh. "I suppose that's good," she says, straightening her spine and folding her hands on the desk.

"It isn't, really. If she's clean as a whistle, where does that leave us with the property bid? Surely, after all this time, you've found *something* we can actually use. Her family is full of murderers, for fuck's sake."

"At least between all the killing, they make a damn good whiskey," Dara adds with a chuckle.

Dax stares daggers over the desk, asking, "And how would you know that?"

"Because I've tried it, of course. How do we expect to beat the competition if we're unaware of what they bring to the table?" She scoffs. "Excuse my brother, he's a bit soft in the head." She snaps to herself, rhetorically asking, "What do you Americans call it? A dickhead?"

Here they go again.

I don't bother responding, because it's no use and I was wrong for assuming the argument I overheard would cease for the sake of this meeting. I'd walk out if I wasn't being paid to be here.

"And Daddy thinks numpty here is the better leader," she teases with an eye roll, all prior anxiousness gone.

"Piss off," he retorts with a scowl. "Twat."

"Not my fault you're a fucking Muppet."

"Are you two done? I don't have all day," I interrupt, my knee bouncing with impatience.

"Ah. Sorry. What else?" she asks, waving her hand as if to move the conversation along.

"I did find something interesting. Her relation to Regina Delvecchio, a crime boss who is well known for being *far* more dangerous than Deirdre. Better known as 'The Devil in The Daylight' for being an unsuspecting terror who hides in plain sight. She's a grieving wife and mother with an alleged affinity for arson and murder."

I decide to withhold exactly *why* Regina is grieving. That information has nothing to do with Deirdre, and I'm not exactly comfortable with it being used against her. Regina's husband, Cidro Delvecchio, disappeared eight months ago after a supposed deal went wrong.

The search continues as a body has yet to be found. Speculation is that she had something to do with his disappearance, but her actions following his death state otherwise.

Dara stiffens, biting her lip as her eyes widen. She asks, "Is she local?"

"No," I assure them, shaking my head. *And it's a good fucking thing she isn't, for their sake.* "She resides in Brooklyn but travels here often. Rumor is she's interested in opening a casino right here in Austin."

They stare in horror, and I resist the urge to snort. *Mira los maldito blanquitos.* Scared that their antics will actually have consequences.

"Absolutely not. All the more reason we need you to get Deirdre to withdraw her bid," Dara states, lifting her chin in indignation.

"Maybe we should consider making an offer to buy her out of their current location? If they don't have business here, we could put a stop to that casino early. What do you think, César?" Dax suggests, staring expectantly at me.

Their uncle would have never suggested something like this. He respected this community and enjoyed being a part of it. Livelihoods shouldn't be toyed with just because you're at risk of losing something you don't even need. But of course, the Hales throw money at any issue without a care in the world.

"This isn't my fight, but it's worth considering the economic impact an acquisition could make. And they may not even be willing to sell. The Klarkes were here first and have contributed more to this community than y'all have. Do you plan to displace their current employees? Or offer them gainful employment? I'd suggest the latter. Otherwise, people will likely come after your company."

I'm surprised at my cool response, but I refuse to bite my tongue, opting to keep it as professional as possible despite my anger. They have the audacity to come to a country that's foreign to them and speak as if they have a say over who *really* belongs here. They *almost* sound like white Americans.

Regina opening a casino here would bring a lot of job opportunities and money to the area. Crime would also follow, but it's already here. The Klarkes and Piñeros are the most powerful families in Austin, and if the Hales even attempt to fuck with their current ecosystem, they'll have a lot more to worry about than losing bids.

I eye my watch and excuse myself, seeing we almost went over time. "I have an appointment I need to make, so I'll get going."

"Alright, mate. Thank you. Cheerio," he says, pushing his chair in to see me out. As always, we part with handshakes.

I get one foot out of the door and stop myself, choosing to give them another piece of advice. They don't deserve it, but if these idiots get themselves killed, that affects my livelihood.

"I think you need to call Theo for insight on how to handle things in this city. He took the time to learn, and you should, too."

Dax nods in agreement, and Dara stares contemplatively.

"I'll reach out with any new findings, and we'll schedule another meeting. Take care," I say before closing the door behind me.

11 / mind yours

Deirdre

9:21 p.m. | 8 days after 'the incident'

I wrap myself in a terry cloth robe as I step out of the shower and begin what I like to call my nightly rounds of self-care. It ends with me curled up with a book until sleep eventually takes me.

My tedious skincare routine has me groaning at the thought of it, but tomorrow I'll be thankful that I put in the effort tonight. My skin is improving greatly thanks to my new esthetician and products to target my hyperpigmentation.

Maybe someday soon, if I'm lucky, I can leave the house makeup free without a care in the world, hoping my dark spots continue to fade. As far as the skin picking goes, I can't make any promises, but focusing on one thing at a time is the best I can do for now.

Once I look like an extremely glazed donut, I retrieve the small mirror at my vanity and begin my search. I tilt my chin upward to check for hairs, and sure enough there are *plenty* despite the fact that I plucked them all a few days ago.

It's only one of the annoying symptoms that come with having PCOS. When Alora was diagnosed with endometriosis a few years back, it actually led me to my PMDD and PCOS diagnoses.

After I had opened up to her about my irregular periods, weight fluctuation, mood swings, and annoying chin hairs that I couldn't stop plucking, she recommended I make an appointment with her OBGYN, and I'm glad I did. After handfuls of appointments and some lab work, I found clarity and began treatment for both. It was extremely validating to finally speak on what I was battling and be heard, rather than being told I simply needed to lose weight.

Finding a doctor you can trust as a Black woman is a different kind of struggle. Especially when you're experiencing infertility issues and would like to have a family someday. The maternal mortality rate for Black women is exceptionally high and is enough to scare the thought of motherhood right out of us. But I am grateful to have found a good doctor, one that I don't mind hopping on a plane back to New York for, but I am glad she'll still treat me virtually between my regular checkups.

I grab my tweezers, angle my magnifying mirror to get a close up, and start yanking out every hair in sight. Medication can help to slow the growth, and I suppose it does a tad, but I secretly enjoy removing them. Strange, I know.

As I flip the mirror to the magnified side, a faint red flash somewhere behind me catches my eye, and I freeze. The volume of my heartbeat increases until it's all I can hear. I turn to find the source, and it's above my closet, giving a view of my entire room and facing my bed.

I knew he planted more than mics in the house and have been determined to find them, but didn't find any until now. Of course, it's while doing the one thing that I should be able to do in the privacy of my own home.

I return to the vanity and continue my routine, tweezing while facing the camera and waving with a fake smile. I hope he can see me right now. I don't care that he has the displeasure of witnessing me pluck my lady beard. That's exactly what he gets for not minding his fucking business.

I'm sorry that I'm not used to being watched, but the least I can do is make his view unpleasant. As if he has a wire hooked up in my brain, my phone chimes with a text from him.

SCAR

So…

What are you doing?

Minding my own damn business. You should try it sometime.

SCAR

So, she bites in the nighttime too.

You don't have anything better to do?

I'm sure my dad didn't hire you to watch me in my bedroom.

SCAR

🙄 You got me there!

Anyways, can you respect my privacy for ONCE?

SCAR

I'm afraid not.

You're really not scared of him, are you?

SCAR

I don't have anything to worry about when I do my job well.

I beg to differ, Sir.

I have yet to see you do this so-called job.

SCAR

That's because my job is none of your business, even if it's keeping a watchful eye on you.

I'll give you something to keep an eye on.

I stand from the stool and drop my robe, prepared to finish my nightly routine completely naked. I unmake my bed, tossing the extra throw pillows onto a nearby chair, and climb under the blankets. I fish for my Kindle, pulling it from under my pillow and settling in before I send off another text to him.

Have fun telling my father what I just did.

Goodnight!

SCAR

Wait…

My shoulders shake with laughter as I leave his text on read and silence my phone. This is my life now, and it doesn't appear to be changing anytime soon.

12 / the fairy godmothers

Deirdre

3:40 p.m. | 10 days after 'the incident'

My phone buzzes on my desk, tugging me from my thoughts. A notification appears on the screen.

1 unread attachment.

I swipe up, opening the group chat with my best friends, Alora and Skye. Photos of a vibrant lavender gown, one that I can only assume Alora created, leave me stunned. It's gorgeous, and she never ceases to amaze me.

LO

Shipping it tomorrow. You'll have it by the end of the week.

Alora Hannon lives, eats, and breathes style. She's a fashion director for Delphine Bloom—a world-famous bridal designer—but loves to sew and upcycle thrifted finds in her spare time. I happen to be lucky enough to be her muse, even though we're thousands of miles apart. That woman knows my measurements better than I do. My smile widens as I admire the photos again, imagining myself in this gown.

Since I no longer attend my family's lavish parties, I'm not sure where I'd wear this dress. But gift giving is her love language, and I know better than to decline a present. Thankfully, wearing Alora's designs make it impossible to not see the beauty in every curve.

I'd be lying if I said I never experienced any insecurities about my body, because I'm human. Lawrence would make snide comments about my appearance toward the end of our relationship. And while he didn't say anything I hadn't heard before, that was one of many reasons I decided to leave him.

I always struggled with my weight, but it was never something my family gave me a hard time about. The kids at school were another story, which led to Regina and Darius getting into fistfights for me.

By the time I went to high school, my dad got me into boxing with Regina and her friend, Audrey. Then I began fighting my own battles, literally and figuratively. While I may not be a killer, I'm not against throwing well-deserved punches.

SKYE DADDY

Goddamn, Lo. This is gorgeous!

Make me something next! Please?

I met Skye a few years ago at the LaGuardia airport. I had a layover and grabbed a coffee. When I found her sitting in the café, reading a Lilith Keene book I love, I went over to strike up a conversation. I hadn't expected to leave with a potential friend, but I did.

We were only yapping about books, and I felt like I'd known her for years. We followed each other on Picturegram and kept in touch. Fast forward to now, she's one of my best friends.

I invited her to brunch once when she was in town to meet Lo, who welcomed her with open arms and adopted her into our friend group.

It's always been difficult to date with a family like mine.

Finding genuine friendships are a similar struggle, but I am fortunate to have found them.

After admiring the photos for a moment more, I type a response.

I have nowhere to wear this dress, Lo.

LO

Girl. You better find an excuse.

SKYE DADDY

Somebody's got a birthday coming up!

LO

Throw a birthday party in that big ass house of yours!

I don't have friends here to invite to a party.

And you know how much I don't like company. 😬

SKYE DADDY

You could go on a date! Have you checked your SoulBlend profile lately?

LO

Your back could use a good cracking, if you ask me.

I'd rather take my chances with a chiropractor.

The only one who needs a good cracking is you, Mother Goose. 😂

LO

I am a Silly Goose, thank you very much. 😆

I'll only be a Mother Goose if any of this damn IVF works.

She follows with the fingers crossed emoji. Alora is at a point in her life where she would like to have a child on her own. I fully support her, but she learned the hard way that the adoption process as a single woman is a wash.

Her endometriosis makes conceiving extremely difficult. IVF treatments aren't cheap but are her best option if she'd like to do this alone. She started them within the past year, and while they can be taxing, she hasn't given up hope.

It's likely that I may need to try IVF to become a mother someday, so I appreciate how transparent she's been about her journey to motherhood. My PCOS comes with many challenges and infertility issues are unfortunately one of them.

I'd love to have a family of my own someday, but I try to keep that dream in the back of my mind. If I have anything to say about it, I'd like my children to be able to choose whether they'd like to be involved in the mob or not.

Though I'd rather my hypothetical children *not* live a life of crime.

SKYE DADDY

Oh, it's going to work! Manifesting it. ✌️

LO

Anyways, the dress is coming this week and you better find somewhere to wear it.

Fine. I promise I'll find a reason to wear it.

LO

I miss you two! 😘

I hope our schedules align soon. ☹️

SKYE DADDY

Even if they don't, I got unlimited PTO.

Say the word and I'll hop on a flight! ✈️

We're long overdue for a girls' night. I miss you guys so much! We'll make it work. 🤞

LO

Get some rest and let's FaceTime this week.
Love youuu! 💕

SKYE DADDY

Sounds good to me. Love y'all! 🫶

Looking forward to it. 💜 I love you too!

13 / sundays aren't for stalking

César

4:44 p.m. | 14 days after 'the incident'

I round the dinner table to set it the way *Mami* prefers. Dinner is nowhere near ready and will take a while longer since we ran out of *cubanelle* peppers. Dad wanted to make *carne de res guisada* and volunteered to pick up some more.

Growing up with both Puerto Rican and Dominican parents, there was always a blend of cultures in everything we did, especially family meals.

Deirdre crosses my mind, and I wonder if she was close to her parents before she moved here. The thought of her not having anyone to rely on while she's so far from home bothers me.

The urge to sneak off to check her cameras overcomes me. I have strict rules about not allowing work to spill into my off days and haven't had an issue sticking to that until now. The distraction I desperately needed comes in the form of my nickname being called from upstairs.

"Chuki! We need a tall person," *Mami* shouts from somewhere in the house.

"Can we borrow your height?" Mariana follows up with.

"Sure," I yell back, laughing to myself as I follow their voices.

Frustrated huffs and bickering lead me to the guest bedroom closet. I find Mariana and *Mami* standing on their tiptoes reaching for the top shelf that's at least a foot higher than their fingertips.

"What are y'all doing in here?"

"*Mami* wants to show us some old photos, but we can't reach the boxes," Mariana grunts out.

"I got this," I reassure them, standing outside the door as they clear out.

Moments later, I exit the cramped closet with several boxes I retrieved.

"Show off," Mariana teases.

"*Gracías, mijo,*" *Mami* says, taking a few boxes from me and lowering herself to the floor to sit cross-legged as she sifts through them. My sister and I follow, removing lids to find what must be hundreds of photos in each one.

"Is there anything in particular we're looking for?" I ask, ready to take on a task that gets my mind off of Doe.

"Yes. Pictures of Mariana as a baby."

"I'm doing my clinicals for labor and delivery, and I delivered my first babies this week. I love it," she says with a hopeful smile. "I think that's what I want to do if emergency medicine becomes too much for me."

"That's amazing, Mari."

"Anyway, I was telling her that some of the babies came out big enough to handle bills, and she swears that I was ten pounds when I was born," my sister nearly yells.

"I remember. Your head was as big as a *guanabana,* too," I tell her with a sigh, a smirk quickly following. "You never did grow into it."

"It was not," she argues, slapping my arm.

"How would you know? That's why we're searching for proof now."

Mami cackles to herself as she sorts through the stack of

photos in her hand. We stay like this for a while. Stopping to ask questions and listen to mom's stories behind the photos.

"I don't remember us having a sloth as a kid."

"*¿Qué?* We never had a sloth," she says, her brows crinkling as she sits up on her knees to peer down at me.

She lets out a surprised gasp when she spots that I'm actually looking at my sister as a toddler. I burst into laughter when she snatches the photo from my hand, pressing her lips together to avoid smirking, and resumes her search.

After I settle down, I lean toward Mari as if I have a secret to share.

"I must be overdue for an eye exam, because that wasn't a sloth, it was you," I taunt.

She glares at me and continues flipping through stacks of family photos.

"Found them," *Mami* exclaims.

She scoots in closer and shares baby pictures of Mariana and me, proving that she was indeed an abnormally large infant and reminding me of the Sesame Street obsession I had as a kid. A photo circulating of me surrounded by at least fifteen different stuffed Elmos is a nightmare of mine. My friends would never let me live it down.

I offer to put everything away while they join *Abuela* in the kitchen to help her prepare dinner. I place the lids back on the boxes, setting aside the stacks of photos *Mami* wanted to hold on to.

My dad returns with shopping bags in hand and meets me at the foot of the stairs, handing them to me.

"I went to two different stores for these," he grumbles.

My eyes scan the bag before I set it on the kitchen counter, and I scrunch my face at the amount of peppers inside and back away.

Not my business. I'm gonna let Mami *deal with that.*

She immediately peeks into the bag and shakes her head in disbelief. "*¡Isidro! ¿Qué es esto?*"

"*¡No me importa!*" He shouts his response as he steps into the kitchen, waving his hands. "Freeze the extra so I don't have to go back."

His arms wrap around her, and he presses a loud kiss on the top of head and whispers something in her ear. She rolls her eyes playfully and starts washing off the peppers in the sink.

This dinner was just what I needed after this week. I always feel recharged after spending time with my family. Mariana kept her word and didn't mention the shooting to *Mami,* or I would've been asked about it all night long.

After everyone is finished eating, I volunteer to do the dishes as usual. I circle the dining table, stacking the plates and utensils atop one another, and tread into the kitchen when my phone buzzes in my pocket. Before I can dry my hands to peek at it, I hear footsteps approaching, followed by Mariana calling out for me in a sing-songy voice.

"Chukiii."

I glance over my shoulder to find her filling a plate with left-overs to take home. "Grab a plate for me, please?"

She nods and retrieves another plate from the cabinet, setting it aside. Once her plate is full, she disappears into the pantry, returning with a roll of aluminum foil in hand.

"I was about to tell you to bring a lot of food back. Don't need to be worrying about you starving through those clinicals."

She stares incredulously at me and says, "*Abuela* is the one you have to scold for missing meals, not me," she says rubbing her soft tummy. "I can't get shit done on an empty stomach. Even if I am seeing things every day that make me queasy."

"How are you feeling now that it's almost over?" I ask, looking over at her as I try to decide whether to check my phone or not. Better not, I tell myself, returning to scrubbing the dishes.

"Relieved and nervous. I'm happy to be graduating, but I still have to pass my board exam before I can start looking for work," she laments, a struggle I can empathize with.

"Ugh, boards. I had to do one to be a PI. Hated it, but I

passed, and you will, too. Thankfully, you're a far better student than I was. More expensive, too."

"Yeah, because Google university isn't my only source for information," she teases.

"Hey, at least I look shit up before I ask stupid questions," I retort with a chuckle.

"I'll give you that. You're still a dummy, though." She pauses. "Seriously though, I wouldn't be graduating if it weren't for you. Thanks for taking a chance on me." Her voice wavers with emotion, but I can't handle that shit right now.

"Don't mention it. Whether you wanted to be a physician's assistant or a clown, you'd have my support. Plus, I won't have to go to the ER ever again because of you," I joke, lightening the mood.

"Speaking of, how are things going with that girlfriend of yours?"

I open my mouth to respond when *Mami's* voice shrieks from behind me.

"*¿Qué? ¿Tienes una novia?*" my mother exclaims, her hands together as if in prayer.

"Oops. I'll be seeing myself out," Mariana mutters with a wince.

"Nope, you're staying." I say, grabbing her arm with soapy hands to stop her.

"What's her name? What's she like? How did you two meet? Tell me everything, Chuki," *Mami* says, her face lighting up, and it makes me feel like shit.

I have to lie because she needs this right now. Something to look forward to, a distraction from worrying about *Abuela*. I'm a shitty liar, but I tell myself I can keep this up for a while. Say it didn't work out after I close the case and she doesn't have to know.

I swallow, turn to grab a towel, and face her. A hopeful smile graces her face, one I haven't seen in a while and would do anything to keep it there.

"Her name is"—I pause to glare at my sister—"Deirdre. She's a whiskey distiller who recently moved here from Brooklyn."

Mariana gasps, cutting me off. "I was talking to Daya the other day. You know she does tattoos in Brooklyn now. Broke up with that *pendejo*, too, and seems happier."

I do want to know more about what led to my cousin leaving her long-time boyfriend, but I'll ask more once I'm no longer in the hot seat. We all hated the guy, so I know Mari won't spare any details about it.

"I didn't know that," I say before returning to the topic at hand, my eyes meeting *Mami's*. "It's still very new. We met not too long ago and have only gone on a few dates. She is not my *girlfriend*, but I enjoy spending time with her."

Mami raises a brow, and the question I was dreading comes out of her mouth.

"When can I meet her? She's welcome to dinner anytime! Please bring her," she begs, reaching over to touch my arm.

I mull over my response, because there is no way in hell I can bring Deirdre to meet my family. As much as I want to make my mom happy, I can't promise anything. My presence in her life is temporary, and what has transpired between us is rooted in dishonesty.

She doesn't know who I am or why I'm following her, and if she did, she damn sure wouldn't agree to meet my parents. I suppose she'd introduce herself at my funeral after she killed me, since mobsters tend to do that sort of thing. Finally an excuse flies from my mouth.

"She travels often for work and our schedules don't always align, but when it feels like the right time, you'll meet her," I say, hoping that ceases any further questions.

"Okay. I'll give it a rest. I'm happy you found someone, son."

"Me too," I murmur. "Me too."

14 / the geminis

Deirdre

6:28 a.m. | 18 days after 'the incident'

SCAR

Good morning, birthday girl. 🖤

I'm sorry that you're a Gemini. Happy birthday, though!

Thanks, asshole. What's your sign since you're talking shit?

SCAR

I love when you talk dirty to me. 😉

I'm a Cancer. No slander allowed.

You're crybabies.

SCAR

Are we crybabies or just in tune with our emotions?

Speaking of crying, you've got surprises waiting.

If you took the day off from irritating me, I'd cry tears of joy.

SCAR

You'd miss me if I took a day off. But you'll see!

We shall see. You didn't have to get me anything. 👀

SCAR

I'm not arguing with you, Deirdre.

Go brush your teeth. We'll talk when you get out of bed.

huffs hot breath through the phone 😂

SCAR

😵 You might as well speak at my funeral.

Bye, Scar. 😜

I roll out of bed and start my morning routine of showering, skincare, and styling my hair. Even though I don't plan to leave the house for anything other than redeeming my hoard of birthday coupons from restaurants and local stores, it doesn't mean that I can't do that while also looking cute.

They say when you look good, you feel good, and I'd like to see if there's any truth to that since I haven't been feeling too great lately. My back has been aching terribly for the past few days. I've been disinterested in reading, cooking, Pilates, and even self-care, which are usually things I look forward to.

Honestly, I wouldn't have been able to convince myself to leave the bed if it weren't for work. So when I checked my period tracker app the other day, sure enough I was predicted to start my menstrual cycle within the next few days.

Unfortunately, my period being on the horizon makes my PMDD—otherwise known as Premenstrual Dysphoric Disorder—rear its ugly head, making my life hell on earth while I wait for the dreaded cycle to begin.

I have the absolute pleasure of being diagnosed with both PCOS and PMDD. Meaning on top of having excessive hair growth, infertility struggles, and irregular bleeding, my periods last longer than normal.

Oftentimes, I should be out of commission for the first few days, but I refuse to sit at home and would hate for my family to do one of their unannounced drop ins during a time where I've called out. So, I power on thanks to over-the-counter pain relievers, comfort food, and lunch break naps.

I know it's ridiculous, especially since I fought against my relatives on the board for all Divin employees who menstruate to have paid menstrual leave and won. All for this to be an employee benefit that I don't even allow myself to indulge in simply because I feel guilty for taking time away from work. As if a day or two off would set me too far back on my dreams for the company's future.

After my shower, I throw on some comfy lounge clothes and plop back into bed while I snap screenshots of all the special birthday discounts I need to use today. On the menu are free coffee, ice cream, donuts, desserts, and other sweets. I'd really love a cake, but I don't see the point in picking one up without having anyone to share it with.

Armed with an organized list of businesses who offer birthday freebies, I gather my things and head out.

While I'm running around, my phone is bombarded with texts and voice messages from my family and friends, wishing me a happy birthday. That's something I actually love about this day. No matter how unseen I feel at times, this is a day I can always count on to be reminded of who's thinking of me.

I return home, needing to make multiple trips to ensure I don't drop anything on the way to the front door. The more I thought about it, the more I realized I deserve to indulge in my craving, so I grabbed a small marble cake. What's the point of all this free ice cream I got if there's no cake to pair it with?

I sit at the island with a fork to dig into it and reach for my phone to dial my brother. And in true twin fashion, his name pops up on my screen with an incoming FaceTime call. I swipe to answer, prop my phone against the empty cake lid, and wait for the call to connect.

He appears on the screen with a lazy smile and red-rimmed eyes barely open. *High indeed.* A definite perk of working around our marijuana farms upstate.

"Happy birthday, Sis."

"Happy birthday, punk," I say with a chuckle, pointing at him with my fork. "I see you've already been celebrating."

"Damn right. Did you get the package I sent the other day? Wanted you to try some new hybrid strains we've been working on."

"Mmhm," I hum while my mouth is full.

"I want some cake," he whines, making a pouty face.

He's so childlike when he's high, reminds me of when we were kids and didn't have to be so serious all the time. I miss those days.

"Have one of your little girlfriends buy you one," I tease, using my fork to cut another piece before bringing it to my mouth. I close my eyes to emphasize how delicious it is, laughing when I open them again.

He chuckles. "Maybe I will. You sound like mom, by the way. Remember when she used to say she ain't one of our little friends," he recites, mocking her voice.

I cackle, staring down at my plate. "Look at her now. She tries *real* hard to be one of our little friends."

"Be all in our business like she is a little friend," he continues, and I glance up at him.

"How is she, by the way?"

"She's good. Misses you. For real, though, she doesn't shut up about you," he complains, running his hand over his face.

"Not sure why when you're the favorite child."

He rolls his eyes at my griping. "They treat me differently because I'm a man."

"Uh huh. You're the favorite. It's cool, I accepted it a long time ago. Keep up." I shrug as I lick some frosting off my fork.

"Shut up, man. What's been going on in good old Texas?"

"This bidding war is moving slowly, as expected. But I have a lot riding on this…I'm just trying to keep my head up and my hands clean. That's all."

Fuck. Why did I say that? I don't need anyone worrying about me.

"And how's that going for you?" he asks with a quirked brow.

"It's been a challenge, but I am hanging on. That's all I can do."

"If you've got a problem, tell me. I'm serious, Dee," he says in a firm tone that sounds exactly like Dad's.

I don't respond, unsure of how to navigate this conversation, and it's not like I'm very good at lying to him. Darius can always sense when something is wrong with me.

He continues, "Need I remind you that the face of the brand *never* dirties their hands. That's what *I'm* here for."

"I find that funny, since you're the *preferred* face of Divin and there's blood on yours," I retort.

"My image is as important to me as cleanliness is to you, but any blood *I* spill allows for *you* to stay clean. You're welcome, Dee," he scoffs.

"How could I ever forget to thank you?" The sarcasm rolls so easily off my tongue.

"Dee, you never give it a damn rest," he huffs, like I'm ruining his high. "Smoke some damn weed and enjoy the day off. I mean it. Might fuck around and put you on a mandatory leave if you don't relax."

"You would not," I challenge, leveling him with a stare.

"I fucking would. Try me, Sis," he says with a smug smile.

"Fine. I'll open up your care package and see what it's hitting for."

"I can't believe you haven't opened it yet." He gasps dramatically, pressing a hand to his chest. "Texas *has* changed you."

"Shut up, punk," I mutter, taking another bite.

"My mama ain't raise no punks."

"She raised *you*," I taunt.

"You know what? Imma let that slide because it's our birthday," he jokes, and I'm faced with his smile. It looks the same way it did when we were kids.

"You're a fool. I miss you, Dare," I say softly.

"I miss you, too. You're always welcome home, you know? Could always hide out at my place to avoid Mom and Dad. I won't tell," he whispers the last part conspiratorially.

"Thanks, man. Enjoy your day. I love you," I say, taking another bite of cake.

"I love you, too, Dee. It's still *our* day, no matter what. See you soon," he says with a wave before the screen goes black.

Once I finish my slice and ice cream, I wander into my office to retrieve the goodies I've been ordered to indulge in. I open the door, and the care package from Darius waits on the floor.

Carefully, I slice through the tape to find an array of edibles and airtight jars of various strains, labeled with their names and benefits. Under those there are some of my favorite snacks and pre-rolled joints.

Always looking out for me, I think as I sift through the pre-rolleds to find an energetic hybrid to enjoy. Something calming for me to unwind, but not too much that I fall asleep.

I find a shaded spot out back near the pool and settle into a lounge chair with my Kindle and fire it up. I quickly silence my phone before getting lost in my latest read. The slow burn is *finally* about to heat up.

* * *

A WHILE LATER, I migrate back into the house to sprawl out on the couch. I've been devouring this book and the spice did not disappoint. I take a peek at my phone and am surprised to see just how much time has passed since I started reading. What is the saying? Time flies when you're reading smut or something like that?

"Motion detected. Motion detected. Front door camera," sounds from my phone.

I rise to my feet, reaching for the gun I keep in a small drawer on the side of my coffee table before I even pull up the camera feed. An unfamiliar blue car is parked in my long driveway, and two women exit, popping the trunk to retrieve luggage as they approach my door. As they get closer, I realize I couldn't be more relieved to see them.

Alora and Skye. Thank God.

The doorbell chimes, and my phone pings with the notification: *You have someone at your door.*

"Honey, we're hoooome!" They sing their arrival in unison.

"Hot and ready at your door," Alora says with a chuckle.

Pressing the microphone button to speak, I say "I'll be right there!"

I rush up the stairs, realizing I now have to stash the pistol in my other hand somewhere they won't find it. *Fuck.*

"Just a moment. Sorry!" I yell out, buying myself time.

Frantically I scramble to hide the weapon, shoving it inside a drawer in my home office. It makes me more comfortable to have one in most of the rooms, but I can't exactly explain to them why I would *need* to. I bolt back down the stairs, wondering if Scar is watching me run around like a headless chicken.

With a deep inhale that I hold, I wipe the beading sweat from my forehead then exhale. I open the door to welcome my friends inside, and between screams, they wheel in their luggage. Skye nearly tackles me to the ground once I'm in their reach, with Alora jumping on top of us. They take turns squeezing me in hugs, and their touch is healing.

I've missed them.

While random pop ups stress me out, my girls are always welcome. Lo flew in from Brooklyn and Skye from Houston. I couldn't be more relieved they're here.

"It's cute how you think we can't tell when you're sad, because you have your tells. So, we're here to get you away from work and outside to party," Skye says with a huff, pushing her hair out of her face.

"Now, where can a girl find a decent drink around here?" Alora interjects, her curls piled in a messy bun on top of her head.

"Or a decent man?" Skye adds with a smirk.

"I'll let you know when I find the men, but the drinks I can provide."

I give Skye and Alora a tour of the place and show them my spare bedrooms for them to settle in before I give them a tour of my room. The moment I swing the door open, Alora heads straight for my bed, plopping down.

Skye's eyes catch on a large vase of flowers waiting on my vanity that wasn't there before I left to get birthday goodies. A vibrant bouquet with florals in shades of pink, red, and purple.

I squint to focus on them, believing that it's the high and I am just seeing things. I must be seeing things.

Are those celosias? On a Thursday? Oh my God.

She climbs atop the bench and retrieves a note from the large bouquet.

FOR THE BIRTHDAY GIRL.
I HOPE YOUR DAY IS AS BEAUTIFUL AS YOU ARE.
CON AMOR, SCAR :)

"Ooh. Who's Scar?" she asks with a raised eyebrow.

My mind races for an excuse that would make sense, because I can't exactly tell the truth without them freaking out, can I?

Scar is a tall, dark, and chiseled pain in my ass.

"So, a funny story about that. I have a secret admirer," I try out, with a forced smile.

"Really now? Is it somebody from work?" Skye asks, her brow raised.

"I suspect it's someone on our payroll, and I'm the boss so nothing can happen anyway," I say with a shrug.

Good one! Not a complete lie either.

"Right, but celosias? Dee." she says dramatically, her face wearing an incredulous expression. "You *gotta* fuck him. At least once. I don't make the rules."

"I can't date anyone that's a part of my staff, so, that's a no for me."

"Bullshit. You've shit where you've eaten before, with—" She pauses, her lips forming a thin line. "I'm so sorry," Skye apologizes, her eyes wide.

Alora chimes in, breaking up the awkward moment. "That's completely understandable. Dee is a professional and has a lot on the line that she wouldn't throw away for dick."

"Thank you very much," I say, grateful for the save.

"So, when did it start?" Alora asks, staring expectantly at me.

"A few weeks ago."

Her brows knit, and she shares a look with Skye. I know that look. It's the *this girl is lying and thinks we must be stupid* look.

"What are you not telling us?" Alora asks, crossing her arms over her chest.

I'm too high for this shit, and I won't make it through this interrogation.

"Nothing. I don't know the guy," I rush out, wishing the conversation were already over.

"But he had flowers sent to your *house*. Not just any flowers either. Are you sure you don't know them?" she asks, staring expectantly.

"It's my birthday, dammit. I don't want to play a game of questions," I whine, now mad that they're ruining my high.

"Well, that's too damn bad, ain't it?" Skye says with a cackle.

Here we go.

15 / cherry smash & a chaser

César

9:38 p.m. | 26 minutes before 'the second incident'

So, I dragged my boys Emiliano, Anthony, and Tyler out tonight. I work so damn much that they asked if I was okay when I invited them to hang with me. I suppose I'm not, since this outing doesn't have a damn thing to do with work *or* taking time off. Deirdre is celebrating her birthday with her friends, and I'm keeping an eye on her. That's all.

Speaking of, the lavender dress she's wearing is hugging her lush curves in all the right places. The smile across her face is genuine, and for tonight, the sadness has dissipated from her usual demeanor. It's refreshing to see her beaming around those who make her feel right at home.

"Shots!" my friend Tyler yells out as he greets the hostess carrying a serving tray loaded with rum shots. "Man, I thought you'd bumped your head when you hit us up earlier," he teases.

"You look stressed. Here," Emiliano says, grabbing two shot glasses and handing me one.

"Yeah, what's gotten into you, C? You even dressed up. When's the last time you got some?" Anthony asks before downing his own. So much for "cheers."

If I told them why I came out, why I look stressed, and why I dressed up, the answer would be one name: Deirdre.

If I confirm that I am here tonight hoping to make a connection with a woman for sexual purposes, my constant staring will not be seen as weird but appropriate. Unless one of them realizes I keep staring at the same woman all night.

Tyler and Anthony have been my best friends for most of my life. I met Tyler back in grade school and Anthony in junior high. I met Emiliano in college when we were both studying criminal law, but for different reasons. He's an esteemed attorney, and I'm nosy for a living. He's also a Cartel prince, so of the three of them, he'd probably be the least shocked.

I know my friends are open-minded, and if I could tell anyone the ridiculous shit I've gotten myself into and never speak on it again, it's Anthony, Tyler, Emiliano, and *mi abuela*.

Abuela has always valued and cherished a good secret, while also enjoying *bochinche*. Nowadays she says, *"Tell me secrets. I'm old and need stories to entertain me in my grave."* Using death to guilt trip us into telling her our business is right on brand for her and not the least bit surprising.

"I mean, I wouldn't mind meeting someone tonight. It's been a few months and Tanya hasn't visited in a while," I lie, scanning the club as if I'm scoping the prospects.

Tyler scratches his beard before saying, "It's been a minute since you mentioned her."

"Tanya's a lovely woman and our arrangement has been nice, but I don't know. I think I want something more permanent."

Also, a lie. I don't want something permanent.

I'll admit, Tanya is great, but she doesn't keep me on my toes quite like my Doe.

"Y'all aren't exclusive, so if you ask me—" Anthony adds.

"But he didn't," Emiliano chimes in, cutting him off. "If the casual thing isn't working, there's nothing wrong with trying something new."

If only they knew.

"That's all I was gonna say, but he just had to get the last word. Lawyer shit," he says with a chuckle.

Tyler nods. "Agreed. You can date whoever you want. Tanya doesn't want a relationship, so why not?"

"Have your fun, *güey*. The night is young, and we're aging better than our classmates," Emiliano jokes.

"I don't know how with our demanding careers, but I agree."

"Ain't that the truth?" he adds, lifting his glass. "To César getting some tonight. Or whatever the fuck it is he wants."

He shrugs, and we tap our glasses together.

"*Salud*," we say in unison.

I tilt my head back and swallow the shot I'd been holding. I only make a twisted face for a moment. It's been a while since I've been out with my boys.

I spot Deirdre in the crowd again, and it seems she's been hiding from me. When she was distracted, I put her and her friends on my tab, ordered her a cherry smash, and tipped the bartender nicely. Asked her to use Divin whiskey only. A little nod to her family and her favorite fruit.

I shouldn't want her to know that I am here, but would it be so bad if she did? Yeah, she could see my face, but I'm starting to wonder if that even matters anymore with how many lines we've crossed from the moment we discovered one another.

She's making eyes across the floor at something or someone. Her finger lifts to beckon them to her and like a lost puppy, this guy drops everything for her call.

As he should.

I study their interaction with pure curiosity. It's unfamiliar seeing her around other men, and I don't know why it bothers me. I only know Deirdre alone and in professional settings, but this is new. I dig through my pockets for my phone, opening up our text thread, and my fingers fly across the screen to distract her. I tap send and watch closely, but she remains focused on him.

My jaw ticks at the sight of his hands on her body, as if

they've earned that privilege. I bet he's a pretty boy who's more concerned with himself than complimenting her. She *is* the main event and exudes that.

He's not a bad dancer, but I'm better. There's no *sazón* with this guy, and she needs someone who can match her energy.

It's apparent in the way he moves that he can't take control in the way she needs. He's rigid and uncertain, hesitant in his every step, and it's clear she isn't going home with him tonight.

She turns around, faces the crowd, and grinds her plump ass on him. A view I could do without seeing, but I can't look away now. His stupid grin widens as he takes in curves he isn't worthy of. I bet he thinks he's getting lucky tonight. Not if I have anything to do with it, I decide.

She can do better than this fucking clown. I shake my head as he palms her hips cautiously, failing to steer the wild ride that she is.

He has no idea that the meek act is a ploy to reel in what she *really* wants. Often erring on the side of caution when she craves small doses of danger and immense pleasure.

What if she didn't have to ask for it? What if this is *her way of asking for it?*

I wonder if she has any idea that I see what she's too afraid to vocalize. I worry about what her interests have awakened in me and if they'd exist beyond this case.

If I had her on this dance floor, she'd melt into me, following my lead and swaying that perfect ass to every tempo. I'd lose track of time getting lost in her with a possessive hold on her waist to leave marks for my eyes only. She'd be a needy, begging mess by the end of the night, desperate to be claimed before we even made it home.

A man who sees her for all that she is and wouldn't think of hiding her. *That's* who she deserves, not a goofy wallflower giving her a lackluster homecoming dance as if she's a child. She's a grown-ass woman with needs that can only be fulfilled by a grown-ass man.

As irritated as this guy makes me, Deirdre can shoo him all on her own. But I'm here if she needs assistance. I'd just prefer that she doesn't see my face, should I need to intervene.

I'm not proud of the texts I sent in my fit of jealousy, but what's done is done. I wouldn't be surprised if this is one of her games to provoke me.

If I react, she wins, but the night isn't over yet. I lie to my friends about using the bathroom and sneak off to the bar to ask the bartender to keep the cherry smashes coming as long as Deirdre asks for them.

They exit the dance floor after a few songs, and my stomach drops at the possibility of her leaving my sight. I zero in on her until they stop at the bar and she grabs a seat to rest.

The bubbly bartender speaks to her, and she begins scanning the room for me. The clown returns with water for her, and he's leaning in again, likely inviting her to his place.

She won't say yes. She has better taste than that. Plus, she has her friends visiting.

Her gaze tracks down as she searches her bag, pulling out her phone to take his number.

She won't be needing it.

After they part ways, I observe as he cuts through the dance floor to return to his section. The velvet rope lifts, and his gaze prowls the space, likely for another woman to attempt to seduce.

Good riddance.

I do something reckless as hell, continuing to dance over the line of impropriety like it's a mere suggestion. I get up from my seat at the bar, keeping her in my line of sight as I begin to follow them, maintaining a good distance. Anxiously waiting for an opportunity to approach her, because she thinks I won't. Normally, I wouldn't react or provoke a subject in a public place. Especially a woman. She could scream, fight, have me attacked or thrown out of this bar, but something tells me Deirdre Klarke wouldn't do that. Not to me.

If dangerous pleasure is her nightly craving, it'd be rude not to offer a taste. It's her birthday after all, and I promised surprises.

I am nothing if not a man of my word.

deirdre

10:04 p.m. | 'the second incident'

Even though I am always working since I moved to Austin, I asked my assistant Brian about the local nightlife and was recommended a spot we're sure to enjoy for girls' night. I hope this spot lives up to the hype, because I don't think I have it in me to bar hop like I once did, way back when.

We hit a bar downtown, and it has the perfect atmosphere. Dark, intimate, and the music is perfect. The dance floor is littered with sweaty bodies, unabashed and in love—or at least for tonight. Mild jealousy settles in my stomach. It must be nice to have someone to go home with, even for the night.

But enough of that. Let's not be a downer when the night is still young.

I escape the crowd and climb atop a barstool, suddenly overcome with the feeling that I'm being watched. A feeling I've grown familiar with, but tonight he feels more present. As if he's in the building right now.

What if he is?

My heart rate picks up at the thought of him watching me in plain sight. My curiosity piques as I swivel on the stool to search the crowded room for a similar build but come up short. If I can't even get a day off from being stalked on my *birthday,* I will be livid. There's *no* way he'd risk being seen without his mask.

Or would he?

Of course I wonder what he looks like beneath his mask, even going as far as wondering what's underneath his clothes. I won't pretend that I haven't dreamt about him or what those muscles would feel like on top of me. Because I have, *many* times since the break-in.

His gruff voice in my ear, pained and desperately encouraging me to let go, is a frequent thought, which I'm not ashamed to admit…to myself. I'll attribute that to my recent audio erotica and audiobook interests. Adding in the fact that it's been a while since I've enjoyed any type of attention from a man, and it's a recipe for lusting after my stalker.

Toys are amazing, but sometimes you just need rough, calloused hands on your body and piercing eyes staring into your soul as you succumb to their every grip, lick, and thrust.

Whew. These are not thoughts I should be having here or about him.

A melodic drawl yanks me from my fantasy as the bartender speaks, sliding a tumbler across the counter to me.

"A cherry smash. For you, ma'am."

"Huh?" I ask with knitted brows. I've been drinking amaretto sours all night.

I didn't order anything. Did I?

"From the gentleman over there," she adds, pointing to a now empty stool to her left. "Oh, well, he *was* there a moment ago."

She chews on her lip as she eyes me and leans in close, as if she means to tell me a secret. "Between you and I, that man was fine as hell. A face I'll never forget."

I stifle a laugh at her enthusiasm before responding, "If he was fine like that, I hope I see him too."

"You'll know when you do. Enjoy yourself, hun! Holler if you run into any trouble."

"Will do. Thank you," I add with a smile, returning to my friends gathered around a cocktail table.

"Girl. That man has been looking at you all night," Alora says into my ear, tilting her head toward a group of men seated in a VIP section.

Back in Brooklyn, when I'd go out with my girls, I wasn't usually the center of attention. However, since I've moved to

Texas, my full curves are greatly admired and appreciated. It's taking some getting used to, though, not that I mind it.

"Who?" I ask, whipping my head in that direction.

"Don't make it obvious, shit. Ol' boy over there." Skye jerks her head, looking even more obvious than I did.

When we lock eyes, he flashes a devious grin, and to make matters worse, he has dimples. He *is* fine, but I can tell by his build that he's not Scar, which leaves me slightly disappointed. He's tall and broad, but Scar is larger in stature and without a question could toss me around.

Nope. Let's unpack that later.

Another thought crosses my mind, a dangerous one. But it could be fun. If Scar *is* here tonight, a dance with this guy could bring him out of hiding, giving me a chance to see the man behind the mask.

Confidence swells in my chest, causing me to crook a finger and invite him over. I'm not sure where the bravery came from, but I'll blame it on dark liquor.

His brows shoot up, and his grin widens. My heart is racing in my chest as the velvet rope lifts and he starts toward me. My skin heats, likely from the alcohol or from the possibility of *two* sets of eyes on me.

As he makes his way across the dance floor, the girls squeal in unison, and I stifle a laugh because they're so damn silly. He greets me with a mischievous grin, closing the distance, and suddenly my phone vibrates in my clutch bag.

Could it be?

I ignore it, keeping my focus on him as he introduces himself.

"Hi. I'm Xavier," he leans in to say, speaking over the music.

"It's nice to meet you. I'm Dee."

His infectious smile widens, and I mirror it, peering up at him expectantly.

Skye shouts loudly enough for him to hear, "The birthday girl needs to dance."

"Does she now?" he asks in a smooth drawl, tilting his head

toward me with a look that makes my cheeks heat. He leans in closer so I can hear him better.

"Would you like to dance, birthday girl?"

"Yes," I say, giggling in his ear.

He takes my hand as he leads me to the center of the dance floor. I tuck the clutch under my arm and steal a peek at my girls, wearing knowing looks as they sip their drinks.

The song switches to an upbeat track with sultry lyrics, and Xavier's palm splays across my lower back, gently inching me closer to him as I take his free hand. He leads this song, and every time I meet his hungry gaze, I consider if a one-night stand is a good use of my time tonight.

When my thoughts become too loud, I turn around to press my ass against him, winding my hips to the beat as I scan the venue for any sign of my stalker. No luck, but the inkling of his presence intensifies alongside the buzzing phone beneath my arm.

A few songs later, we head toward the bar for him to grab himself another drink and a water for me. I'm having fun and he's sweet, but I'm now in the mood to climb into my bed. It's obvious we're not in college anymore, but it's even more apparent when I start yawning, and last time I checked my phone it was only ten at night.

Desperate to rest my feet in these heels, I grab a free seat at the end of the bar as he orders our drinks. One of his friends approaches, distracting him, and I search my clutch for my phone. But I'm interrupted when the bartender spots me, a knowing grin stretches across her freckled face.

"The guy from earlier came back and said to put whatever you want on his tab."

"You're serious? I ask, staring incredulously.

She nods assuredly. "Friends too, he said. Another cherry smash?"

"Yes ma'am."

"Coming right up," she shouts, turning away to grab a new glass and a bottle of Divin whiskey off the shelf.

"Some guy, huh?" Xavier asks in a hesitant voice as he reemerges.

"I have no idea. I'm just the birthday girl," I say with a shrug.

He smirks and meets my gaze, leaning in close. "That you are. How are you feeling? Would you like to head back to my spot?"

He's cute, but I just want to go home.

I shake my head. "I came with my girls, and I'm leaving with them."

"I respect that. Can I give you my number?"

"Of course," I answer, retrieving my phone from my clutch. I unlock it to find a number of notifications, and I rapidly swipe them out of view before handing it over to him.

He enters his number and saves it as Xave, flipping it to show proof.

"I hope to hear from you soon," he says, placing the phone back in my hands and holding onto my gaze.

"You will. Have a good night."

"You, too, beautiful." He winks and parts with a wave, returning to the section where his friends are seated.

Alora and Skye join me at the bar right as the bartender slides the cherry smash across the counter, and I tell my girls if they want something, it's on me.

"You're not paying for anything on your birthday," Skye argues.

"Someone said whatever we'd like to drink is on their tab. So, technically, I am not paying. My secret admirer is."

Alora raises a brow but proceeds to order a root beer anyway.

Skye excuses herself to the restroom, but we follow. The buddy system is an unspoken rule between us, like texting when you've made it safely to your destination. I'm itching to check my notifications in hopes that my suspicions were right.

I trail them down the dark hallway, and they step inside

when a recognizable scent captures me. Followed by a large hand gripping my waist, their touch resembles an open flame igniting my dress. I yelp as an erection presses against my ass, heat pools in my lower belly at the sudden intrusion.

I bite my lip as that familiar voice warns, "Doe. Don't make me chase you, 'cause you can't outrun me."

Fuck.

I still, my core clenching in response. As quickly as he appeared, he's gone, a cool rush in his wake.

Lust overtakes me, intwining with fear and stolen breaths. I imagine that grip on my throat, goading me to climax as he gambles with my life. I'd beg him to tap dance on my grave for that euphoric reward, and he'd oblige, anxious to redeem himself as a worthy partner in our dance with death.

The lion thinks he's won, but we're just getting started.

16 / stalker daddy

César

11:48 p.m. | 1 hour and 44 minutes after 'the second incident'

Tonight was risky, following her without some sort of disguise. Not to mention, I let myself get far too close. She is without a doubt a very attractive woman, and her insistence on driving me up a wall is entertaining.

I thought I was immune to her charm, but it turns out she's too damn good at drawing me in. Oftentimes without even trying.

Seeing her dancing with that guy infuriated me. I never considered myself to be a jealous man, but from what I've read in some of Doe's books, it can rear its ugly head with the right person.

She is a single woman enjoying her life, and who am I to stand in the way of that? Especially since I can't be the man she needs.

While my ability to hide in plain sight serves as a superpower in my career, it's been nothing but a hindrance in my love life—or lack thereof.

Is my loneliness to blame?

No, there's no excuse for my behavior tonight. So as I get

cozy on the ride home, I type out several apologies, but can't decide on the right words. Rather than sounding like a *mamao,* I give up and leave it for tomorrow.

"I can't believe it isn't even midnight yet," I say with a yawn.

"Being the designated driver is easier when the drunks don't need to be babysat and are sleepy by ten o'clock," Emiliano responds from the driver's seat, chuckling to himself. He allowed himself the one shot and sat back, checking his phone from time to time.

My phone vibrates in my pocket, and I fish it out to see notifications of Deirdre texting me back to back. My palms are sweating as I refrain from opening it. Since I'm not sure how I'll react, I won't risk having to talk about her or our current situation.

"You good, man?" Emiliano asks as he slows in front of my house, turning to look at me once he parks the car. "You seemed on edge most of the night."

I shove my phone back in my pocket and decide, *fuck it.* If I tell someone, it may as well be the man who has plenty of secrets of his own. Some of which he'll take all the way to the grave.

We have this in common.

"It's nothing—" I stop myself from the lie that I've even tried to convince myself of. "I kinda met someone." The words feel foreign, giving weight to something I've forced myself to deny for weeks now.

"Really?" His eyebrows shoot up, and when I give him a look, he clarifies, "No, I just don't know how you found the time."

True.

"I met her through work," I start, staring at him as I await his secondary questions. I know they're coming.

"Through work or…*through work.*"

I nod at the latter, and he snorts a laugh.

"You know—"

"Yes, I know, *baboso,*" I interrupt, using an insult he's often referred to me as. I don't need to be reminded of how fucked up this can get.

"As long as you're careful," he reminds me, leaning his head back, fatigue in his voice. "Get your ass inside. I gotta work in the morning."

Shit, so do I.

We say our goodbyes, and I step out of his car, my phone pressing against my thigh like it's reminding me that I have messages waiting for me.

My hands shake with excited anticipation as I approach the front door to let myself in. I kick off my shoes, loosen my belt, and undo my shirt. I don't even make it to my bedroom before I unlock my phone.

From Doe: 3 unread messages

From Doe: 1 movie

I tap on the screen several times to see what she sent me. A *video*?

DOE

You've got some fucking audacity.

Anyone could've seen you.

I'm glad you were jealous. Mission accomplished.

I press play on the video, and it starts with her fresh face wearing a flirty smile and giggling to herself from her balcony. She's wearing a purple silky robe, and her cleavage has me drooling.

"I'm high right now," she says, pausing to take a drag from a joint, jealousy rearing at the sight of her plump lips wrapped around it. She releases the smoke in a steady stream before speaking again.

"You wouldn't know that I get *really* horny after I smoke. Sadly, there's no one to take care of me. And what you did at the bar before you left wasn't very nice. What happened to southern hospitality?" she asks, mocking me with a chuckle, and takes another drag.

I resist the urge to respond because she can't hear me. I try to ignore how hard I am from hearing her talk like this. But it's fruitless, knowing it'll end up in my hands.

"It's not polite to leave a girl soaked and needy like that. Have you no manners?" she chides with a deep chuckle that makes me palm my dick through my pants. "Now, I have to go and take care of what *you* did. I hope you're proud of yourself, Scar."

She hums, ashes the joint, and steps back into her room, holding the camera out in front of her.

"You know, if I didn't know any better, I'd think that you like me. Do you like me, Scar? My dad is firmly against fraternization. He'd kill you for fucking me. Does that only make you want it more?" she taunts, her voice breathy and low.

The camera follows her movements as she holds it in front of her face, navigating her bedroom in the robe that's loosening with every step she takes.

She halts, leaning forward to prop the phone against something, and I'm distracted by her peaked nipples and full breasts swaying before the camera. They're seconds away from being set free as that flimsy belt struggles to conceal the deadly weapon that is her generous frame.

Coño.

The view widens as steps back enough for me to see all of her, pulling her straightened hair back into a messy bun before lowering to her knees to retrieve a box from under the bed. She returns to her height, setting the box on her bed, and sifts through it. She busies herself, setting aside a pink case and something green that I can't make out.

What is she doing?

"Hmm. Oh well. It's not like you'll act on it anyway. You're too scared of my father, and that's a shame," she tsks. "If you're a professional and I'm wrong, you *won't* watch me through that camera as I make myself come. You'll turn that feed off and go to bed like a good boy, won't you? Or not."

She shrugs, untying her robe to reveal a lacy purple lingerie, and I groan in response. My dick is painfully hard as she struts toward the camera, her gorgeous face in view as she holds the phone up.

"And if I'm right, you'll watch, hoping to hear your name on my lips, and come with my name on yours. You can, *if* you want. *Or* go be a good little spy for my father and rest," she says playfully with a pout. "Goodnight, Scar."

The recording ends with those doe eyes staring into my soul.

Fuck.

This video was sent twenty minutes ago. I shouldn't pull up that feed to see if she's touching herself. I shouldn't. Even if she said I could. My mind wars with my dick, desperate for relief and to watch her squirm as she chases her pleasure.

A need that I inspired. Whenever she starts her meticulous routine of setting the mood before she gets herself off, I check out. Cutting the cameras and giving her privacy. Not once have I even listened to her moan or whimper, despite my curiosity. But tonight is different. She knows I'm here and is inviting me into this fantasy. A peek won't hurt, and the birthday girl gets what she wants.

I review Deirdre's bedroom feed, finding her in bed with spread legs, writhing beneath a vibrating wand. Soft buzzing fills the room, quiet enough to not disturb her guests. Her moans are hushed and breathy in an attempt to keep this session private. I envy the vibrator teasing her needy clit as it lures every moan from the depths of her throat.

Quickly, I undo my pants, freeing my hard dick, working it in my palm as precum drips down my shaft. My palm smooths over the tip, dragging the wetness down the base as I fuck my hand to the sight of her grinding against that wand.

I imagine I'm on top of her, earning those whimpers as I drill her into that mattress, slow and deep while she moans into my mouth.

I'd fuck her like a dirty little slut while she fights the urge to scream about how good her secret admirer feels. Pain and pleasure etching on that pretty face as she stretches around me. Training herself to take me like a good girl.

She'd whimper as my tongue traced every inch of her perfect body and fist the sheets so hard she'd break a nail. I'd cater to her swollen clit and toy with her until she begged for relent. She'd clench around my dick at every hint of praise and degradation.

She comes with lifted hips, hushed curses, and my name on her tongue. Pleasure seeps from her aching pussy and puddles around her.

She just fucking squirted for me.

My orgasm is immediate at the sight of her making a mess, and I don't silence my moans when it hits me. She earned them, and I wish she could hear what she's done to me.

I observe her closely as she shuts off the soaked toy, bringing it to her open mouth and licking it clean like the good little actress she is. I'm awestruck and hard all over again.

My Doe would think twice about taunting me since she'd be too cock drunk to think of anything but being filled.

I would coax her curiosity out of hiding just to devour it. If I unleashed her dark desires, she'd be out of commission for a week. She has no idea how badly she'd crave me after a meager taste.

Tonight the deer and lion are tied, spent, and satiated. Tomorrow is a new day.

17 / cuéntame

César

9:21 a.m. | 3 days after 'the second incident'

I was ten minutes early for this debriefing with the Hales and sat waiting for them to arrive on their usual bullshit. That's not what I'm currently faced with as we sit here. There was an awkward energy in the room after they entered, and it's only grown since. No bickering, and they were surprisingly on time.

Dara arrived first with her usual shyness, but Dax's demeanor is different from the norm. His arrogance has taken a backseat, and stress is drawn all over his face. Makes me wonder if they took my advice and called their uncle before they got themselves in the middle of a war with the local crime families.

To make things more uncomfortable, I trade in my stoic face for a fake smile and start the conversation. Picking up where we left off, I slide a folder across the table for them to review. The deafening silence urges me to speak faster in hopes of getting out of here quickly.

Abuela has dialysis this afternoon, and while I don't look forward to it, I do enjoy the time we spend together and would much rather be there than here.

As the briefing concludes, I ask if there's any further information they're interested in moving forward with, and it'll be prioritized before our next meeting.

Dax clears his throat and folds his hands in front of him. "Thanks, mate. This is all very good, but I have something to add before we part."

I lift a brow and remain seated, gathering all my documents as I brace myself for whatever bullshit he's about to share.

Let's hear it, Dax.

"We spoke with Uncle Theo. He disapproves of our idea to buy them out in hopes they'd leave town."

Of course, he does.

Dax continues, "This expansion, regardless of who wins the property, benefits the community and brings more jobs. Theo informed us that the Klarkes are known for hiring more people of color, making up half of Austin's population and…we do not," he says looking down, lips forming into thin line.

Mmhm. Knew that, too.

Dara interjects, "I did some research on Regina and the Delvecchios casino empire. They *also* employ more women, people of color, and veterans than other *white*-owned casinos in the state. I understand that the locations she currently oversees are Black owned, and those are rare."

"Yes, they are rare. I've never seen a Black-owned casino," I concur.

"Regardless of their personal beliefs, he emphasized that in order to do business in a community, you must immerse yourself in it by getting to know the people you serve. We could do a better job of that," she admits.

"Mmhm," is my only response.

"He didn't say the Klarkes deserve the property more, but he didn't have to," Dax adds with a shrug. "Theo also said that we don't stand a chance going against them and would be doing ourselves a favor by aligning with them instead."

Makes me wish he was still in charge.

I nod in agreement. "That's exactly what I expected him to say. How's he doing, by the way?"

"He's good. Happy. Looks younger since he stepped down."

I chuckle with a shake of my head. "I bet."

It's good to hear he's still the voice of reason in this family, but I'm not yet convinced they'll take his advice. Or at least Dax won't.

I suppose if they do step on a landmine with any of the Austin locals over this deal, it's a good thing I have other clients with deep pockets.

* * *

"TELL me something about your week. Find anything fun on a stakeout? Is that what you call them, or are my shows lying?" *Abuela* asks, her frail hands clutching a pencil and a word search book.

I glance over my shoulder to find her dark-brown eyes waiting expectantly for an exciting story and her long, silver locks coming undone in a braid that rests over her shoulder.

I'd make one up if I needed to, just to hear her laugh.

"No, *Abuela*. I don't do stakeouts," I inform, standing to fix her hair. "We call it recon, and when we follow subjects, we are tracking them." I take it down, using my fingers as a comb to loosen any tangles and braid, crossing each section over the other until I tie it off at her ends. We can thank Mariana and all the tea parties we had with her dolls as kids for me knowing how to do a basic three-strand braid.

She rests her hand on mine, expressing her gratitude, and I press a kiss to her temple before returning to the recliner beside her.

I think to myself about my recent cases aside from Deirdre's. "I unfortunately found a subject that has a second family. Telling my client was rough. It was giving telenovela."

"Chucki! ¡Cuéntame! I can't watch my stories when I'm dead," she adds with pleading eyes.

"Of course that's the case that sparked your interest," I say with a cackle.

Drama from my work stories serves as her entertainment until it's time for her telenovelas and she drifts off to sleep soon after they end, as always.

Once I hear her snoring, I drape a knitted blanket over her and grab my phone to check on Deirdre. I don't have anything set up at her job to monitor to avoid setting off any alarms when it comes to her family. It's a family-owned operation, after all. So I've limited my hidden cameras to her home only, for now…and a GPS on her car. For safety, of course, and my peace of mind.

Speaking of, I did something new when I last visited her home after the birthday incident. My usual routine of eliminating tasks has become a common dance, with me dodging her housekeeper and landscaper. But I took it a step further this time.

I wasn't there for long, but I dropped off some prepared meals, swapped the water for her flowers and…stole something. It was impulsive and reckless as hell, *pero* like, she's to blame, not me.

When I was leaving her bedroom, I spotted dirty clothes in the hamper and threw the load in the laundry. While I was separating colors from darks, I found that matching lingerie set she wore the other night.

What surprised me most was instead of tossing the thong into the wash, it ended up in my pocket. *As if by magic,* I think with a smirk.

But I wonder if she'll notice.

Mami didn't raise a thief. She also didn't raise a man to invade a woman's personal space.

So what *Mami* doesn't know, won't hurt her.

I've done more than I'm proud of and haven't been the most respectful of her boundaries. The most egregious prior to the panty stealing was hacking into her home surveillance system and wire-tapping her devices.

Truthfully, she could benefit from being more careful and stop using the same damn password for everything.

In my true caretaker fashion—at least when it comes to Doe—I know I've got to do something about that.

Note to self: Tell her to update her passwords.

18 / bullseye

Deirdre

5:28 p.m. | 'the third incident'

Please don't make this weird, I think as I place my driver's license in the hands of the attendant. I'm not sure if I'm reminding myself or hoping he doesn't. I don't miss his crinkled brow or the double take as his eyes flit back and forth from the card to my face.

I can see those wheels turning and offer a soft smile to confirm his suspicions.

I am one of those Klarkes.

He nods and returns my identification, clearing his throat. I glance at his name tag. Jeb.

What kind of day are we about to have, Jeb?

"Alrighty. What're you in the mood for, ma'am? Bullseye or silhouette? Handguns, rifles, shotguns?" he asks, pointing over to the guns displayed behind him.

"Paper bullseye, and I brought my own, actually." He looks at me expectantly, and I clear my throat before I say, "A nine millimeter handgun."

"Ahh. Good one. Need bullets?"

"Yes, please?"

He nods assuredly, reaching beneath the counter to search the case below.

"115 or heavier?"

"115 FMJ is perfect," I glance around as I try to speak low enough so only he can hear.

His brows raise, and his hands feel around the case before landing on the target and my preferred brand of ammo. I nod, confirming my selection, and he returns to full height, setting the bullets and rolled poster on the counter.

"You know your stuff."

"I do," is all I offer in response.

He announces the total, and I reach into my handbag, thumbing through bills. I hold two twenty-dollar bills out for him.

He hands back the change, slides the box of ammunition across the counter, and watches me gather my things.

"Thank you, Jeb. Have a great night," I say softly, placing my earplugs in my ears as I catch his response.

"You, too, darling. Holler if you need anything." He tips his chin in the direction I'm meant to go.

I offer him a small smile and follow where he gestures toward the entrance to the range.

It's spacious with many vacant stalls, and I walk past several, trying to decide which one I'd like to use once I secure my things in the locker room.

I slow to a stop when a familiar scent permeates, causing my brain to damn near short-circuit. My heart rate elevates, and I speed forward, not bothering to search for the source.

I'm not fucking stupid.

Whether it's him or not, I'm here to shoot. I enter the locker room and quickly put my personal items inside.

On the way back out, I glance at the mirror, taking a moment to adjust my earplugs and the protective goggles I brought with me. Content with my safety equipment, I make sure my gun is secured in the holster on my hip and exit with my ammo and poster tucked under my arm.

The furthest stall calls for me, and I set down my things. It's not my first time at a gun range, but it has been a while. Regina's father, Angelo Biavati, is an arms dealer with shooting ranges back home. It's where Dad taught us how to shoot.

Long before I became so against the ways of the family business, I used to love shooting with him. The pause before each shot felt like the world was standing still. But things are different now.

The weighted pistol rests in my hand as I load the magazine, cock it, make sure the safety is still switched on, and set it back into my holster. The target stares back, waiting to be used, as I will the thoughts in my head to cease.

My chest rises and falls as I part my feet, take my stance, and retrieve my gun.

I stretch my arms out in front of me, focus my aim, and pull the trigger, only to miss the bullseye. By a lot. For some reason, my shots are veering left, nearly missing the poster entirety. I release a breath, roll my shoulders back, and try again. Another miss. I double tap this time, and my grouping is a fucking disaster. I'm all over the poster, at this point. Everywhere *but* the center.

Fuck.

Frustration boils in my gut at my rustiness. Clearly I wouldn't stand a chance against an attacker at this moment. And my couch can vouch for that.

Darius's voice repeats in my head, *"It's not like you're willing to catch a body. You're not a killer, Dee."*

I don't want to be a killer, but I don't like being seen as weak either.

I blink away the tears threatening to fall, securing the weapon as I try to clear my head.

My thoughts are halted when a finger taps my shoulder and startles me. The cologne I've become far too familiar with fills the space, causing me to look back and glance over at the source with annoyance.

It's an aggressive scent, but oddly comforting, reminding me of thoughtful gestures and a smart ass mouth. My brow lifts as I turn to assess him from head to toe.

He's a tall man, wearing a dad cap and sunglasses. With a smile, he motions to his earplugs like he's taking them out. His facial expression seems foreign, as if he's as out of practice smiling as I am when it comes to shooting.

I study what's visible of his face; deep-brown skin, a full, neatly trimmed beard, and a deep scar through his upper lip.

Scar.

I take in his broad shoulders, big chest and arms. He could be ex-military, a retired football player, or an undercover Fed.

Except my family would *never* hire a fucking Fed.

Good job, Dad, I think to myself.

Whether he's been hired to spy or protect me, at least he's sexy.

Fuck me.

His brow arches over his sunglasses, and he smirks down at me.

Shit. Did I say that out loud or does he have a wire recording my thoughts?

Is that even possible?

I rush to apologize, but we speak over each other. The deep timber of his voice sends a chill over me, bringing me back to the other night when it was in my ear.

"Sorry to bother you, Miss. I didn't think you heard me." He pauses to lick him lips. "I couldn't help but notice your form and wanted to offer some tips, if you're interested."

Miss? So he's going to act like we don't know each other.

Cute. I'll bite.

A breathy laugh escapes me, lacking humor. "Thanks, but I—"

"Are you a new shooter?" he interrupts. "Sorry to cut you off again. My manners escape me when I'm passionate about something."

I bet, you nasty mother—

I shake my head to keep me from falling down that rabbit hole.

"If you plan to mansplain shooting, I'm not interested. Not a rookie, by the way. Just out of practice," I tell him, trying not to roll my eyes.

He narrows his eyes as he works his jaw.

"You're not hitting the target, because you're shifting your weight to your heels. It's your balance, the aim is fine. Try again, but stand a bit taller and widen your stance to shoulder width. Don't be afraid of your weapon. You're the one in control. You're always in control," he orders in a gruff tone, eyes now on my feet.

I'm not a fan of obeying, but something about his voice makes me want to. I rationalize that I'm here to practice, so I may as well take the advice. I follow his instructions, positioning my body as directed.

"Chest out. Good g—" he stops and coughs.

What was he about to say?

"*Coño*," he says softly. "*Bueno*. Now, shift your weight forward. On your toes. You want to be able to move if need be while maintaining your balance and control. That recoil'll fuck you up if you're not careful. May I?" he asks, tilting his head toward the target.

I nod, giving him permission, and he approaches with caution, as he should. I am the one holding a gun right now. He settles behind me and palms my waist for a moment, and his touch singes me. As if he can feel it, too, he rips his hand away before I can react.

He has a surprisingly calm presence, despite how annoying he can actually be. When his touch graces me again to straighten my arms, I stay focused on my form and aim at the target.

"How's that feeling?" he asks, his voice a near whisper.

When I don't respond, he leans in closer and blows on my ear, sending heat to my core.

He's diabolical.

"What cologne is that?" I blurt, ignoring his question.

For a moment, I think he's going to ignore it, but he responds, "Dark Embrace by uh—I can't think of his name, but he's a liquor heir."

"Like me?" I ask, cutting him off.

"Stay focused," he urges in a firm voice, releasing me from his hold. He puts distance between us and expels a long breath behind me. "Go ahead. Take the shot."

I remain on my toes and fire continuously, emptying the mag. Time slows as the bullets pierce the target, hitting the bullseye until it's a gaping hole.

A relieved sigh escapes me as I switch the safety on and tuck the pistol in my side. When I turn behind me expecting him to be there, he's nowhere to be found.

That motherfucker.

I tap the button to retrieve the poster, tossing it in the trash once I'm back in the locker room. With a huff, I snatch my things from my locker and dash out of the building.

Wearily, I peer around the parking lot, pressing the panic button on my key fob to draw attention to myself in case he's waiting for me, but it seems like I'm alone.

I open my car door, peering into the backseat, and it's empty, as is the passenger seat.

I slam the door shut and settle in, turning on the car before I whip out of the parking lot. That was him, without a doubt. A scar on his lip and that sexy fucking cologne. My hands grip the steering wheel roughly as I unpack this encounter.

That motherfucker knew exactly why I was there and offered tips on how to successfully shoot him.

At this point, I need to use my family's resources to put some pieces together. I'll just need to be vague.

"Call Angie," I state, and the Bluetooth dials my cousin.

Angelo Jr.—Regina's older brother—is a consigliere, and if anyone is a vault in this family, it's him.

"Deeee. Haven't heard from you in a while. How you doing?" His jovial greeting fills every crevice of my car. I turn the volume down as I head home.

"I need you to look into someone for me," I say, focusing on the road.

"What happened to your fucking manners? You greet someone when you call them," he barks, his New York accent is very thick.

He's not *actually* pissed, but he's half Italian and was raised to be far more polite than I was, apparently.

I huff, "Hello, Angie. I need you to look into someone for me."

"That's better. You got a name, date of birth, or plate number?" he asks, keys clacking in the background on his end.

"I don't, actually, but I do need your help."

"Are they local? Work in the area? Gimme a physical description," he suggests.

About that…

"I don't know what he looks like. His face is always covered," I confess in a low voice as the click of my blinker fills the space.

"What? The fuck do you want me to do, then?" I wince at the incredulity in his tone.

Fuck it.

I think of something else I need to know.

"Um, is there anyone assigned to look after me in Austin?"

"Yeah. A couple of guys, actually. The Piñeros. Regina's people. Is anyone giving you trouble?"

"Not exactly, but—wait. Regina hired them? Not my dad?" This may not be the information I called for, but it's definitely enlightening.

"Nah. Uncle El says he's backing off. So, Gi stepped in. The guy you're asking about. Do you like him or is he a problem?"

he asks. "Cause this is different, cousin. The Piñeros don't fuck around. We can't just take one of 'em out like we do in our city."

Fucking Gi.

"Um. I don't think he's *that* kind of problem. He's pleasant, but annoying. Since Regina vouches for them, he must be all right," I reason, more to myself than Angie.

"They're good people from what I've heard, but the Cartel goes by a different set of rules than we do."

Ya think?

"Yeah. I get that, but the Cartel thing makes me nervous."

I really don't understand that. How can I want to go legit and fuck around with somebody in the Cartel? I literally can't.

His tone softens as he says, "Look, I can hear the wheels turning in your head. Do me a favor and don't do anything stupid. Get me a phone number to trace, an occupation, or a car make and model? I'm good, but I can't pull something from nothing. So, help me help you, okay?"

"Okay."

"Promise me you won't fuck him before I do a background check?"

"I promise," I lie. "I'll get more information and send it to you."

"Right on. Love you," he says.

"I love you, too, Angie."

The line disconnects as I pull into my garage. I don't waste any time shutting the door behind me and walking inside. I peel off my clothes on the way to the shower, thankful I live alone, even if I have an audience. When I finish, I trot around in my robe and resume where I left off on my latest audiobook. I'm soon distracted by my phone lighting up with text messages from him.

SCAR

I didn't follow you, I promise.

Lie again.

SCAR

Seriously, I go there whenever I need to blow off some steam after a long day.

I tried to leave you be, but you're a terrible shot when you're anxious.

I've never seen bullseye posters with couches on them but one of those might help. 😜

You want to help me be a better shot so I can do more than clip you next time?

SCAR

You could've done it right there and didn't.

Don't tell me you're having second thoughts?

🤔

🙄

SCAR

Speaking of thoughts...What did you imagine me doing when you came the other night?

This man is an absolute idiot, and I don't know how to respond to that. I had a feeling he watched me, but hadn't mentioned it until now.

Go fuck yourself, Scar.

SCAR

That's not what you said earlier. Lol

I cannot help the chuckle that escapes me at how ridiculous this man is. I mean it, I'll miss his stupidity when he's gone. My phone chimes with another message.

1 attachment from Scar.

He wouldn't send a selfie, but still my heart races at the

possibility. My index swipes to open the thread, and it's a photo of him in his balaclava.

A familiar sight, however, it's rolled up to his nose with a pair of...I zoom in to make sure my eyes aren't deceiving me, because that *can't* be panties in this man's mouth. Surely, not *the* panties I haven't been able to find recently.

Except those *are* my panties.

Oh fuck.

Heat rushes over my body, and I clear my throat to snap out of it. The other night was a one-time thing, and I can't let him think it'll happen again.

I can't have a relationship with this man. I don't even know him, and the last thing I need is for a man to derail me again. I feel somewhat better that he's one of Regina's guys, but what if he's more murderous than she is?

Another text rolls in, grabbing my attention and withering at my restraint.

SCAR

I wish they were the ones you're wearing now,
but these will do. Goodnight, Doe.

I know what I'll be dreaming about.

You're a nightmare.

SCAR

Keep telling yourself that, mi beba.

I set my phone on the nightstand to charge, draping the blankets over myself when it hits me that I do sleep better when he tells me goodnight.

I'd rather not read too much into that, but if the circumstances were different, maybe we could've had a shot. *If only.*

19 / sisqo & sancocho

César

6:41 p.m. | 3 days after 'the third incident'

It's been a few days since the gun range incident, and while stalking is my job, I don't know what the fuck I'm doing when it comes to this woman.

The other night at the shooting range was unplanned, but I impulsively approached her—while she was wielding a weapon. Practicing her aim for next time, I'd assume. And here I thought we were starting to hit it off.

First she shoots me, then comes with the name Scar on her lips, though I wish it *was mine,* but I'm the bad guy once again. I accept that I probably took it too far with those texts and the selfie. Reasonably, I've taken the hint and stayed away for the past few days.

I've been surveilling from my car and phone, at semi respectful distances, and may have changed my mind about hacking into her webcam at work.

Sometimes, I still find myself waiting outside her window. I'm playing with fire, but I've never encountered a flame more tempting than this.

I've been spending time at my parents' today and have made good on my "no work on the weekends" rule, until *mi abuela* kicks me out of the kitchen and boredom strikes. Curiosity floods my mind, and I tell myself a quick glance at her feed won't hurt.

I pull up the app and zero in on the movement in her kitchen. She appears to be having a normal day, wiping down her countertops and gathering cutting boards. Deirdre squints at her iPad, scrolling with her knuckles as she follows a recipe online for *sancocho*.

Sancocho*? Is she trying to seduce or poison me? Maybe both.*

Her hips sway as she gathers all her ingredients on her spacious kitchen island. Curious about what she's listening to, I fumble through my pockets for my AirPods, and to my surprise she's listening to "Thong Song" by Sisqo.

Haven't heard this one in a while.

It quickly reminds me of the very thong in my nightstand that I used to taunt her the other night.

Plantains, yuca, potatoes, corn, squash, and seasonings crowd around her as she moves to the sink to wash and chop her vegetables. Afterward she focuses on the stew meat and chicken thighs, cleaning and patting them dry before dicing into small cubes. She scrapes them off the cutting boards to brown in the stock pot on the stove.

She seasons it correctly, pausing to retrieve the *sofrito* I left her in the fridge, and I smile to myself as she adds it in per my instructions.

Good girl.

My breath catches when she disappears off camera, returning with the *pilón* I gifted her. I study her as she uses it to mash the potatoes and yuca to thicken the base. My brow lifts in suspicion, because that tip is not in the recipe she's using.

Let me find out she knows some other Puerto Ricans.

I'm mesmerized as she dances around the kitchen cooking, and intrigued that she is learning to make it after I mentioned it, and using my gift.

Deirdre is seemingly unaware that I can see everything in her search history, but she isn't naive and certainly has put two and two together.

And judging by the gun tucked into her waistband, she's awaiting my return. Possibly even baiting me with this little cooking show, *if* she suspects I'm watching.

She thinks I'm stupid enough to come running because she makes some Puerto Rican food? Maybe she's right, but it's more fun to prove her wrong. Especially after her little stunt with the video.

She said it herself, *"lions like the chase."* I've never been one to entertain a game, but this one keeps me on my toes. Maybe that's her game. Being prey is a farce, only to reel you in for the kill.

Is it so bad that the thought entices me? There's pleasure in chasing her, but what if she succeeds in catching me first?

I wonder if the pain she'd inflict would be slow and savored or quick and painless. And after all that's transpired, if she'd be the one to end me or leave it to someone else.

Should I survive all that she is, will I ever be the same? Do I even want to go back to the way things were?

* * *

Saving some sancocho for me? 👀

DOE

I planned on it. I made too much to eat all by myself.

Who taught you about the plantain balls? You got other Puerto Ricans or Dominicans in your life?

I thought I was special. 😔

DOE

Lol, Scar. I'm from fucking Brooklyn. Of course I know other Puerto Ricans and Dominicans.

Though, you hold the crown of the ONLY one who pisses me off on a daily basis.

I'll proudly wear that crown.

And Thong Song? Really? Funny that you're wearing one right now.

DOE

Now, wait a minute. That song is a certified classic that aged incredibly well.

Next, since you insist I'm wearing a thong, what color is it?

Not purple. 🤪

DOE

Fuck you.

Whenever you think you're ready for that, mi beba.

DOE

¡Nunca!

Well, that was sexier than just saying no. Gotta turn that never into siempre.

DOE

I'd like to see you try.

Say no more.

20 / normalcy announcement

Deirdre

9:15 p.m. | 30 minutes before 'the fourth incident'

A FaceTime from Alora lights up my screen, and I swipe to answer and am greeted by her rosy face and glassy eyes. As if she's been crying.

"What's wrong, Lo?"

"You know how I said I wanted to try again? The treatments finally worked. I'm pregnant, Dee," she shrieks, waving a pregnancy test in the air. "I'm going to have a baby!" Her eyes well with tears as a soft smile stretches across her face.

I gasp. "Lo, it's really happening."

"You're going to be the best auntie ever!" she exclaims.

"Seriously, I can't wait. What did your moms say?"

"I still have to call them, but I had to tell you first since this wouldn't have happened without your help," she says, her voice breaking.

"Don't mention it, babe. I hate that I'm not there celebrating with you," I respond with a pout.

"Hey, you're chasing your dreams right now. I know how it is. Come down whenever you can. I'll be right where you left me, just pregnant!" she squeals.

I chuckle. It warms my heart to see her so happy. She's going to be the best mother, and I can't wait to meet the little nugget.

"I love you. Go call your mamas and tell them I said hi."

"I will. I love you, too. Thanks, Dee," she beams before the screen goes black.

My best friend is having a baby, and I miss her so much. I miss home so much. It's moments like these that really suck. Watching everyone live their lives without me, because I'm so set on proving a point. Is it even worth it when I'm missing out on such important moments?

I swipe to open my calendar app, checking if my schedule allows for a weekend trip back home, when the tears I held in on the call finally burst, dripping onto the screen. The emotional dam I've worked so hard to build breaks, and steady streams fall, soaking my shirt.

This is a reminder of how different our lives are. It gives me hope that if IVF worked for her, motherhood could happen for me someday. But reality hits like a ton of bricks, reminding me of the danger I'd be bringing a child into. I'm embarrassed for mourning something I haven't even experienced, and it makes me feel like a bad friend.

We both struggle with infertility and have had these conversations because they're normal. Jealousy isn't the word for it, because I am *so* thankful that she's pregnant. Proud, as if it were me.

At the same time, it would be incredibly selfish if I started trying, due to circumstances out of my control. Alora lives a normal life, free of crime, stalking, break-ins, and threats.

She has a career of her own and is fit to parent in ways I'm not. I can hardly make up my mind, am too stubborn to ask for help, and since I don't exactly have the best support system, what kind of mother would I be?

The dream of legitimizing dealings with Divin have always been rooted in the future I hope to have.

My childhood was *unique*, but still privileged, so I know

better than to complain. My normal wasn't like Alora's normal. She was adopted as a baby to a lawyer and a therapist who were well-off. Really good people. We both faced challenges from the outside world because of how our parents were judged, but people didn't fear for their lives when *her* parents entered a room.

They went to work every day to provide her with everything she needed and fully supported every dream she's ever had. My parents ensured we never had a need for anything. Never missed a recital or sporting event. They were always present and affectionate. So, at least we shared *that* kind of normal.

At sixteen, she got her first job, working at a clothing store in the local mall. Whereas I was groomed to lead the organization and cleaned my first crime scene when I was sixteen.

Cici needed to run an errand after church one day. I waited in the car with her driver who told me to cover my ears to drown out the noise, but I still heard the gunshots. She was on the phone when she returned, and I'll never forget her words.

"Klarkes don't deal in bribes. We don't exchange gifts for threats. Money is expendable, and once you offer it, it's spent. Death is a debt paid, and I like my debts paid in full."

She was so calm, that same eerie calm that Regina has. If anything, she was more upset about the blood spatter on her Sunday's best than the life she took. Cici then instructed me on how to properly dispose of a body, because I was old enough to "get my hands dirty." Darius was a bit younger when he got his start. It changed us and not in a good way.

Sometimes strangers would come over and we'd be introduced, only to never see them leave the way they came. I remember the screams of agony coming from the basement, the sounds of my dad throwing punches on victims, the blood residue in the sink, and that same mirrored calm on his face.

The scent of bleach still makes me nauseous, and I refuse to own a home with a basement. Kinda funny that I have a thing against basements while working with whiskey. Though I'm not afraid of basements or whiskey cellars, I don't enjoy spending a lot of time in them.

I recall Dad holding my hand as he'd walk me into school with wrapped knuckles. When I'd ask about him being hurt, he'd say, *"I'm okay, baby girl. We were just boxing."*

Sure, Daddy. Sure.

There were plenty of hushed conversations after dinner that we weren't allowed to sit in on because it was "grown folks business." Except I'd listen anyway, because I'm so nosy that I couldn't help myself, only to overhear things I wish I could scrub from my mind.

I don't want my children to live in similar conditions, and I remind myself *that's* what I'm fighting for. *That's* my dream, and if I stand a chance at parenting with minimal trauma, I need to pull this off. Probably would be best to find a therapist, because bottling things up makes for violent explosions under pressure, and I am *always* under pressure.

So, should I fail and prove my family right, I'll concede, accepting leadership on their terms. Because I'm honestly tired of screaming into the void, and it might just be safer to own a dog. The hope I'm holding on to dwindles a bit each day, but I need to believe in something or I'll lose my fucking mind.

21 / masks on

Cèsar

9:45 p.m. | 'the fourth incident'

Nothing could have prepared me for the sight of Deirdre like this, and I hate it. She just got off the phone with her friend, Alora, who shared she is pregnant, and she seemed so happy, but is now sobbing in bed with her face in her hands. Her shoulders shake as she succumbs to the emotions, and I'm not sure what to do or if I should let her know I'm here for her.

This is a private moment, and I'm already invading her space by watching, texting her will only make it worse. There's nothing wrong with crying, it's healthy. And however she needs to express herself, she should.

I want to comfort her. It's difficult for me, as a fixer, to see a problem and just leave it alone. As much as I intrude and have taken interest in finding solutions to her problems, I'm tempted to check in anyway. I understand that may only make things worse, but Deirdre is alone in more ways than one, and I can't just sit here without offering to help.

My thumbs scurry across the keyboard as I go back and forth testing various messages to send and delete. I'm unsure of the right words to say but am overcome with the need to say something.

Hey.

You can tell me to fuck off, but can I come over?

Her sobs are halted by the sound of my messages, and she turns to search for the phone she tossed in the mess of sheets. Once it's in her hands, she sniffles and unlocks it, staring at it for a moment before her thumb hesitantly hovers over the screen. I decide to push her, which could end badly *or* help lessen the awkwardness of what's happening with us right now.

You're taking a little long to type two simple words. "Fuck" and "Off"

She snorts and begins typing.

DOE

Fuck off.

Come over and do what?

Drink your tears, of course.

Or hold you, but I understand how weird that sounds.

DOE

If I said yes, which would be incredibly stupid, could we agree on something?

Easy answer. I agree.

DOE

You don't even know what the question is. 😂

If I invite you into my space, will you respect it, keep your hands to yourself and never mention this to my family?

I know you don't know me, but you've gotta give me more credit than that.

Why would I mention this to your family? It doesn't make me look good either.

DOE

Because it's your job to snitch on me. Fucking rat. 😂

I'm sure this would be a good thing to report.

That couldn't be further from the truth, but at the same time, I can't exactly share the real reason I'm here. I'm certain I'll come to regret this later, but for tonight, I'll pretend that another little white lie can do more good than harm, when used appropriately.

I promise, I won't mention it.

You have my word.

DOE

Fine. You can come over, BUT you're not staying the night.

I could use some company, that's all.

My keys are in hand right away, jingling as I lock up and beeline for my truck. I settle in and fire off a response before she feels embarrassed and revokes the invitation.

I'm on my way.

I turn up my music to drown out the thoughts telling me to turn around and go back home. The drive is a blur until I turn onto her street.

Coming to her home without sneaking around is…different. Do I pull into the driveway or park on the street as usual? Do I ring the doorbell or let myself in? Could she be waiting on the other side of the door to finish the job, or does she really want to talk? Of course, I didn't consider any of this until now.

But if I am nothing else, I'm a man of my word. I choose to park in her driveway. *As an invited guest should,* I think, killing the engine and almost getting out. *Shit, my mask,* I remind myself before I grab one of my many balaclavas in the glovebox and pull it down until it rests comfortably on my face.

I flip the sun visor in front of me for a good look in the mirror to ensure my face covering doesn't reveal any part of myself that I don't wish to be seen.

I'm standing in front of my truck when I text her.

Here

My heart races as my eyes follow those three dots blinking on the screen. She can change her mind, and I'll respect it. There's nothing remotely normal about what is happening or could happen here.

DOE

I'm upstairs.

Please remove your shoes at the door.

Yes ma'am.

Reluctantly, I stand at the door while my mind and body war with each other. My mind wants to give it more thought, but my body disagrees as the key turns the lock.

Slowly, I open the door and peer around, fully expecting an armed woman awaiting me, but finding an empty entryway instead. Darkness greets me as I shuffle into the foyer, removing my shoes and setting them aside.

The house is silent, and the staircase seems a mile long. Of all the times I've explored her home before, this feels uncertain. As if the space I could navigate blindly in is now uncharted territory, every step feels fatal and ominous, each footfall potentially bringing me closer to my demise.

I stop outside of her bedroom and knock softly, awaiting her invitation. "You can come in," she says, defeat in her voice, followed by a sniffle.

I twist the doorknob to find red-rimmed doe eyes staring back at me. She beckons me over, patting a space on the mattress beside her, and I oblige. The bed sinks beneath me as I stretch my arm behind her, and to my surprise, she scoots closer.

A relieved sigh escapes her plump lips as she settles into my chest, enveloping me in her decadent fragrance of cherry, jasmine, and vanilla.

We sit in a comfortable silence as I rub small circles on her back. For a moment, this feels natural, as if it should always be this way. I've never known what it feels like to come home to someone after a long day and embrace them. If it's anything like this, I have been missing out.

"Can I ask you something?" I ask, cutting through the silence.

"No," she answers abruptly.

"Alright then."

I expected that and won't ask for more than she's willing to share. It's a wonder she even wants me here right now.

"Scar?"

"Hmm?"

"Do you have children?"

"No."

"Do you want them?" she inquires, peering up at me.

"Yeah, but my career makes that difficult. Takes up so much of my time and wouldn't be fair to a kid. That's why I don't even have a dog. What about you?"

"I do, but I am having a hard time accepting that may not be possible," she says softly.

"And why is that?"

"Many reasons. Like the man who stalks me," she quips, pulling from my grasp to sit up.

I miss the contact immediately, as if her touch soothes me in the same way. *Enough of that,* I think, returning to the conversation with a comeback in hopes of lightening the mood.

"I disagree. If a baby is what you want, I could provide. So, *that's* not a valid reason," I tell her with a chuckle.

Her hand playfully slaps my arm as her laugh swells. An intoxicating sound that I vow to add to my daily responsibilities during my time with her.

Make her laugh, if nothing else.

"You are really annoying. You know that?"

"I could say the same about you," I add with a quirked brow.

"Feeling better now?"

She nods and clears her throat. "I am," she says with confidence. Whether it's false, I'm unsure.

Oh. The job is done, then. I should leave.

"Well, I'll get out of your hair, then," I state, shifting off the bed and heading toward the door.

"Wait," she says, stopping me in my tracks.

"Yes?" I turn to face her.

"Would you stay? I don't want to be alone tonight," she murmurs before quickly adding, "I understand if you have plans."

I almost never have plans.

The words fly out of my mouth. "I can stay. Don't think I should sleep in a mask, though."

"I agree. You might suffocate to death."

"You'd like that wouldn't you?" I tease.

"I don't know anymore," she replies, avoiding eye contact as she rifles through her drawers.

She retrieves a pair of pajamas and disappears into the en suite.

"Make yourself at home," she orders, followed by the sound of running water.

"I'll be back," I call out.

She pokes her head through the doorway with a toothbrush in her mouth. "Where are you going?" she asks around a mouthful of toothpaste.

This is all so domestic and not at all what I expected the night to be.

"I need my overnight bag," I inform her, pointing my thumb toward the door.

"Okay," she offers her garbled response and ducks back into the bathroom to resume brushing her teeth.

Fresh air greets me as I walk back out of her house, and I hope I come to my senses soon, because once again my mind and body aren't on the same team. It's not like I wasn't hugged enough growing up. Thankfully, I am surrounded by affection, but she triggered something that I'm not ready to part with just yet.

So, I open my trunk and sling the duffle bag over my shoulder to return to whatever the hell this is with Deirdre. She ripped the mask off tonight, and she's not at all what I'd expected her to be.

Strolling through the house a second time is easier than the first. The air is still heavy, but the energy is lighter.

I enter her room to find her in a bonnet and lavender silk short set, setting out her outfit for tomorrow morning. Her generous curves and smooth brown skin are on display, and I avert my gaze when she catches me staring.

This is the most unprofessional thing I've ever done.

Awkwardly, I slip past her to head to the bathroom, shutting the door behind me so I can get ready for bed. I often get hot at night and opt out of a shirt, but I don't think being both shirtless and maskless is a good idea in this situation, so I put on a white tee and some sweats. Thoughts run rampant through my head as I brush my teeth, so many questions I don't have answers for.

When I step out of the bathroom, I witness her doing the nightly routine that I've familiarized with through a screen. She pulls the curtains closed, circles the bed to unmake it, and climbs in on the left side. Usually, she lies in the middle of the bed, but with company, she appears to prefer the left side.

Noted.

The silence makes me nervous. The entire night feels like I've stepped on a landmine. Accompanying her to bed, even innocently, *will* be something I pay for.

Here I am doing it anyway, regardless of consequence.

I blurt, "I was thinking of a way to not scare you whenever I drop by. I'll do a *coquí* whistle whenever I'm around, so you'll know it's me." Anything to offer her even a semblance of comfort.

"What's a *coquí?*" she asks softly, tilting her head.

"It's a frog that's native to Puerto Rico. Their mating call is a whistle, and they sing at night. I love hearing the *coquí* frogs whenever I visit."

She watches intently as I whistle, giggling to herself after a failed attempt at it. I can't help but smile at her, and it's a good thing she can't really see it.

She is absolutely beautiful and can't whistle worth a damn.

"You can take off your mask. I won't look at you, if that's what you're worried about," she suggests.

"And how do you suggest I avoid being seen?" I question, not fully trusting that she'll manage to keep her eyes closed.

She holds up a finger and turns to sift through her bedside drawer.

"This," she states, holding up a pink silk eye mask.

That is *a good idea.*

"Okay, but don't expect anything kinky to happen with that blindfold. I know you have *unique* interests," I tease, climbing in beside her.

She rolls her eyes playfully. "Says the peeping Tom."

"Call me by another name again, and I will take the couch," I threaten, but there's no bite to it.

"Anyways," she says, pulling the sleep mask over her eyes,

turning opposite me. "Goodnight, Scar," she says through a yawn.

"Goodnight, beautiful," I whisper, yanking off my balaclava in the dark room.

Dios mio. It feels amazing to be out of that hot-ass mask. I glance over, fully expecting her to be stealing a glimpse, but she hasn't moved. I tug the blanket over my legs and turn to face her back. Instinctively, my arm wraps around her waist, bringing her closer. Soft snores interrupt the silence, and I smile to myself as I drift off to sleep.

Tonight, the deer wins, but the lion cradles her in his arms as consolation.

22 / losing game

César

10:16 a.m. | the day after 'the fourth incident'

Staring across the table at the Hales after spending the night with Deirdre Klarke has me on edge. I've answered all their questions without sweating. Except the deeper ones, of course.

Last night, something shifted, I fear. Her mask dropped and so did mine, in a way. They hadn't requested for me to be as *hands on* as I have. Literally.

I'll admit I have a tendency to romanticize things, but after this case is closed, what if there's a possibility she could forgive me? For the stalking, flirting, *and* eventual blackmailing. Should she develop feelings for me, dropping the bomb that I'm only here to blackmail her would be the ultimate betrayal.

Yeah, not happening.

We can't have a future after this, and if I suggested it, I'd be deserving of whatever she gave me. I'd expect a punch, drink to the face, or another gunshot wound. But since Deirdre has a flair for the dramatics, I'd say all of the above.

The Hales have a few questions about Regina Delvecchio that I quickly answer, carefully curbing the obvious ones about her missing husband. Assuring them that while there's speculation that she played a role in his disappearance, there's no evidence to confirm this.

But of course, that doesn't matter to them since they're always looking for a reason to be afraid of non-white people. I could probably shout "boo" at this table right now and scare the fucking shit out of them.

Not going to do that, but it would be entertaining.

By the end of the meeting, I'm tasked with acquiring more information on Regina, since Deirdre really is the "good girl" she claims to be on paper.

Her cousin, on the other hand, is an interesting character who keeps herself very busy. The intel I could pull on her alone would draw this case out while unfortunately providing enough information to lengthen these meetings. Which I am not looking forward to.

And the way they speak about Regina bothers me. As if she isn't a human being but an irrational killing machine. I don't disagree with her being a killer, but they shared that same kind of implication when presenting Deirdre's case and they couldn't have been more wrong.

A thought crosses my mind that makes me question if I have truly lost it. The deep dive into this family has me wondering what really happened to Cidro Delvecchio. Billionaires don't just drop off the face of the earth, *especially* not ones in the mob.

What if I proved that I'd be useful to her family? It could be what saves me from a similar demise as her ex, and after all, she's convinced that I'm *already* working for them.

If her family did hire me, I'm certain I could find more answers through skip tracing and finally give them some much needed closure. Something to keep in the back of my mind should I need it after the case, because I'm not certain I'll agree to another assignment from the Hales moving forward.

My mind flits back to last night with Deirdre. She didn't have to tell me anything that she didn't want to. Her allowing someone to be there for her was out of character for her. At least for the character that she often stars as.

I did manage to get some sleep while holding Deirdre in my arms. She stayed in the same spot and didn't appear to have left the bed at all.

Still I ran out of there before sunrise.

The risk was already too high, and I needed to hear myself think. I don't like that I ran out on her, but maybe she'll understand. I sent her a text that I needed to come into the office early, but she hasn't responded.

She was vulnerable, and so was I. Maybe it would be best to just leave it at that.

I've fucked up and have found more ways to do so on a consistent basis now. At this point, I should speak up and remove myself from this assignment. That would be the right thing to do. I'd just need to come up with a good excuse. But it always comes back to money. I *really* need that money. My family really needs that money, and that's why I'm here now.

What if I withdraw myself just enough to put a pin in this? I can do that, right?

That's easier said than done until I'm rewarded with a flashback of her crying and my stomach drops. I can't be the cause of more tears.

But becoming involved with a subject is not only frowned upon, it could end my career—or even my life—if I'm not careful.

I'm aware of how ridiculous it sounds to even consider a possible future with the woman I've been stalking and lying to. Knowing I'll need to stay far away from her after this is all over unsettles me. That idea seemed a hell of a lot easier before I knew what she felt like in my arms.

We both have our secrets, but at this point, I'd do anything to keep them between us. Because if they got out, we both stand to lose what we've worked so hard for.

Deirdre will have a backup plan and a career even if she loses this expansion opportunity, but if I lose my private investigator license, I don't have an alternative at the ready to ensure my family will be taken care of.

That's reason enough to distance myself in preparation for the end of whatever this is.

23 / washed & dried

Deirdre

6:32 a.m. | 'the fifth incident'

The first three days of my period are the exception to my beliefs around murder and violence. I can overlook a lot of things when I'm on my cycle.

Might even volunteer to do shakedowns as a way to blow off steam *if* I participated in that side of the family business. Unfortunately, due to my moral high ground, I settle for being bitchy instead.

SCAR

Good morning, Doe. 😊

It is *not* a good morning, more like terrible. I woke up feeling like I'd been hit by a semi-truck that backed up and ran over me enough times that I became one with the pavement.

"Fuck," I grunt.

I could hardly get comfortable and spent most of the night tossing and turning. Not too long after I'd finally fallen asleep, I woke up before my alarm to discover that my period came a few days early. All over my white sheets.

Love that for me.

After a slew of curses, I clean myself up, strip the bed, and toss everything into a giant pile on the floor. I scoop up the pile and start for the laundry room, nearly tumbling down the stairs with all the bed linens.

Fuck this.

I chuck the bundle of linens at the foot of the stairs, leaving it for later. Thankfully, Flora is off today, so I don't have to worry about her stumbling upon it. I'd prefer to clean up my own mess and plan to, just not now.

Begrudgingly, I stomp back to my room, make the bed with fresh linens and climb in, wrapping myself in the blankets. My head is pounding, my back is in excruciating pain, and the cramps feel as if I am being clawed from the inside out.

I slept so wild that I have no idea where my bonnet is, and I hope it isn't wrapped in that pile waiting downstairs. I doze off, later awakened by my blaring alarm, reminding me it's time to start my day. My hands fumble around for the phone and the sound is coming from under my bed.

Lovely.

I flick on my bedside lamp and crawl out of bed, following the sound to discover my bonnet lying right beside it. My finger taps the screen to shut off the alarm, and darkness absorbs the room when I switch off the light before securing my bonnet onto my head.

Welp. I guess I'm up now.

As much as I hate to do it, I have no choice. My team will live, and I will too if I start giving myself a break. Nobody should have to be around my miserable ass today. I am calling off.

Alert the media.

I pull up my text thread with my assistant, informing him I won't be in today and that he'll need to lead the meeting in my place. As expected, he's concerned, and I assure him I will be fine and am taking a day or two to catch up on rest.

Then I fire off a text to my brother, so my absence is recorded. He responds immediately.

DARE

Period or you sick?

It's none of your business, boss.

DARE

Ah. Period.

Do you need anything?

Nah. I need more sleep.

And pain relievers, but I've got some.

DARE

Take all the time you need, Sis.

We shall go on.

Thanks. I love you.

DARE

I love you too. I'll call later.

Darius must've been onto something when he threatened to place me on a temporary leave, because my cycle heard him and said, "bet."

For once, my curtains are shut, and I couldn't be more thankful. It's dark enough in here that it looks like it's nighttime, and that's exactly what I need to go back to sleep. If I'm not working from home, the least I can do is catch up on sleep and my latest read.

Before I forget, I list the groceries I'll need to restock on to get through the next few days. And set a reminder to order takeout, because I am not cooking. I roll over, yanking the blankets over my head, and drift off to sleep.

* * *

A PUMPING HEARTBEAT sounds in my left ear, waking me up. Scar's cologne envelops me, and I'm convinced I'm still asleep, but I blink my eyes open to find that I'm lying on his chest. A large hand rests on my lower back, the other holding my e-reader.

The title atop the screen reveals it's a why choose novel. One of the *filthiest* ones in my possession, and here he is just eating it up. I'm a why choose girlie, and have no shame about it.

My eyes trail downward, and the outline of a thick erection steals my attention. A *very* thick erection. In gray sweatpants.

Of course, his dick is big. It better had been with his fucking attitude.

While this isn't the worst sight to wake up to, I am not in the mood for his antics and prefer to be left alone as much as possible during my time of the month.

Curiosity overtakes me, and I try to peek without moving my head, hoping to sneak a glance at an unmasked Scar, but no luck.

What is up with the mask? I doubt he's unattractive, so what is he hiding?

I break the comfortable silence, glancing up as my head rests upon his chest. "Scar, why are you here?" I ask, sleepily.

When his whiskey eyes return my gaze, there's a softness in them that makes me feel less annoyed that he's broken into my house yet again. Let him tell it, he's a guest.

He's a charming pain in my ass.

"First off, I have ten minutes left in this chapter, and they're about to fuck," he says, seriousness in his tone. "She has *three* holes and there are *five* guys," he informs me, using his fingers to emphasize each number, and I resist the urge to laugh. "I'm invested and need to know how this is going to work."

"I can assure you they make it work and it's *very* hot."

"No spoilers," he scolds. "Secondly, good morning to you, too. Thirdly, you didn't text me back *or* go to work. Then I saw you nearly broke your neck on the stairs, so I rushed over to check on you, but you were sleeping."

I stare incredulously at him, unsure of how to respond.

"And lastly, I washed *and* spot treated your sheets. They're in the dryer now. Groceries and takeout are on the way. *De nada,*" he adds.

"*Gracias.*"

"I could teach you better Spanish than that, but you'd have to be a good girl, and you're not," he teases, booping my nose.

"I could show you what a good girl I am, but you'd have to stop breaking into my house and you won't," I mock.

"If you don't want me here, change the locks, Doe," he challenges.

Maybe I don't want to keep you out, I think.

"You're annoying," I say with a deep sigh.

"*¿Tú sabes? Deja la jodienda,*" he mutters under his breath.

"*Qué?*" I ask with a cackle.

A chuckle rumbles through his chest. "I said, 'stop fucking with me'. Because I'm trying to read and you're insulting me. Now, if you don't mind, I'm going to finish this chapter. Then I'm going to take care of you."

"Why would you do that?"

He places a finger to his chin through the mask, as if he's thinking. "Deirdre?" he asks sweetly, looking into my eyes.

"Hmm?"

"*Vete a dormir.*"

I stare inquisitively. "*Dormir* means sleep."

"Yes, it does. Do it," he advises while adjusting my bonnet.

"Fine," I resign with a pout. "Only because your chest is comfortable."

"I know. Now, please let me read my smut," he says, splaying his hand on my lower back and pushing me closer.

He kills me. Now it's his *smut?*

He's lucky I'm exhausted. I settle back onto him and start dozing off moments later.

* * *

"I'D LIKE to run you a bath before I go. Do you like your water at a temperature that compares to *hell*? Most women do."

I try to hide my disappointment that he's leaving, but he's got a life to get back to.

"Now, Scar, I do like my water hot as hell, but I'd be a little jealous if I learned you're drawing baths for other women. I thought I was special," I say in my best southern accent.

He chuckles. "That wasn't bad. You are special, Doe. And I do draw baths, but only for *mi abuela*. She's my best friend, and I take care of her as much as I can," he informs me, bending over to plug the tub.

Wow. It is possible for him to be even more attractive.

I steal a glimpse at his ass and avert my eyes before he catches me in the act.

"She's lucky to have you."

"Thanks," he says, and I wish I could see if he smiled or not.

He places his hand under the running tap to check the water temperature, wincing as it heats up.

With a step back, he wipes the water onto his sweats and faces me. "I can confirm that the water is underworld hot. I hope it meets your expectations."

He squats down, opening the under-sink cabinet to retrieve a container of Epsom salt that wasn't there before. His large hands twist off the lid, taking heaping scoops before adding them to the running water.

I tilt my head curiously in question as he returns the container below the sink.

"It's for your cramps," he tells me, shifting to shut off the faucet. "I read that it could help. I hope it does."

He asks me to give him a moment and shuts the door to the en suite. I gather pajamas to change into, setting them neatly on the bed.

"All ready," he announces, opening the door to reveal a candlelit bathroom. Dim and cozy, exactly how I like it.

"Oh, wait," he gasps, like he's forgotten something. "I

warmed this up in the dryer for you." He returns with a folded terry cloth towel, placing it on a nearby stool with my e-reader atop. "And I thought you might want to read."

My heart swells at his attentiveness, and I'm unable to hide my smile. "Thanks, Scar."

"I'm glad you like it. I'll leave you to it," he utters with a nod and closes the door.

I undress, tossing my clothes in the hamper, and carefully step into the clawfoot tub. My hands grip the sides as I lower myself, and hot water caresses my achy muscles as I submerge my body. A relieved sigh escapes me as I rest my head back.

A light knock raps on the door, I hum and sit up, not bothering to hide my naked body.

It's nothing he hasn't seen before. He doesn't have to admit he accepted my invite to watch. The stolen panties confirmed it.

Scar opens the door a crack, standing in the doorway as he asks, "How're you feeling?"

"Better. Thanks for today," I add, meeting his gaze.

"Anytime. Do you need anything else?"

I shake my head in response as his dark eyes drink me in, and I bask in it, smirking to myself.

He clears his throat. "Goodnight, Doe. I'll lock up."

"Goodnight," I sigh, sinking deeper into the tub.

Dare I say, I was reluctant, but I thoroughly enjoyed his company today. As much as I argue that I don't need saving and can take care of myself, he still insists on being here.

He cooked, ordered groceries, and did the laundry unprompted. All because he wanted me to take it easy.

Even brought me this portable heating pad that resembles a fanny pack. It looks strange, but it's so helpful.

Still, he hung out here all day with a mask on and refused to share why he even wears it. I'll admit it's weird, but it's growing on me.

24 / skye daddy

Deirdre

8:16 a.m. | 5 hours before 'the sixth incident'

Skye Daddy!!

I need a book rec. Preferably an audiobook.

SKYE DADDY

Heyyy now! That I can do!

What are you looking for?

A dark romance. Maybe mafia or stalker?

SKYE DADDY

The fact that you willingly read mafia romance is hilarious to me. They're not triggering for you?

Sometimes, but I remind myself it's fictional.

SKYE DADDY

Stalker...hmm.

Spicy or Mild?

Spicy! You already know! 😂

SKYE DADDY

I'm so glad you said that because I have got the book for you!

A golden retriever that posts masked thirst traps online stalks one of his top followers.

STOP. Sign me the fuck up!

Send the link!

SKYE DADDY

On it, Sis!

She follows up with a link; I click and purchase immediately. I'll be diving in after my morning debriefing. Curious as to whether or not it's good for me to listen to something like this as someone who is currently being stalked. Only one way to find out.

25 / daddy downer

Deirdre

8:52 a.m. | 5 hours before 'the sixth incident'

I'm dreading the catch-up work that comes from being out of office, but secretly looking forward to being left alone while I settle in. There's a new proposal waiting for me to review, and I will be indulging in a new audiobook while I lock in.

From the moment I step foot inside the distillery, the usual energy is off. Everyone has their heads down, and I brace myself because I have no idea what I am walking into, but I wouldn't be surprised if I've earned another drop in.

Dad's been rather quiet lately, and while Angie mentioned he's been wanting to back off, I don't buy it. He *never* lets go of the reins when it comes to me. I haven't seen Dad since I moved here, and I'd like to avoid him until I have good news to share.

Then again, with how unpredictable my father can be, I must stay ten steps ahead so he never catches me slipping.

I hope that Darius will give me a heads up beforehand. My brother has the luxury of being a free bird who has earned his trust. Regina is the spitting image of Cici. And then there's me, the odd one out.

It's not that I don't love this family or being a part of it. I'm grateful for our history and understand how hard we've worked for all we have. I'm not naive to the sacrifices we've made for success or survival, nor am I embarrassed. So my family has buried some skeletons along the way, who hasn't? Except when civilians say "skeletons," they don't *actually* mean bodies.

But we do.

The closer I get to my office, the looks on everyone's faces tell me all I need to know. Visits from my family *really* kill the mood around here. My guess is Darius, Regina, or Dad. My money is on the latter. I'm not sure why anyone needs to check on me now that Scar is here studying my every move and likely sending daily updates to them, even if Regina's the one who hired him. Surely his updates go straight up the pipeline to my parents.

I'm greeted by an awkward silence the moment I step off the elevator, and I brace for impact. The Klarke on the other side of this door is gonna ruin my fucking day. I take a deep breath and turn the knob to find none other than my father seated at my desk, wearing a hopeful smile that has indeed ruined my day.

"Hi, Daddy," I say, attempting to sound excited.

"Hey, Dee," he croons, getting up to wrap me in a bear hug. It's a far cry from the abrupt phone call we last had. But this is the cycle. He hovers, we get into it, he comes crawling back after my mother catches wind of it, and then it starts over again from the top.

His deep baritone voice is soothing as he holds me tight, bringing me back to moments when I was a child and he still cherished the softness within me. It's the same softness he now wishes I didn't have.

"I miss you so much," he whispers, pressing a kiss to the top of my head.

I want to ask him if Mom sent him to make nice, but I already know the answer.

"What are you doing here? Where's Ma?" I opt to ask instead.

"Getting straight to it, huh?" He chuckles, stepping back to say, "Your mother stayed back. It's just me. I told her you'd be disappointed."

We stand there for a moment, and I finally find the nerve to ask, "She sent you down here, didn't she?"

"I know that look, Dee. Believe it or not, I'm not here to give you a hard time. I was in town to sign off on some things, and hoped I could take you to lunch before I flew back. Are you free this afternoon?"

He avoids answering, but I know.

Mom can't force him to be the father she wants to be. That's probably why she sent his ass here alone to grovel.

"I can be," I sigh, trying to go through my mental checklist to make room for someone who couldn't even call in advance. "I'm playing catch up today, but I'll have Brian move some things around."

After hinting at my workload, I maneuver him toward my office door, my hand on his upper back. He nods, stepping out in time for me to catch some of my staff averting their gazes.

Sometimes it's easy to forget who my father is.

Elgin Klarke is no ordinary man, nor is he the face you wish to see before closing your eyes for the final time. Or in my case in my office.

To me, he's my grumpy dad who's still so in love with my mom that it feeds the hopeless romantic in me. He hates everyone but her *and* us, and he's proud of it.

My parents are polar opposites in every sense of the word. My mom is to blame for my gentle heart. I attribute my mother's calm demeanor to spending so much time around plants.

Plants absorb energy, release it back into the world, and breathe life into us. My mother is no different, a true breath of fresh air and balance for dealing with a personality as strong as Dad's.

Not to mention she could salvage *anything,* nursing it back to health with love and attention. Even her smile could mend the cracks in a broken heart.

So it makes sense that not only is she able to rein in the powerful Klarke patriarch, she also has the power to get his ass on a flight to make nice with his daughter.

I shut my office door behind him and mutter, "Thanks a lot, Mom," under my breath.

12:15 p.m. | 60 minutes before 'the sixth incident'

The waiter brings us our meals, and I wait until he's out of earshot before addressing the elephant in the room.

We don't discuss the family business around civilians.

"Alright. Let's talk shop and get it out of the way."

He unravels his napkin, eyes fixated on me as he sits up straighter. "Deirdre, we don't talk shop over meals, and that isn't why I asked you to join me."

I resisted the urge to call my mother and ask her why she sent him here with his tail tucked between his legs, but now I want to tell her to come and get her husband.

Instead, I twirl my fork in the pasta and opt to play nice. "What did you want to talk about?"

"How are you adjusting here?" he asks while slicing into his filet mignon.

Sorry, Dad. We're talking shop during this meal whether you like it or not.

I sigh. "I'm doing okay. I've always loved this area. Here, I feel important and optimistic in a way I don't back home. My input has value with this team. I don't share many updates on this venture, because if there isn't a win to share, it's not worth celebrating." *To you all,* is the part I can't say out loud.

He chews slowly; eyes that were once staring at his steak trek up to meet mine. And when he parts his lips, he slides his speared steak into his mouth, rather than engaging in this conversation.

Don't say anything, Dad. It's not like we were having a serious conversation.

I huff. "Tell me why you trusted me to lead Divin through an expansion in another country, but won't support me doing it here? The success of the cognac launch had *nothing* to do with Lawrence. I volunteered to spearhead that project to get away from him."

By the time I'm finished, my fork is pointed in his direction and I have to remind myself that we're in public. I take a breath, waiting on his response.

He gently sets down his utensils, wipes the sides of his mouth with his napkin, and breaks his silence. "Dee, I—" He takes a beat, exhaling. "I am damn proud of what you accomplished in France. You'll notice I haven't denied any funding for the bid, nor did I give you an issue on partnering with Gi," he reminds me, leaning back in his seat.

I take a sip of water, debating whether or not to air out my other grievances, and decide why not. Since he wanted to fly here unannounced and fuck with my workday, let's take it all the way there.

Fuck it.

"I know Regina offered that contract out of guilt, not because she believes in me. I'm grateful for the opportunity and exposure for our brand, but it was busy work to shut me up. If that was the goal, she succeeded."

He tilts his head as he assesses me. "Baby, I don't like hearing that you feel this way, but I can assure you that you earned that opportunity. As for Regina, I have no say in how she handles her business. She does whatever the fuck she wants, and the only person who could level with her isn't here anymore," he says with a frown.

We don't talk about this, so the fact that he let it slip into our conversation has me smoothing my napkin over my lap and staring down at it as I try to find the words to say.

Maybe hurt people hurt people. And even though I wasn't in

love with him anymore, it still broke all of my trust in her. I miss the trust more than I miss him.

"I know. I don't think I ever looked at it that way, like we're both grieving," I murmur, meeting his gaze again.

"What happened with Lawrence," he starts, pausing to consider his response. "I know you didn't want *that* for him, but an example needed to be made. Do you understand? He hurt my daughter and stole from my family. I'd order that hit again, and he was lucky Regina let him go out with some dignity, because I wouldn't have been so kind," he adds, keeping his voice low.

He didn't have a lick of fucking dignity, and damn sure wasn't deserving of kindness.

Frustration builds in my gut, and I ball my fists in my lap in an attempt to hold my tongue.

"But I got accused of it, *not* her. They walked *me* out of Divin headquarters in cuffs, Daddy. I've never been more afraid in my life. She hasn't even fucking apologized for it," I lean in to whisper-shout.

He rubs his jaw. "Now, I'm disappointed to hear she hasn't even apologized. Nobody thought it would come back on you, and it shouldn't have. You had a solid alibi and were released quickly. Thanks to the lawyer she called in. Uh—what was his name?" he asks himself, snapping his fingers as he attempts to refresh his memory. "Piñeros. Emiliano Piñeros. That's it."

"Piñeros? Why does that name sound familiar?" I glance at the ceiling, willing my brain to remember.

"Oh, they're looking out for you down here. Have you met them yet? Good people."

"Dad. Seriously?" I shake my head, urging him to get back on track.

"As I was saying, signing off on your ideas isn't the same as showing up. I never intend to make you feel stifled or silenced, and for that, I am sorry. You're my gentle child and thrive with TLC. You take after your mother in that way. Those damn plants," he says as he chuckles. "I love you more than you even know, and I worry about you. You're so different, which isn't always a bad thing. But I'm relieved to hear that you're happy here."

I pat away the tears threatening to fall and clear my throat. "I love you, too. And as much as I miss you, can you at least call before you drop in? You scare my staff," I tell him before I snort at the ridiculousness of the situation.

"I can do that. Will you visit soon? Your mom will kill me if you don't," he grimaces as if he can hear her now.

"Well, we can't have that, huh?" I joke. "Thank you for listening. Don't tell Mom we talked shop the whole lunch."

He shakes his head, shoulders bouncing as he laughs softly. "I knew you were going to do it anyway, but it's just us. You know better than to pull that shit with your mother back home."

We don't discuss the family business around civilians or *at the dinner table.*

26 / pokerface

Deirdre

1:02 p.m. | 'the sixth incident'

SCAR

How was lunch?

I don't even bother asking myself how he knows about my lunch because of course he does.

Better than I expected.

SCAR

Glad to hear it.

Got something for you.

Should I be afraid?

SCAR

Only if you don't follow instructions.

What is that supposed to mean?

SCAR

Tell me when you get to your office and lock the door.

Careful now.

I don't take kindly to orders.

SCAR

That's a lie. I know the filth you listen to.

I'll have you know that listening to men whimper has increased my productivity by at least 80%. Thank you very much.

SCAR

Sure it has. Freak.

When I get back from lunch, I find a small pink gift box on my desk, topped with a bow and a note that reads, "open me for stress relief." This is the perfect sentence to lure me into a white van. Of course, I'll bite.

The door is locked.

SCAR

Good girl.

Open the box and give me an answer.

I remove the lid and silk drawstring bag to discover a small red toy with a clit and a G-spot stimulator inside that makes me gasp. There's a tiny remote in there, too, and my face flames under the notion of us not only crossing this line, but happily orgasming over it. I peek over my shoulder as if someone could see and set it back down to text him back.

Is this because of the video I sent the other day?

You can't expect me to use this right now.

SCAR

That's exactly what this is about.

What's your answer?

You can say no.

I don't want to say no, but if I say yes, what am I agreeing to? The video I sent was only to tease him back. Maybe I took it too far. I'm not usually that bold or comfortable, and I should've known it would come back to bite me in the ass sooner or later.

My eyes flit back and forth from the toy to my phone. I shouldn't, but goading him is so much fun. And I reason that letting him get even *is* fair. Hmm…

Yes.

Give me a moment to put it in.

SCAR

Excellent choice.

Right now, I am grateful to have an en suite in my office. I beeline for the bathroom, clutching my phone in one hand and the toy in the other.

My heart is racing as I lift up the hem of my dress, sliding my cheeky panties to the side and resting my foot onto the counter. The image of my panties in his mouth overtakes me, filling my core with need.

My lips part when the silicone bulb grazes my clit. I spot myself in the mirror, wetness glistening on my pussy. At that moment, I reach for my phone, snapping a picture I'm not certain I'll send.

I quickly insert the toy with an inhale and press the lips on the other end gently against my clit. Releasing the breath I've anxiously held, I pull my panties back in place, adjust my dress, and take one last look in the mirror as I wash my hands. Nothing will be the same after this little game we're playing, and I try to tell myself I'm okay with that.

We'll find out, won't we?

When I return to my desk I pull up emails, scrolling back to my last day in office and text him to confirm I am ready to start.

What do I do now?

SCAR

Whatever I say until you're ready to stop.

What's your safe word?

A safe word? Fuck.

Taking a moment to consider a good word to use, I opt for something easy to remember that won't feel silly to say.

Cherry.

SCAR

Cherry it is.

If it becomes too much at any time, please say the word. ¿Me entiendes?

I understand. I'm ready.

SCAR

Headphones are needed.

I'll be playing the audio simultaneously on my end.

I put my AirPods in and wait patiently as I review my inbox, sending out delayed replies until my phone lights up with a new message.

1 Audio File From Scar

I press play on the audio, bracing myself as his deep timbre shares his exact plans for this game. His voice commanding my body has me squeezing my thighs together already.

"Hi, Doe. I'm going to play with you while you focus on your work, because you're a good girl and you wouldn't want anyone to know that you have a toy inside you that I'm controlling, right?"

Oh fuck.

"That remote doesn't have a charge, but I've got it from here," he says with a chuckle that sends a shiver down my spine.

Shit.

To ensure I am paying attention, he activates the toy, causing my breath to hitch as the suction on my clit intensifies then suddenly halts.

Motherfucker.

"See? Mmm. I can see how good I'm making you feel through that webcam, give me a wave, Doe."

I'll probably come to regret it later, but I flip off the camera instead of waving at him.

He continues, "You will address me as Sir. No matter what I do or say, you cannot react, moan, or scream. If you do, game over."

I nod in agreement, though I worry I may have bitten off more than I can chew.

"Mmm. One more thing. You cannot come until I say so. *¿Tú me entiendes?*" he asks, leaving a pause for me to answer.

Umm. Nope.

"Yes, Sir," I say, eager for the game to begin.

"Good girl. I'll let you get back to work," he says as the audio ends.

That's it?

Knowing that he can hear me, I keep my reactions to myself and proceed with clearing out my inbox. Of course, once I get in my zone, a buzz between my legs throws me off-kilter.

He leads with mercy. Low, steady vibrations radiate my core, and I breathe deeply through the pleasure. When I can resume my work, he adds pressure to my clit, matching the speed against my G-spot, and my head swirls with desire.

"Fuck," I breathe, hoping he doesn't notice my reaction.

As if he can read my mind, a text rolls in that I'm nervous to look at.

SCAR

Do you want more?

A simple question and a double-edged sword I'd love to impale me. He already knows what I want, getting me to ask for it is his game.

I can imagine him wearing a stupid grin on his face as he enjoys a front row seat to my power struggle.

Yes.

SCAR

Yes and?

Yes, Sir.

SCAR

Carry on.

As the text lights my screen, the pulsing on both ends picks up and doesn't relent. The urge to abandon my workload and hide under my desk is strong. My legs tremble as I struggle to keep a straight face. My lips part, but no sound escapes them. I *am* a good girl, after all. I take a deep breath as I tip my head back into the headrest, and the pulsing stops.

SCAR

Throwing your head back is a reaction.

Let's try again.

My lips form into a pout. I want to groan in frustration so badly, but the power is in his hands, literally. I won't admit how much I'm enjoying it either.

Incoming Call From Scar

I hesitantly swipe to answer. Both nervous and excited for what's in store. His gruff voice greets me with demands I'm anxious to obey.

"If you want to come like I know you do, you'll do as I say. Nod your head slightly. Don't react," he orders in a firm voice, and the buzzing returns.

I nod, training my face to remain calm as my breath quickens.

"You're off to such a good start."

Game on.

"I want you to imagine lying back on that desk, lifting those hips to remove your soaked panties and spreading those legs as I drink you in. Show me that pretty fucking pussy that's weeping for my mouth. Would you let me taste what belongs to me on company time, Boss?" he asks, and I can *hear* his smile.

I shudder at the thought of him here, staring up as his tongue takes over. Those big hands roaming my body in appreciation as I display myself for him.

"You're not allowed to argue, but I know you want to. It became *my* pussy the moment you put that toy in for me to control," he taunts, switching the toy on, quickly increasing the speed and pressure to test me, and I will not fail.

I breathe through my nose, taking a break from my typing to ball my fists into my lap.

"I don't trust you to keep quiet, Doe. Especially since I've heard just how loud you can get by yourself. Would you let me gag you with those panties? You wouldn't want anyone to know you're so desperate to be tongue-fucked that you can't even wait to clock out," he mocks.

Oh my God.

"You want to come, don't you? Have you earned that right, baby? I don't think so."

Delicious pressure builds in my lower back, and I'm near tears. My hands wrap around the armrests in a tight grip for leverage when that pleasure is ripped away at the press of a button.

Goddamn it.

"Soon, Doe. Let me enjoy this. You're so pretty when you're angry."

My eyes shut to prevent a reaction in front of the webcam as I await more of his sweet torture. I'm so sensitive, and he resumes, edging me with the lowest setting.

"Hold on to that anger. I like it rough," he murmurs. "Imagine my tongue flicking your clit as you watch me lose my mind at the taste of you. I don't think I'd be able to pull myself away. Fuck."

Jesus. How can I not scream right now?

I fight to stifle my moans, hoping he'll let me come soon, because I don't know how much more I'll be able to take.

"Imagine me bending you over that desk to punish you for those empty threats. I need to grip your hips and feel that ass bounce against me."

He trails off, and I can hear his hand moving up and down his shaft, the wet squelch of lubricant as he thinks about fucking me. I cover my face as I internally scream.

"If you wanted me dead, you'd have already made that call, but you want me to fill you so badly. Is that because you know I'll give you exactly what you need? What you're afraid to ask for? Nod if I'm right," he boasts between his teeth, pausing for me to respond.

He is, but fuck him for this.

He doesn't know me.

But he kinda does.

He turns the speed up a few notches as he awaits my answer, making it even harder to keep quiet, but I nod begrudgingly. The pulsing returns to a steady pace, and I squirm in my seat, desperate to come.

"How would it make you feel to know I'm in your bed right now stroking my dick? Hmm. Would you like that, Doe? To watch *me* for a change?"

I would like that very much.

My eyes widen at his admission, I envision him in my bed, hard body on display, dark eyes piercing me as he strokes his thick dick. It's been a struggle not pushing up against it the few times he lay with me.

"Since you aren't here, I'll paint the picture. I'm in the same spot you were in when I watched you squirt for the first time. Do you know what I would've done if I'd been there? I'd lap up every fucking drop of the mess you made for me. *Coño,*" he grunts.

Well, fuck.

"I'd curl my fingers inside of you until you drenched my fucking beard. I'd quench my thirst and coax another orgasm out of you. A greedy girl like yourself would love that, wouldn't you?"

My chest rises and falls as my pleasure builds. I grip the seat of my chair and close my eyes as I fight back tears.

"Please," I beg softly.

I need to come. Please let me come.

As if he can hear my thoughts, he relents, "Are you going to come at your desk for me, baby? You have to stay quiet if you want to be rewarded. Come for me, Doe. Fall apart on my dick. Please?"

Don't mind if I do.

"Come for me, *ahora. Ahora mismo."*

My body obeys. Pleasure sweeps through like an undertow, dragging me as I come back to life.

Never have I experienced anything like that. Help. ¡Ayudame!

"Where do you want me to come, *mi beba*? Undo your top so I can paint those big, beautiful tits. Mmm," he orders, huffing out his next breath as his strokes quicken.

His breath hitches as he strokes even harder. Without another thought, I rush to unbutton my top, yanking it open to reveal my lace bra, my full breasts on display for him through the camera.

Anything to hear him come.

He groans, guiding me through his climax, and it's music to my ears. His staccato breaths, my name on his lips, the sounds of him fucking his hand. It's enough to make me come again, but as the sensations build, the buzzing halts.

"Asshole," I say to myself.

"That was a good game, Doe. Thanks for playing. You up for a rematch?" he asks with a chuckle.

Does his mother know she raised a fucking villain?

27 / empty threats

César

2:08 p.m. | 66 minutes after 'the sixth incident'

DOE

You're eviler than I thought you were.

I don't know what you're talking about.

I tap the remote once more to frustrate her, and I can't help but laugh. Pissing off Deirdre Klarke has become my new favorite pastime. Though, I've tortured her enough today and decide to give her a break, shutting it off.

DOE

Fuck you.

I just did. 😏

You can take it out now.

DOE

Thank you. You better not be at my place when I get back.

Or what, Deirdre? What will you do?

DOE

Don't try me.

Another empty threat. You aren't ready for the real thing, but that's okay. 😌

DOE

Keep telling yourself that, Sir. 🖕

28 / oops (oh my)

Deirdre

6:08 p.m. | 4 hours after 'the sixth incident'

I couldn't be happier when the workday comes to an end. While it was eventful and productive, I'm spent. Between lunch with Dad, Scar's teasing, and tackling a heavy workload, I am ready to blow off some steam. Eager to get home to my toys and pl…Fuck. I forgot to charge them. Shower head it is.

Note to self: charge my damn toys.

I pull into the garage and enter through the side door, slightly disappointed that the house is empty.

Without preamble, I undress, trailing to my bathroom, humming softly as I turn on the shower. As I go over my mental checklist I remember to grab my toy chargers and plug them in. To my surprise, the lights don't blink, indicating a full charge.

He did not.

I'm not mad about it, because I don't stay on top of charging them my-damn-self. A clear sign that this man is *very* attentive to my habits *and* needs.

Speaking of need, replays of his commanding voice urging me to come hijack what should be a relaxing shower into a pregame session.

I aim the detachable shower head downward, applying the perfect amount of pressure to my clit. The thought of him handling my toys turns me on more than I care to admit. The delicious combination guides me to the cliff, and I tumble over in ecstasy.

I complete my nightly routines for my skin, hair, and body and finish up as I massage the vanilla-scented lotion into my skin. I'm admiring my body in the mirror when an idea comes to mind. Not a good one, but since he played with me all day, I must return the favor.

He wanted me to play and I will.

I wrap myself in a robe and head downstairs to fetch a pre-rolled joint from my office stash before dragging my step ladder into my room to retrieve the camera above my closet. I place it directly in front of my bed before stepping onto my balcony for a few puffs to calm my nerves.

Once the high hits, I put the joint out, dim my bedside lamps, and pick out a crotchless cranberry teddy to slip on. I don't wish to obstruct his view, because tonight, I *want* to be seen. To thank him for helping me get my mind off the unexpected visit, I'll give him a show he can't resist.

I grab a vibrator from the box underneath and climb onto my bed, a strong wave of his scent takes over, as if he's here, but he must've sprayed his cologne on my pillow.

Cute.

I position myself into the camera's view, picturing his broad build and whiskey eyes on me. This may be the wildest thing I've ever done. While all signs point to no, I still send a text to Scar.

Bedroom camera.

Tell me what you see.

Moments later, my phone pings with a response I'm nervous to open.

SCAR

I see a greedy girl in need of my attention.

Oh my God.

Is that right?

SCAR

You tell me.

Better yet, show me.

Yes, Sir.

I GRAB the violet dual-sided toy, one end reminiscent of a tongue and the other a vibrator. I hold it up silently, asking him to choose for me.

SCAR

Option 2.

Good choice.

Watch and learn.

A low hum fills the room, and I spread my legs, revealing my soaked pussy. My eyes lock with the camera as the toy kisses my clit, but I don't stop.

Moments later, chimes fill the air, breaking my lust-induced haze. I peek over my shoulder to find **Scar** flashing across my phone screen, ripping the air from my lungs. I swipe at the screen, eyes darting to the camera.

"I don't remember giving you permission to touch yourself, but go off," he says with a groan.

I scoff. "Are *you* touching yourself?"

He chuckles softly. "You look so fucking good, can you blame me?"

"I can. This is supposed to be my moment," I argue.

"Claim it, then."

I imagine my nipples between his teeth, grazing the soaked vibrator across my sensitive buds, and a hushed "fuck" escapes his lips. The deep rumble of his voice sets my body on fire as I drag the vibrator back to my clit.

"That pussy needs to be filled. Show me how you'd take me. *If* you could, that is."

"Oh, please. I can handle you, Scar."

"*Sir*. Prove it, baby."

I tease my entrance before inserting the vibrator. My needy pussy welcomes the intrusion, tightly squeezing around it.

"*Coño*. Good girl. Now fuck yourself like I would."

I'm certain I could come just from him speaking to me.

I part my legs wider, sinking the toy deeper until it bottoms out, increasing the pressure as my hips grind. I arch my back at his whimpers as he fucks his hand for me.

"You're going to come whenever I say so. *¿Me entiendes?*"

"Mmhm," I manage between breaths, wriggling as the pressure builds, arching my back in anticipation.

"*Cuéntame*. Use your words."

"Yes, Sir."

I've never felt sexier in my life, on display for his eyes only. My hand rubs soft circles around my clit as I taunt him with breathy moans, waiting for further instruction.

"You're taking it so well, baby," he praises.

The sound of his moans spurs me on, making me a whimpering mess when I'm close.

"Fuck. I'm going to come for you," I breathe.

"Come, *mi beba*. Come with me."

The pleasure overtakes me, and I buck my hips against the vibrator, chasing every spark. I catch my breath as I come down, decreasing the vibrations before shutting off the toy. Gently pulling it out as my pussy clenches, excited breaths are all I can hear.

"*Bueno*. Taste yourself."

I raise the toy to my lips, moaning as I suck it clean, wishing it was him instead.

"Mmm. *Quiero comerte,*" he says in a gravelly tone that sends chills through me.

I cannot believe I just did that.

"You were so good for me. *Buenas noches,* Deirdre," he says and disconnects the call.

I'm still reeling as I clean up. *What a day,* I think when I slip into bed, recalling how it felt to have an audience and follow orders with a purpose. He was right, I like being watched as much as he likes to hide.

But today was a shift for us both, my shadow stepped into the light before retreating into the night. I won't tell a soul; this was just for us, and I like it that way.

Scar has become a dirty little secret, one I don't mind keeping. My little secret, kept in good taste. Damn good taste.

29 / get off my lawn

Deirdre

12:06 p.m. | 3 days after 'the sixth incident'

This audiobook recommendation from Skye is unlike anything I've ever read, and I cannot stop listening to it. Every free moment I have, I've been locked in.

I even slowed this book down to 1x speed, so I don't finish it too quickly. I'm on the edge of my seat with every chapter, and another spicy scene is coming up.

I'm hoping I can get to it before I make it to the site visit with my realtor.

I've got about fifteen minutes before I make it to Spicewood, that should be enough time.

Traffic slowing down ahead makes me nervous about arriving on time. At least I left early and could get further into this book before it picks back up.

As if the universe heard my excitement, the narrator's voice quiets and the Bluetooth speaks. "Motion detected. Motion detected."

"What is it now?" I say to myself, swiping to unlock my phone, secured in a mount on my windshield. I tap the camera app in time to find the source: Scar entering my garage as if he lives there.

He'd argue that he does.

"What the fuck is he doing?" I ask myself, squinting to make out what he's up to.

Moments later, he lifts the garage door and emerges on my riding lawn mower. Dressed in a long sleeve shirt and dad hat, covering his face with sunglasses and a neck gaiter.

But below the waist, he's wearing what Skye calls "hoochie daddy shorts." Could he crush a watermelon with those thighs? Or my head? Both? I'm curious now.

My mouth waters as I admire this infuriating man tending to my yard. Either this book has got me hot, or lawn mowing is sexy when he does it.

He eventually looks toward the camera and waves as he passes by on the riding lawn mower. Like he knows I can't resist an opportunity to observe him. *He's so annoying,* I think, but oddly charming. We've embraced these fleeting moments at a respectful distance with tampered boundaries that've only increased the excitement of the danger we are to each other.

If things escalated, I'd have the same concerns that I always do. How much time would we have before the mask came off? Not the mask he *physically* wears, but the one that holds his guard.

The inevitable slip of the tongue in a state of comfort is how it begins, always ending in a familiar demise. My love is lethal, unintentionally violent, and incredibly hopeless. For his safety, I shouldn't pursue him.

I can't even explain what's transpired without them going all Klarke, killing first and asking questions later. I've learned my lesson, and moving across the country hasn't absolved me of their sins.

He doesn't deserve to walk into a burning building that he won't exit. I know what I attract and grant in return. Partners aren't allowed to make mistakes and move on.

At least not when they know too much and pose a threat to the organization. However, the possibility of him working for my family only increases the chances of him not making it out of this alive.

That's why I haven't entirely ruled out Xavier, though I must admit he doesn't excite me the way Scar does. He's a pretty boy, and I get the feeling that he only wants sex, but I also wouldn't mind that human contact, even if just for a night.

There are rules when working for the Klarkes, and one is that no one is allowed to touch me. I assume he's been so creative with my pleasure due to this very rule, but regardless, I do have needs. Needs Xavier can fulfill without a death sentence.

Does Xavier know about the significance of celosias on Thursdays? Of course not. Would he take care of me during my period? Or make sure I have time to read after a long day?

My guess is none of the above, but he's the safer choice. That is, if I stand to protect Scar from ending up like Lawrence.

My Bluetooth speaks again, serving as the perfect distraction from my thoughts.

"Incoming call from Skye. Answer it?"

"Answer it."

"Heyyy," she sings.

"Hey, girl. What's up?"

"I'll be in town this weekend for the Techy Awards and wanted to see if we could have lunch?"

"Of course! I miss you," I admit, excitement now filling my voice. A visit is just what I need to keep my mind off of my stalker and the lackluster dating pool.

"I miss you, too, and you better finish that audiobook so we can talk about it!"

"I'm trying to, but you interrupted me."

"Well, shit." She chuckles. "Love you. Bye."

"Bye. Love you, too!"

30 / our lawn

César

2:11 p.m. | 3 days after 'the sixth incident'

You should fire your landscaper.

He fucking sucks.

DOE

And you're any better?

I am SO much better and you'll see when you get home.

DOE

Will you be there?

I can if you want me to be. 😏

DOE

Without the mask? 👀

No can do.

DOE

The masked man shit isn't sustainable, you know?

You still want to fuck me and have never seen my face.

I'd say it's working well for me so far.

DOE

When have I said I wanted to fuck you?

Didn't have to. My job is to know things.

DOE

Anyways.

Thanks for tending to my lawn.

Our.

DOE

What's that?

Our lawn. You had a typo there.

I was just helping you out.

DOE

Oh. I hadn't realized. 😂

Get the hell out of my house.

Already gone.

Drive safely, Doe. 😚

31 / spill

Deirdre

10:25 a.m. | 4 days after 'the sixth incident'

"You said you had some tea for me. Spill it," Skye sings from across the table, giggling over her mimosa, never ceasing to make me smile. She stuns in an orange off-shoulder maxi dress as her brown skin twinkles with shimmer beneath the sun. Some people may shine, but Skye *glows,* lugging that heavy light and kindly sharing it with us.

I know it's only been a few weeks, but I missed her.

Living in Austin has felt as if I'm on an island all by myself, until Scar. Thankfully, Houston isn't far, and I least get to see Skye from time to time.

My long-distance relationships with the girls weigh on me at times, but we make an effort to meet up whenever we can.

I gulp down my mimosa to prepare for this conversation.

Whew. Here goes.

"So, you remember that guy I told you about?" I start, dragging my eyes to meet hers.

"Scar? The secret admirer?" She gasps.

"I—uh sort of met him not too long ago," I opt to share instead of confirming.

My eyes dart around the patio in search of him and come up empty. But I know that doesn't mean he isn't close by.

"Excuse me? Why am I just now hearing this?" Her head jerks back in surprise, her earrings swaying with the motion.

"Well, I wasn't exactly sure how to bring it up. You know that book you recommended with the thirst trap stalker?" I say in a hushed voice.

"Yeah. Did you like it? And why are you whispering?" she asks with her brows drawn, taking a sip of her mimosa.

"I loved it, but I'm being stalked. Right now." It's the first time I've ever said it aloud to anyone else. And I feel like I'm talking about the fucking Boogeyman and not the man I think about every time I come.

"What?" she splutters, choking on her drink. She coughs into her elbow and holds up a finger with her free hand, signaling me to wait as she gets herself together. "I understand I cannot drink for this conversation. Go on," she urges.

"I'm certain that he has my phone tapped and can hear everything I say," I inform her while taking a bite of my French toast.

She raises a brow. "Are you serious? Dee."

I nod as I swallow, my hair tickling my back with the aggressiveness of the motion, and her eyes widen. When the shock wears off, she'll want an explanation, which I'll give.

Then again, Skye is the "no judgment friend." The one you call if you need to hide a body. She'll pull up with an array of shovels, no questions asked. The one you can confess your sins to, and she'll root for the chaos.

"So, is he your secret admirer? Or do you have two potential stalkers at the same time?"

"Thankfully, I got a two-in-one special," I say with a wince.

She blinks at me. "You are electric sliding too fast, and I can't keep up. Give it to me at turtle speed. Now," she orders, leveling me with a stare.

"Okay. It's the same guy, and I've seen him around my house."

"Fuck. Is this connected to your family?" she asks, throwing her hand over her mouth.

"That's the thing, he kinda is. But he's supposed to be looking out for me."

"Like a bodyguard?"

"Uh--kind of. I guess." Except he's also seen my pussy and came on my bed.

"What's he look like? Show me a picture right now," she whisper-shouts.

The only picture I have of him comes to mind, causing me to squeeze my thighs together.

"Sooo…I don't have one? I've never seen his full face because he wears a mask."

I brace myself, because now that I'm saying this out loud, it's even more ridiculous than it sounded in my head.

She scoffs. "You're fucking with me right now. *My* Deirdre doesn't live life on the edge. You need an itinerary for every adventure."

She isn't wrong.

"I know, but this fell into my lap unexpectedly," I add, taking another bite of my food.

"Have you? Fallen into his lap by chance?" she asks with a smirk.

The waiter approaches the table wearing an awkward smile as he refills the mimosa pitcher. "How is everything?"

There's no way he didn't hear that.

But us women are notorious for having the most outrageous conversations in public.

"Amazing," we rush to answer, our voices overlapping each other.

"Great. Need a refill on that water? " he asks Skye, eyes dropping to her empty glass.

"Yes, please. Thank you so much," she answers.

When he leaves, I blurt my response, knowing he'll be returning soon.

"Not exactly, but I may have let him talk me through it…and use a toy on me at work."

Her jaw drops. "You nasty girl. I am impressed. Does Alora know?"

Uhh. About that.

We're interrupted once again by the waiter returning with a frosty pitcher to refill Skye's water. We wait for his exit to continue.

"Not yet. She has so much going on right now, and I don't want her to worry."

Alora isn't judgmental in the slightest. I attribute that to her being raised by a lawyer and a therapist. She's the "airtight alibi" friend. The "use her whiteness to keep you out of trouble" friend.

They're both ride or die in their own ways.

"So, you want *me* to worry instead?" She giggles. "Well, we have to tell her eventually. Shit. I'll do it with you," she cackles over her words.

"Thank you. This isn't an easy thing to share. Given how strange it is," I add, trying not to feel shame over my questionable choices.

"Wait. What about the guy you met at the club? Have you talked to him?"

I nod. "Xavier. We're going out next weekend," I say hesitantly, knowing Scar may be listening.

"How will, uh, what's his name, feel about this?" she whispers, taking to glancing around as well, as if she knows what he looks like.

"I guess we'll find out soon enough," I reply before sipping more of my drink.

My phone chimes expectedly, and I flip it over, anticipating a text for confirmation that he's listening right now. Sure enough, he is.

2 Unread Messages From Scar

SCAR

You're telling people about us?

I told Mami about you.

I tried to give you some privacy, until I heard my name…and his.

Jealous, are we?

SCAR

No. You can do better is all.

Enjoy your time with Skye. Tell her I said hello, since I'm no longer a secret.

I smile as I read his messages, tilting the phone toward Skye for proof that we indeed have an audience.

"Hi, Scar." She snorts and waves at the screen. "Girl. You really weren't lying. I'm gonna need time to process this, but I wish you had a damn picture. I gotta know what he looks like," she laments.

"You and me both," I tell her with a sigh.

32 / word of advice

César

1:37 p.m. | 7 days after 'the sixth incident'

I'm gathering intel for another client who suspects their partner is cheating. The usual, meeting up at a hotel on their lunch break. Another CEO fucking his secretary that convinced his wife to give up her dreams while he pursued his.

I hope she takes him for all he's fucking got, I think as I snap photos of them exiting The Orlov Hotel looking flushed and disheveled. These cases tend to be cut and dry for the most part, but the emotional aspect? Not so much.

Catching a subject in the act never gets old. While some are more discreet and creative than others, they always leave breadcrumbs behind. I dread sharing those findings with my clients, because no matter how much they think they can handle what I find, the devastation guts them every time.

It's one thing to suspect infidelity, but having actual proof is something you can't come back from. Helping my clients find the truth they deserve is worth the trouble, but it also serves as something normal to share with *mi abuela* whenever she asks about work.

I stay a few car lengths back as I tail him, veering off when he pulls into the office parking garage.

"Scumbag," I mutter as I send a text to my client, requesting a meeting to share an update on her cheating husband.

As I await her response, Deirdre's upcoming date with Xavier crosses my mind, and it bothers me more than it should. I believe she should find someone to date that isn't me, but she's too good for him.

Not to mention he's fucking boring.

Xavier Arnez Coleman Jr. is a twenty-nine-year-old Black man from Atlanta, Georgia, who is a physical therapist that lives alone in a studio apartment and has a three-year-old Shih Tzu named Carl. He has a 660 credit score, drives an electric smart car, and plays basketball with friends every Saturday at a local gym, but *always* gets dunked on.

Like I said, *boring*.

His conversation skills are juvenile, leaning on the question game to learn her ins and outs. He only knows what she wants him to, which is basically nothing. How could they have a lasting relationship if she doesn't feel like she can be herself with him?

My phone pings with a response from my client, informing me she's available to meet at my office tomorrow morning at ten.

Now that that's handled, I tap open my camera app to check in on Deirdre. She's mindlessly snacking on cherries while she reviews an HR training on compliance in her office. I distract her for a moment, because I can't help it.

You seem bored.

DOE

Very bored, but at least I have a snack.

Thanks for removing the pits.

Cherries are one of few fruits I've seen her eat. Her fragrance even smells like them, with hints of amber and vanilla. A scent that lingers in the air and in my mind. Kinda like her. A craving that cannot be fulfilled.

Anything to stay in your good graces.

DOE

Lie again. 😂

There's something about her that unnerves me in a way that makes me feel out of control. Almost as if I'm the one in front of the camera instead of her, and that makes me question my sanity. I'm long overdue for a couch session and should get on booking one right away.

A pulse check with my therapist may help me sort out some of these warring feelings between Deirdre and my career as of late. I've always felt rewarded by my work and prideful for the opportunities it's granted me. I'm grateful to be able to provide for my family in ways I never saw possible.

I spend more time with my work than I do with my family, and now that my subject has become more of a fascination than simply a task to check off my list, I'm second-guessing myself.

I'll break the law within my bounds for the right case and price point, but how does that make me any better than my clients? Or the subjects I'm hired to provide intel on?

Not one time have I sat in on a debriefing and willingly withheld information necessary to propel the case forward. But every time I sit down with the Hales since the meeting that went awry, I find myself rehearsing in my head what to share and what not to.

I'm simply a mortal compared to the beguiling and destructive Deirdre Klarke. She's threatening to dismantle everything I've worked so hard to achieve in a matter of weeks, and doesn't even know it.

You don't have to believe me, but I'll let you get back to work.

DOE

Alright.

Will I see you around later?

Maybe.

I'll remember to whistle.

DOE

I appreciate it.

I looked up the coquí and they are so cute!

They really are. 🥺

I stop my hands from typing anything further. I nearly suggest bringing her to Puerto Rico someday to see them in person, but I can't say things like that. She doesn't deserve to be lied to any more than she already has been and will be hurt enough when the job is done.

* * *

"HE'S JUST gonna stand there all night?" I ask, swirling my rocks glass as the ice mingles with my whiskey. Divin, of course.

"That's what he's paid to do," Emiliano confirms, his hand on his own glass. Of course, this fancy *pendejo* suggested this swanky bar, not too far from his office. This place is too quiet for me to lose myself in, which I guess is a good thing. But the urge to whip out my phone and watch the woman on my mind has me swallowing down more liquor. The shits *good*.

"Feel free to start talking," he nudges, glancing at his watch. It easily costs more than what the bartender will make in a year, but he's otherwise dressed like just another stuffy asshole.

"Like you've got anywhere to be," I mutter. I clear my throat and throw caution to the wind. "Remember that I told you I've sort of become intrigued by my latest assignment?"

"Which never happens, so this woman must be something." His words oddly comfort me after weeks of second-guessing myself. I'm not hurting for pussy, I don't need to find connections through work, and I've never jeopardized my career for infatuation.

Still, I swallow, preparing for our worlds to collide in a way it never has. Even when his older brother—who happens to be the head of the largest Cartel division in America—outsources me to find people, it's never gotten as messy as this has the potential to be.

Because through my own fieldwork, I've learned that Regina Delvecchio is one of Emiliano's current legal clients.

Yeah, this motherfucker's brother is the head of the Cartel, and he's a fucking attorney. *Que jodienda.*

I look at the man who's been my friend since our freshman year of college and say, "Her name is Deirdre Klarke."

Emiliano stares at me, his brows furrowed as he glances away, sorting through his mental rolodex. After a few moments, his eyes widen, and he meets my gaze again.

"This is how you're choosing to die, *güey*?" The way he fights a smirk pisses me off. But I'm not done yet.

"I know you're representing her cousin, Regina Delvecchio," I reveal, holding my hands up when he opens his mouth to respond. "I'm not asking you to breach any confidentiality agreement. I'm just putting all the shit out there."

"The Hales hired you?" His eyes squint a fraction, and he downs his drink as he waits for my response.

"Yeah, but I can handle them. The last thing I need is for you and Ignacio to get involved," I remind him. Shit can get messy, especially when white people are involved—foreign or not.

"So what are we discussing?"

"You making sure Regina doesn't kill me when shit comes to a head."

Emiliano snorts a laugh, shaking his head.

"What? You can't save my ass?"

"Nah, it's not that. She actually just asked if I knew anyone who could help her track down her husband," he admits, quirking his brow at the timing of it all.

"The one who went missing?"

"Yup," he answers, holding his glass of ice up so the bartender sees. "She's convinced he's still alive."

"So she's insane."

"I don't know," he says with a shrug, nodding when he's handed another drink as the empty glass is whisked away by a server. *Spoiled* cabrón. "She seems perfectly intact to me."

"I'm not sure I can trust your judgment," I start, grinning at his puzzled expression. "You can't even tell when a woman doesn't want your ass."

"*Pinche pendejo*," he quips under his breath, tipping his glass toward me before bringing it to his mouth. "But you don't see me stalking her, César."

He knocks back his liquor, and I follow suit, holding my now empty glass up because apparently that's what these rich assholes do here.

"Then what do you suggest I do instead?" I ask, knowing damn well I'm not about to remove my equipment from her home and office. Still, I'm interested in his perspective.

"Show her who you really are." He cuts his eyes to the side as he scans the room like there isn't a man behind him that would gladly take a bullet for him. "You're loyal, hard-working, somewhat funny, and women find you attractive. Let her get to know you the way you've gotten to know her."

"So give her access to my every waking moment?"

Why do I even listen to him?

"And what about—" I start.

"Your *pest problem*?" he interjects, speaking a little louder than I was. *Shut the fuck up about criminal activity*, his eyes say. "I know of a good exterminator."

I can't have the Hales taken out by the fucking Cartel. *Can I?*

No. I definitely can't.

Another drink is set down in front of me, and before I can touch the glass, Emiliano asks, "Any advice for me?"

"Grow a pair and go get her," I answer, watching him deadpan over the rim of my glass as I gulp down more whiskey.

Hector chuckles, and Emiliano lifts his hand for the check, tired of my shit.

33 / a night at the drive-in

Deirdre

6:45 p.m. | 35 minutes before 'the seventh incident'

One of my favorite memories from my childhood was going to the drive-in with my family. Dad loved movie nights, and we'd have them once a week. He has always been very firm about quality time as a family, and to this day, no one is allowed to contact him for any non-life-threatening reason during his time with us.

So, when I found one not too far from my place in Austin, I obviously had to go. I almost invited Scar but decided against it. It's probably wise that I don't let him join in on something so sentimental. I've learned the hard way with so many memories tainted by Lawrence's presence.

My ex worked in marijuana distribution with my family and was good at it. But then he got greedy and started keeping a little to himself. Had hoped to build up an inventory to eventually compete with us, it seemed.

He'd lie and cheat on the job, then come home to repeat the cycle, not bothering to cover his tracks or fess up to his wrongdoings any time I confronted him.

While he never raised a hand, his words sliced through me,

leaving scars in their wake. My weight was his weapon of choice when he *really* wanted to hurt me, but everyone thought he was such a nice guy. *Charming.* He would've gotten himself killed eventually, believing he was untouchable.

Until he crossed Regina.

"Such a terrible accident," people said. Except *he* was an accident waiting to happen. Lawrence was an abusive, manipulative piece of shit, but he was still a person.

Granted, he wasn't *my* person, but he was meant to be somebody's. That somebody will now live the rest of their life without ever finding him. Some may say good riddance, but I disagree.

An example needed to be made. He was buried in a closed casket, and I sat beside his mother in mourning, rubbing her back as she sobbed uncontrollably. Not one of my proudest moments.

My dad wasn't wrong when he called it an accident. It *was*, but the cut brake lines made it murder, leading to me being a person of interest.

Thankfully, no one else was hurt in the crash. A rare occurrence whenever my family gets to "problem solving."

Similar to how superheroes tear up the city fighting the villain in the movies, that's what my family does. Except we're no superheroes.

césar

7:20 p.m. | 'the seventh incident'

I just left from visiting *Abuela* at *Mami's*. She didn't have much energy today, and it pains me to see her like that. As much as I try to pretend I'm not losing her, I am, and there's nothing I can do about it.

She got a DNR order signed behind our backs and has been firm on her stance. This is what she wants, and no matter how much it pains me, I have to respect her decision. All we can do is make sure she's comfortable and enjoy the time we do have with her.

I was on my way to the shooting range to blow off some steam, but turned around when I saw Deirdre was going to the drive-in. She shouldn't mind me crashing, and I don't want to be alone right now.

I'm unmasked when I arrive to not alarm anyone, and I pay for my ticket, hoping to find her before she sees me. I spot her license plate as she hops out to open the trunk. Her plump ass bends over to reach for blankets, and I resist the urge to gape.

I park a few spaces away, maintaining a distance but staying close enough to keep her in my sight. After tossing the blankets in the backseat, she gets in line for the concession stand.

She better come back with popcorn.

Without another thought, I step out of my truck, make sure I'm out of view, and sound three *coquí* whistles before ducking down, pretending to tie my shoes.

She whips her head around to search for the source, and her lips tick up in a soft smile. If she isn't careful, I'll think she doesn't mind having me around.

If that's true, it'll only make it harder to leave.

I resume to my height, tap the key fob, and when the locks click, quickly make way for her SUV, helping myself into the passenger seat. I retrieve the balaclava from my pocket and slide it over my face. My eyes scan the area as I await her return, but as soon as I hear her footsteps approaching, I face forward.

She opens the driver's side door without looking and tosses small bags of candy at me. She ducks her head as she climbs in, not noticing me and clutching the large tub of buttered popcorn to her chest. She reaches over, slamming the door shut with her free hand.

When she finally turns toward me, she lets out a yelp before leveling me with a stare. I'm the first one to break the silence.

"Really? After all we've been through? You scream when you see me?"

She huffs. "When you scare me, I do."

"I whistled," I exclaim, reminding her of our little agreement.

"Yeah, but I didn't expect you to be in my fucking car. What are you doing here?" Her question is less breathy, gaining volume now as she pins me with her glare.

"I'm here to enjoy a movie. What are *you* doing here?"

She settles her plump lips in a line, and I try not to focus on how gorgeous she is when she's annoyed.

"Minding my own goddamn business. You should try it."

"Can you recommend a book on that?" I tease.

She rolls her eyes, shoving the tub of popcorn into my hands. "I didn't plan on sharing my snacks." She reaches behind her for a fleece blanket she lays over her legs, adjusting her seat so she's farther from the steering wheel and reclining. "And don't eat all my damn popcorn," she snaps, scooping a handful from the tub and tossing it into her mouth.

"I won't make any promises, but I'll replace what I eat."

"Fine. Can I go anywhere without you tagging along? Want to be the third wheel on my date, too?" she asks, staring expectantly at me.

The lights start to dim, serving as the perfect save to avoid this question.

"Shh. The movie's starting. Give me some of that blanket," I add, shoving a fistful of popcorn into my mouth.

34 / a lesson in eradication

Deirdre

9:07 a.m. | 4 days after 'the seventh incident'

After a call with my realtor, anxiety builds in my gut. I toss back my meds with a swig of water and wait for the calm to wash over me. They're not backing down from this bid, and for the first time during this whole experience, I'm nervous I'm going to lose.

I could use some advice, but I'd prefer it from another Black woman instead of Dad or Darius. Mom isn't as cutthroat, and since we're cut from the same cloth, that leaves one person.

Regina.

I check the time before dialing her number. Her kids should be at school by now, so she may pick up. The line rings three times, and when I think it's going to connect to voicemail, the line picks up, but she doesn't speak right away.

After a moment, I hear her voice say, "My bad. I had to put on my headphones."

"Are you busy?"

"Nah, I can talk. What's up?"

It sounds like she's in the car, and I hear something like muffled screams on her end of the phone. I probably shouldn't ask, but it may keep my mind off of this bid for a moment.

"Are you alone? It sounds like someone is screaming over there."

She scoffs. "Noise cancelling headphones, my ass. Goddamn chloroform wore off. Excuse me for a sec," she grumbles, and I hear a thumping sound that I can only assume is her banging on the roof of her car. "Hey! If you don't shut the fuck up, you're getting knocked out again. I'm trying to have a conversation here," she exclaims, her thick New York accent in full effect. After a deep sigh, she continues, "No manners, this fucking guy. Sorry about that. What's going on?"

"Where is Price?" I ask, ignoring her question.

"I shook him. He follows me *everywhere* and claims he's 'following Cidro's orders,'" she admits in a mocking tone, poorly imitating his Scottish accent. "Sometimes, I just want to be left alone. I don't see the fucking issue."

It's no wonder why he ordered that she shouldn't be left unsupervised. Look at the shit she gets into.

"I agree that you don't *need* a bodyguard, but if that was Cidro's wish, it's what he wanted," I mention, hoping to reason with her. After all, Cidro was the only one who *could* reason with her.

"I don't understand why Ro would hire a Scot to work for the Italians. I've looked him up and can't find shit on this guy. But my husband trusted him to look after me in his absence? I call bullshit."

"Um, I don't know. He seems nice and very handsome."

"You don't have him tailing you all day. Please tell me more about his glowing personality, because to me he is a red-headed boulder with teeth."

I snort. "Gi, my God. Please tell me you're not doing a shakedown over there."

"Fine, I'm not doing a shakedown. I'm teaching a lesson."

"What's the difference?" I squeak out, not sure if I want to know the answer.

"I warned him twice about counting cards, and he thought I

was playing. Today was the third warning and you know I hate repeating myself. I got a call from my team. They took him off the floor so I can talk to him when I get there. Tell me why this motherfucker called me out of my name and tried to *spit on me*?"

Oh shit.

"I've had enough of these racist motherfuckers trying me because they hate a Black woman in charge. It is what it fucking is, and if he's got a death wish, he found the right one. So, long story short, he's kicking and screaming in my trunk."

I have so many questions, but for once I can't say she isn't overreacting.

"Why didn't you have anybody help? What if he overpowered you?" Somebody has to be concerned for her safety, aside from the red-headed boulder with teeth.

"I had help. The valet boys put him there. Those kids will hide a body if you offer them cash," she murmurs the last part, as if it's advice I'll one day need.

"Counting cards isn't illegal, Gi," I remind her. But what she's doing *is*.

"It is in *my* fucking house. We'll see how well you play blackjack without all your fingers, *Alfieee*," she sings.

I resist the urge to laugh at her, though it's a challenge. She'd be fucking hilarious if she wasn't dead serious.

"Geez. It's 9 a.m. What are you going to do?"

"Cigar cutter. One at a time then cauterize them," she informs. "You got a better idea?"

Jesus. I love my family. I didn't ask for them, but I love them, no less.

I swallow. "umm. No. I wouldn't know the first thing about that."

"Mmhm. So, why are you calling? You don't call anymore and barely answer the phone for me. What do you want?"

She clocked me. She's really good at spotting bullshit.

"Advice. I have a problem."

Muffled screams filter through her end of the line, reminding us of the company she's keeping.

"Hold on. Enough, Alfred. No one is gonna save you. If you'd been respectful, you'd have some leg room, but instead you ran your fucking mouth. And you better hold your bladder until we get there, I swear. Or you will be cleaning up your own mess with whatever's left of your fingers. I only clean up after my kids."

Silence passes as she waits to hear if he's going to continue.

"I'm back. Sorry about that. If you're ordering a hit, you're gonna have to call Angie. I had to squeeze this errand in before I head back to the kids' school."

"What's going on at the school?"

"Girl, fucking career day. Ro always did this, and it's the first one without him," she sighs. "He was better at this shit than me. A real PTA Daddy, he was. I'm not good with children that aren't mine. You remember when Uncle El used to come to ours?"

I chuckle. "How could I forget?"

"You remember him threatening Joey's dad after he pushed you off the swings?"

"I do. He told him if his son didn't keep his hands to himself, he'd break both of his arms—"

She finishes my sentence, "And if he had to wear two casts, he wouldn't be able to touch a damn thing." She breaks into a fit of laughter at the memory.

"It was embarrassing then, but it is funny now. Joey never touched me again. Wouldn't even look at me," I muse.

"I'm not *that* bad am I?" she asks, her tone serious.

"I don't know, Gi. Have you threatened to break the bones of someone else's child?"

"I can't say I have."

"Then maybe you *can* take on events with the kids. Go be a PTA mom."

She blows out a breath. "That sounds awful, but all I can do is try. Now, whatddya need advice on?"

"Well, I just talked with the realtor and the Hales aren't giving up. I'm getting closer to my cap on this property, and I'll have to concede if this bid doesn't end soon."

"Fucking trust fund babies. I mean so are we, but we're Black. It's different," she grumbles.

"I'm so tired, Gi. They don't even need this property. They just don't want *me* to have it," I add with a resigned sigh. "What would you do?"

"I'd take them out."

"Absolutely not. Gi, why does your mind always go there?"

"No days off. Eradication is my ministry. Life is easier when problems disappear. Like this fucking guy. You hear that, Alfie?" She pauses, and there's no response. "Oh now you want to be quiet," she taunts while I wonder if the guy passed out from lack of oxygen. Can that happen in a trunk?

"Let me rephrase. What would you do without violence?"

"You could keep bidding and see how much you're willing to spend over your cap, if needed. Or…" she trails off.

"Or?"

"You're not gonna like this one, but you may need to throw in the towel with this property and find another because you stand to lose a lot of money fucking around with them. What are you thinking?" she asks.

"I don't know."

"Now you see why I choose violence every time. Quick and easy. The offer still stands. You won't be in a war with them if they disappear."

"No, Gi, they're billionaires. It will be a fucking mess that'll blow back on me," I remind her, only ever wanting designer bracelets on these wrists. "Plus it goes against me wanting to do things the right way."

"It must be nice to have a moral compass. The needle snapped on mine a long time ago," she jokes before continuing. "There's one other thing I'd do if I were avoiding violence. I'd call your dad and schedule a sit down. Let him do *all* the talking, though. I know this is *your* venture, but you need muscle and intimidation. Uncle El will spook them."

She ain't lying.

"I'll think about it. Thanks, Gi."

"Fair enough. The offer still stands, *if* you need it."

"I'm going to get back to work. Have fun with Alfie." I pause a moment before offering words of support. "Oh, and you're doing great with the kids. I don't know if anyone tells you that," I blurt.

A weighted silence takes over the line, and I fear the call may have dropped.

"Uh—Thanks. I love you," she squeaks.

"I love you, too," I say before the line disconnects.

35 / nice watch, run it

César

7:35 p.m. | 70 minutes before 'the eighth incident'

I've been doing a lot of thinking about what Emiliano said, and he's right. *Pero,* I'm not telling him that shit.

Deirdre needs to know who I really am in order to take me seriously and the mask has protected me, but I'm still left vulnerable whenever it comes to her. I raid the weed stash she keeps in her office to give myself a break from my anxious thoughts. This is either going to go better than I planned or be a complete disaster, but a few puffs of a joint should soften the inevitable blow.

I would've appreciated more time to plan a grand gesture, but she went on a date with Xavier tonight and it may be too late for the bells and whistles. It's possible I've convinced myself that she doesn't like him because that makes me feel better about my chances.

She's let me bring her to orgasm, but that's vastly different from dating me in public, where I can't wear a mask. Unless we rob a bank. Though, I'd reserve a robbery for an established relationship, not a first date. *Or* second, if she counts the drive-in as our first.

Now, I'm standing in the kitchen roasting a pork shoulder I've marinated for two days to prepare a home-cooked meal for a woman who's going on a date with someone else tonight. *Pernil y arroz con gandules* can turn any night around.

It's too late to turn back now, and something tells me she'll still be hungry when she leaves a chump like him at the restaurant. I don't want her to have a bad date, but I don't see him keeping her interest beyond a half hour.

All he does is talk about himself and ask her stupid questions. He's probably showing her pictures of Carl, because that dog is the only thing interesting about him. The least I can do is give her something to look forward to when she gets back and a good meal.

I see Deirdre in a way no one else does, and I don't mean what I view through her camera feeds and windows. I see *her*. A flawed, anxious, overworked, and underappreciated woman desperate for success and her family's approval.

My heart aches when I overhear her speaking negatively about herself because her family has led her to believe she isn't worthy of taking on more responsibility.

I see how she runs that company, and it's with pride. She is a leader who empowers her team, supports her peers, and is passionate about her craft.

She's more than a beautiful woman with loads of generational trauma and some *questionable* sexual interests. She is comfortable with hiding layers of herself for the sake of business and her image, but Deirdre is a rare sight when she has even a moment of peace.

Freedom exists behind her front door, where there are no societal pressures, competitors seeking dirt, threats on her life, or blood relatives making her feel inferior.

I hadn't planned on doing anything stupid tonight or intimidating anyone, but I may have followed her GPS to see for myself how their date is going. I threw the *pernil* in the oven to keep warm and since the movie they saw should be ending soon,

I planned on driving by to make sure she was enjoying herself before they continued the rest of their date. But when I spot her walking down the sidewalk, I'm taken aback by how incredible she looks in a vibrant pink dress with a matching trench hanging off her shoulders.

Her dark hair is blown out in loose, voluminous curls like a movie star, and those glossy lips are begging to be kissed. She is radiating.

Xavier is so lucky to have even a moment of her time, let alone a date. Then my eyes follow *him,* and my lip curls in disgust as he allows her to walk curbside.

¡Es un cabrón bien fresco, pa' colmo!

I'm not letting you waste another minute of your precious time, I think as I prepare to do the most ridiculous thing I've ever done. *Sorry, baby. I'll beg for forgiveness later.*

I reach into my glovebox for my balaclava and slip it over my face before grabbing my handgun, tucking it in my waistband when I step out of the truck.

I take a deep breath and do the sign of the cross over myself before following them.

I'm a good distance behind as I trail them, but to not alarm her, I do a *coquí* whistle three times. She maintains her stride with him, shaking her head in disbelief when she hears me.

Good.

It's a quiet night without a lot of people around. I couldn't be more grateful for little to no witnesses.

This is *not* what Emiliano meant when he said to get the girl, but I never said I was wise.

deirdre

8:45 p.m. | 'the eight incident'

I hear three *coquí* whistles in the distance and shake my head. I don't bother turning around so as to not encourage my shadow of a man. My provocations don't drive him away, they only entice him. Scar is a prominent tail I can't lose, and I'm not sure I want to.

Xavier walks to the left of me and is seemingly unfazed by the whistles. We just left a movie and are headed to dinner, as the restaurant is at the end of the street.

Tonight has gone smoothly so far. I enjoyed the movie, but the thing with movie dates is you don't have to talk to each other.

I love that we're heading to the dinner portion of the date, because his behavior will tell me everything I need to know about him. How he treats service workers, whether he tips, or closes his mouth when he chews. If he eats his vegetables, drinks water, or handles liquor well.

The list is endless.

My excitement for dinner dims when a large dark figure looms in the corner of my eye. I sigh in preparation for whatever he's up to.

This motherfucker.

Scar approaches us, cosplaying as a mugger, and I stifle a laugh, hiding it in a cough. He's dressed in black sweats and a hoodie, wearing that damn mask. Xavier shrieks when he *finally* notices him, nearly jumping out of his skin, and I pin him with a stare.

Now I know his lack of situational awareness will get us killed.

This can't be my life.

"Gimme all your money," Scar grunts with a finger gun in his pocket.

I'm convinced he has a wire in my brain, because he proves me wrong when I hear the unforgettable sound of the safety being switched off, but his hand remains in the front pocket of his hoodie.

Oh God.

"Please, I don't have any money. I'd give it all to you if I did," Xavier begs, and any plans I had of giving this man more of my time have flown away in the breeze.

My eyes bounce back and forth between them as this foolishness goes down.

"You don't have any money, but you're on a date? With *her*?" Scar asks, staring incredulously at me. I know he's grinning beneath that mask, and my blood is boiling.

Just because he's supposed to keep tabs on me doesn't mean he gets to scare off my dates.

Scar sizes him up. "Run me that watch, then," he orders.

Xavier removes his watch with trembling hands to give to Scar and raises his hands in surrender.

Why me? I'd love to disappear right now.

"You know what? Never mind. I feel bad for you, man. Keep the watch," he says, tossing the watch to Xavier, who catches it and stares in awe.

He hasn't looked at me once since this occurred. It's like I'm not even here. *What if this was a real stick up? Would he even protect me?*

"You're shaking like a leaf, man. Get the hell out of here," Scar jeers, shooing him away.

As if he remembers I exist, his fearful eyes finally meet mine, staring expectantly for me to join him.

He wants to proceed with this date? This is mortifying. I think the fuck not.

"Don't worry about her. She's better off without your broke ass. Bye," he sounds jovial as he dismisses Xavier.

When he doesn't turn away, Scar jolts toward him, and Xavier scurries down a nearby alley until he disappears from view.

I'm fuming. Bare. Vulnerable. Unprotected. I'm a deer in the headlights, and he resembles a lion admiring its prey, anticipating a vicious kill.

He corners me against the brick wall, enveloping me while his scent sends heat to my core. "Like I said, you can't outrun me, Doe."

"Now, what if he calls the fucking cops?" I ask, changing the subject.

"He won't. Plus he left you here with *me*, the big scary man in a mask. A guy like *that* wouldn't tell a tale unless it makes him look good. So, fuck him," he assures with a shrug.

"You have some fucking audacity. White man audacity," I spit, my anger growing at the sight of him in that stupid-ass mask.

He gasps. "Well I never," he says in a fake country accent. "*Nobody* has more audacity than white men. How dare you insult me like that?" he adds playfully.

I love seeing him loosen up like this, but I'm still annoyed.

"I'm just saying, you either need to shit or get off the pot," I tell him, struggling to avoid eye contact as he encases me.

"I can't," he whispers, his breath hitting my cheek as I try to look around.

"Can't what?" I finally glare up at him again.

"Can't get off the pot because I'm shitting," he answers, his shoulders shaking with laughter.

He's such a fucking idiot.

"Wanna go home?"

"No. I came to eat and that didn't happen thanks to *you*," I argue, booping his nose.

"Lucky for you I cooked us dinner at home."

Dinner at home. I like the way that sounds, but I'm still annoyed.

"Was this little stick up planned, too?"

"No. That was my first time. How'd I do?" he asks, humor in his tone.

"Not bad for your first armed robbery, I guess."

As we exit the alley, he rests his hand on my lower back, leading me to the parking lot. He stops at a large navy pickup truck.

"C'mon, Doe. Get in. I want to take you somewhere." he says, tilting his head toward the door he opened for me.

He holds his hand out for me to take as I climb onto the sidestep.

"Watch your head, *mi beba,*" he warns.

I try to ignore how my stomach flips when he calls me that. Mi beba.

To a passerby, I look like I'm being kidnapped by a masked man. If only they knew.

I settle in the passenger seat when we both reach for the seatbelt, and his large hand rests over mine. We stare at each other for a moment before he leans in closer.

"Allow me," he says, breaking the silence.

He holds eye contact as he extends the seatbelt and drags it over me. My body heats under his gaze, and my heart races from the proximity.

I hope he can't hear that.

The click of the buckle fastening breaks our trance, and he backs up to assess me before shutting the door. He rounds to the driver side and settles in, glances over at me and blows out a deep breath.

He turns on a '00s pop playlist, and I am convinced he's doing it to either annoy me or convince me to sing along.

"You can't get this in an Uber," he croons.

He proceeds to sing, replacing every word of "Fergalicious" with "Deirdre-licious," blowing me kisses on every *mwah.*

I don't know what's gotten into him, but he's sillier tonight. I reach for the volume dial when my hand is swatted away.

"Don't disrespect The Dutchess like that," he says in a serious tone.

"Are you serious?" I ask amusedly.

"*Very* serious."

He turns the music up and continues his one-man show. Shimmying and rolling his hips from the driver's seat, he's now catching eyes at the stop light.

Kill me now. Please?

I stare down the traffic light, praying for it to turn green, and of course, it's the longest red light I've ever been stuck at.

"Turn green now. Please?" I plead under my breath.

Moments later, the light changes, and he proceeds to tap the steering wheel, singing every millennial pop song that comes on, eventually settling down as we get closer to my place.

He reaches for my hand to hold, and I let him. He remains focused on the road, giving my hand a gentle squeeze every few minutes.

The sight of this man driving with one hand on the steering wheel and the other in mine should be illegal for my ovaries.

As I study him with knotted brows, I try to piece together his behavior tonight.

No he didn't.

"Are you…are you high right now?"

"Do you get nervous?" he asks, tossing a knowing look at me. "I say hell yeah fuc—"

"Well, there's my answer," I say, cutting him off. "From *my* stash?"

"*Our* stash," he corrects.

He turns onto my street, peering over at me as if he has something to say, but he doesn't. It isn't until he pulls up the driveway, stopping outside my garage, that he speaks.

"Are you mad at me?" he asks.

"Yep," I reply, staring forward, popping the P as yank my hand out of his and cross my arms.

I suppose Dad was onto something about the whole "acting like mom when I'm angry" thing. Her silent treatment and disapproving looks would make a mime break character to apologize.

"What I did back there was impulsive and stupid. I'm sorry I crashed your date and embarrassed you."

I suppose I have inherited her apology demanding skills.

"I'm listening," I say in a low voice, avoiding eye contact.

"You were settling for him. He wouldn't give you what you need. And if *I* scared him, imagine how he'd react to your family."

He's right. A stinging reminder of why I avoid dating now.

"So, what's the plan? Are you supposed to be velcroed to me forever or is there an expiration date on this?" I ask.

"There doesn't have to be an expiration on it. That's up to you." His words ebb out slowly, like he's nervous.

"Why would that be up to me?"

"You're always in control, Deirdre. Even when you think you're not."

I turn toward him with an incredulous look that reads, *bullshit.*

"I have never been in a situation like this, Deirdre. You make me feel so out of control, and I think you know what I mean."

I know exactly what he means.

"I don't think rationally when it comes to you, and that scares the shit out of me. I need my job. My family counts on me to provide, and whatever this is," he says, gesturing between us, "jeopardizes that. I know the potential outcomes, but I'm willing to risk them if you are. But if I'm reading this entirely wrong, please stop me before I make an even bigger fool of myself?"

"Scar, you're not reading anything wrong. I think we both have our reasons, but mine grow weaker every day. I don't have the best of luck with dating, especially not with men in the life, okay?" I admit, taking his hand. "When I get involved with people, I put them in danger, and I don't mean to. You should know that before you agree to trying this with me."

He can still back out, and I wouldn't even be mad at him.

"I'm going to give you all the power here. Everything you'd need to hurt me, because you should feel safe," he says, removing his balaclava. Once it's completely off, I stare at him, not even blinking.

My breath catches in my throat, and I study him closely, taking in every inch of his face. His full beard, dark curls, and the scar through his lip.

It's the most beautiful face I've ever seen. This is him.

"Your name," I blurt. Not a question or a statement, but I need to know it.

"While I don't mind you calling me Scar, my name is César. My birthday is July thirteenth, and I'm twenty-nine. I'm a finder, and that's what I meant when I said it's my job to know things."

"And what do you know about me?" I tease.

"Everything I could learn without asking."

"What do you wish you knew?"

"What you taste like," he says with desire in his eyes.

I'm aware I shouldn't let him get too close, still my hand hovers over his flame in test. Is it possible to both fear and desire someone?

To wonder how far this dance could go? Because I crave him, unmasked and bare. A vulnerability reserved for me only. I'd take it to my grave.

I love my family, but what they don't know simply won't hurt them. Our empire was built on secrets. Secrets held in good taste. So, what's one more?

He leans over the center console, my gaze drops to his full lips, and time halts between us. I match the distance, hovering my lips over his.

"César?"

"Yes?"

"Kiss me," I whisper.

And he does. Calloused hands cradle both sides of my face as he devours me. His kisses are delicately rough, hungry, and desperate. He swipes his tongue at my bottom lip, a power struggle I succumb to as I moan into his mouth.

We break away to catch our breath, and the need in his eyes sends a shiver through me.

"I need you, now," I pant, crawling over the center console to straddle his lap.

He gulps. "Doe, if you let me touch you—"

"Shh," I say, cutting him off, guiding his hands to my dripping core.

"Fuuucckk," he breathes as he palms me through my panties.

I grind into his large hand, and nip at his neck as need courses through me.

I've never wanted anything so badly.

"Doe, wait. Our first time will *not* be in my fucking truck," he demands, removing his hand to press a button on his sun visor.

My garage door opens behind us, and I shake my head in disbelief. "You have a remote for *my* garage?"

"*Claro que sí,*" he says with a smug smile, holding me close as he parks and closes the door. He steps out of the truck, holding me in his arms with ease as we walk toward the door. "Remember what you asked for," he reminds me with a smack on my ass as we enter the house.

Finally, my shadow has stepped into the light, and I'll do anything to keep him here.

36 / homewrecker

Deirdre

9:17 p.m. | 42 minutes after 'the eighth incident'

We're a tangle of limbs and tongues as we stumble into the house. Our hands roam each other in a race against time, though we finally have plenty.

I've *never* been more desperate to be touched. I kick off my shoes, and he does the same. Even while excited, he still remembers to respect my home.

He'll be rewarded for that.

He breaks our kiss abruptly and takes off for the kitchen in a hurry.

"I ruined your date, I can't ruin dinner, too," he says.

And just like that, I'm a puddle, observing him navigate my kitchen comfortably as if he's always lived here. He carefully removes the dish from the oven and is back to me in no time.

"I made *pernil y arroz con gandules.* Now, where were we?" he asks, and before I can respond, my back is against the wall as he gathers my wrists to hold above my head.

His free hand lifts the hem of my dress, and he studies me as his rough fingers trace my seam, taking pleasure in my mewls for more.

He roughly tugs at my waistband, ripping away the lace clinging to my wetness, slipping remnants of the fabric in his pocket.

As if he needs a memento of this night.

"You're so fucking wet for me," he growls, dropping to his knees, balling the hem of my dress. "I need to taste your pretty pussy," he groans and flattens his tongue over my needy center.

Fiery eyes study my every reaction to his worship. Generous kisses travel from my stomach to inner thighs, taking time to appreciate what's before him.

He savors the moment, pressing his nose against me as he takes in my scent and his effect on my body. His touch is patient and precise, a sweet tormenting appetizer before he devours me.

Even when rough, he's an attentive student, taking notes of pleasure to memorize. His tongue plunges inside of me without warning, and I ride it willingly, working my channel as his nose teases my swollen bud.

He tortures my needy pussy with swirls and flicks before latching onto my clit. I grind my hips into his face as my legs tremble beneath me. Rough, calloused hands hold me steady as my nails claw the wall.

"Right there. Don't stop," I breathe, and he obeys, sucking harder as his thumb toys with my other hole.

"Come in my mouth, Doe," he orders before filling his mouth once more. Moans and hums vibrate against my clit, and I obey, screaming for him as he decorates my sensitive pussy with teasing licks.

When he stands before me, his beard is drenched and it's so fucking sexy.

"You taste so fucking good," he praises, leaning in for a kiss, and I command his mouth. I moan around his tongue as he explores my curves, parting my legs to slip a finger inside me.

"You're so greedy, clenching as soon as I touch you. Did you need this, baby?"

I nod eagerly. "More, please?" I beg.

He inserts a second finger, pumping at a delicious pace as I buck into his palm.

"César, fuck," I weep into his neck.

"Fuck, my name sounds so good on your lips," he moans, adding a third finger and pumping harder into me as his thumb circles my clit.

My eyes roll back while his face is buried in my neck as he sings praises in my ear.

"You're going to come for me as many times as you need to. *¿Tu me entiendes*?" He groans, curling his fingers toward my G-spot.

Oh my God.

"Yes, Sir.

"You gon' squirt for me, baby?"

I clutch onto him when my orgasm wracks through me, tunneling my vision as release runs down my legs.

Oh fuck.

He watches me in awe as I ride the aftershocks against his palm. Showering me with praise and forehead kisses.

"You looked so fucking pretty when you came for me. Bend over, *mi beba*," he orders.

I turn away and bend at my waist, wailing as he fulfills his promise. His warm tongue licks my legs clean and swirls around my other hole, peppering kisses on my ass and thighs.

"You are so perfect. So fucking perfect," he says with a hard smack on my ass that has me throbbing with need all over again. "C'mon, baby," he coos as I return to my height.

"Do you want to have dinner now or?" he asks, glancing from me to the kitchen.

"I—uh actually have an appetite for something else," I suggest as my eyes flit to his thick erection.

My mouth waters at the sight of it, and my thighs squeeze together, failing to dull the ache.

I need him now.

When he catches me staring, he smirks. "I was thinking the

same thing. I haven't quite had my fill," he says, gripping his dick through his pants.

"I'd like to get out of this dress," I whisper, leading him to the living room as I reach to undo my zipper, but he beats me to it.

Sweet kisses grace my shoulders and back, as he unclasps my bra and the dress pools at my feet.

"*Dios mio*," he says under his breath, watching me step around it.

He takes my hand as we enter the room, and when I lower myself, he reaches out to stop me.

He places a pillow at my feet, and I kneel onto it, rushing to undo his belt, eager to see him for the first time. With a tug of his pants, the outline of his hard dick is revealed.

He steps out of the pants and removes his boxer-briefs, and my eyes widen as his thick dick springs free. Whiskey eyes set my skin ablaze, and heat pools between my legs as I stroke his length, spreading his precum over the tip.

I swipe my tongue against him to steal a taste, savoring it as I stare up at him eager to please. "Mmhmm."

He's a walking threat and forbidden fruit, ripe for the taking. A taste I yearn for no matter the consequence.

"Fuck my throat, please?" I state in a low tone.

"You sure?" he asks, searching my face for hesitation and finding none.

"I've never been surer," I assure him, spitting as I jack him off.

"*Coño*. Tap my thigh three times if it becomes too much, okay?"

"Yes, Sir."

I welcome him into my mouth, dying for him to be rough and fuck my face. He starts off gentle, cradling the back of my head, and I hum around him.

I want to make him lose control tonight. I need to see him match my dark desires and give me everything I need.

I flatten my tongue along the side of his dick, relishing every vein and ridge of him. My thick thighs squeeze together, applying pressure to my throbbing pussy. I drip with need as he holds my head, using my mouth to satisfy his needs.

When I spread my legs to rub my free hand over my clit, sparks ignite instantly, and I roll my hips onto my palm.

Flames spread over me as pleasure licks up and down my spine. I arch into my hand and moan around his dick as he thrusts into my mouth.

"Show me what a good girl you can be with your mouth full," he taunts with a wicked grin.

I pinch my nipple with my other hand as he picks up the pace. "Fuck, Doe. Your mouth feels so fucking good," he grunts, pressing himself further in my throat.

I perform beneath his gaze, rubbing my pussy and pinching my nipples. Every sensation is heightened under his stare, and my muffled whimpers drive him wild.

"Make yourself feel good, Doe. Rub that pretty fucking pussy with my dick in your throat," he urges.

My body ignites at his permission and praise, and I chase every last sensation while I come down.

"Ohh, fuck. I'm gonna come. Where do you want me to come, pretty girl?" he asks, and I squeeze my full breasts together, providing a canvas for him to lay claim.

White ropes decorate my brown skin, and I swipe a finger through for a taste. Under his watchful gaze, I suck the digit clean as he admires the beautiful mess he made.

The lion and the deer rest, while Deirdre and César roam wild.

37 / the chiropractor

Deirdre

8:14 a.m. | the morning after 'the eighth incident'

The sun violently shines in from the bedroom window, and I drag the comforter over my head to hide. Until I remember I didn't go to sleep alone. I blink my eyes open to find the bed to myself, the aroma of breakfast being cooked, and Latin music playing faintly from downstairs.

Damn. I slept better than I have in *months*. He wasn't lying when he said it'd be hard to pull away once he finally touched me. I didn't want him to stop, and he didn't until I tapped out.

He spoiled me with aftercare and a bubble bath where he joined me, and as much as I love being independent, dare I say princess treatment isn't so bad?

I climb out of bed and slip into my house shoes to investigate what's on the menu.

I toe down the stairs to find an unmasked and shirtless César dancing Bachata at the stove, who I'm surprised to see has a back covered in tattoos.

Seeing him in his element but still navigating through my kitchen as though it's his, does something to me.

My footsteps are quiet as I climb onto the barstool to observe all that is him.

César, I think. Such a beautiful name for him, and it is very moanable, so that's a plus for me.

He is such a gorgeous man, I wonder why he would he ever cover up that face *or* body, because *fuck.* Wetness pools between my legs as I imagine him naked last night, pounding me into my mattress.

Oh my God.

"*Buenos días,* César. Everything smells amazing," I say to his back, and he doesn't startle at my voice over the music. He turns to face me, like this something we do all the time.

"*Buenos días,* Deirdre," he says with a smile as he rounds the counter to kiss me on the cheek. "Thank you. I thought I'd give you the best of both worlds today. Lucky for me, you're not picky."

He makes a show of presenting the dishes, and it's so cute.

"We have *mangú con los tres golpes,* a Dominican breakfast. Salami, fried eggs, and fried cheese with *mangú,*" he says, placing the plate in front of me.

"I am not a good baker, but my sister found a Latin bakery that sells Puerto Rican pastries, and I know you love donuts and pastries, so I got us some *Pan de Mallorca,* it's sweet bread," he informs me, pointing to a box onto the counter.

"And *café con leche* I made in the *greca,*" he finishes, pointing to a silver coffee maker on the stove.

"I didn't know I had one of these," I joke.

"You do now," he says with a smile. "Trust me, you won't want coffee any other way after this."

"I'll take your word for it," I tell him.

He faces me, and his eyes roam my frame with the same intensity as last night. "That's because you're a good girl," he reminds me with a wink, rounding the counter to pull me into a kiss that would wake me up if I wasn't already.

Damn.

"Should I expect this *every* time I wake up with you? You could make me spoiled," I warn him.

"And? You deserve to be spoiled. I like taking care of you. Haven't I made that clear, already? Because, if not, I have more work to do."

"I suppose you have. Especially after last night," I say, biting my lip.

He shares a look that screams, *we could go again*, and my thighs are clenching together.

"Are you doing anything on Friday?" he inquires, grabbing a cloth to wipe down my countertop.

"No, you got something planned for your birthday?" I ask with a furrowed brow.

"I thought we could go out," he suggests.

"I'm down. You sure you want to go out with *me* for your birthday?"

"With you? *Absolutamente.* How do you feel about being seen with *me* in public?"

I chuckle out my response. "I'm fine with it. You're kinda cute."

"Only kinda? Girl," he says with a playful eye roll.

"Where did you want to go?" I ask before finishing my coffee. I could definitely become addicted to this.

"Somewhere special. I prefer to keep you on your toes when I'm not curling them," he teases.

"Oh really now?" I giggle.

This man. Wow.

"Hurry up and finish your breakfast, there's something to show you in the bedroom," he says over his shoulder.

"You don't have to wait." With a grin, I point to my empty plate.

"Say no more," he says, picking me up, and my house shoes slip off. He places me on the counter, spreading my legs and tugging off my panties as he kneels before me, pocketing them once again.

He adorns me with kisses all over my legs and feet, trailing closer to my dripping core. He grips my thighs roughly and bites my inner thigh, staring up at me with hunger as his tongue parts my lips and twirls around my clit.

"You're going to squirt for me again. That's so fucking sexy to me," he growls.

"I hadn't done it until recently," I admit.

"Don't say it's because of me," he warns, filling me with his thick fingers and curling them toward my G-spot.

I gasp at the intrusion. "Why not?"

Whiskey eyes pierce me, filled with intrigue and desire as his fingers pump in and out of my pussy. His tongue flicks and sucks as his fingers travel up to pinch my nipples. I toss my head back, and when I squeeze my thighs around his head, a growl escapes him that vibrates through my core.

"Oh fuck. Right there," I sob.

He maintains his pace, his gaze encouraging me to let go, and I fucking shatter on this marble countertop at his silent command. Groans follow as he greedily laps me up with no desire to stop until he's satisfied.

He leaves gentle kisses on my legs as he helps me off the counter, gripping my ass possessively as my feet touch the ground.

* * *

Ahem.

I declare that I finally got my back cracked last night, and this morning.

Spoiler alert: and it wasn't by a chiropractor. That is all.

Will report back soon!

SKYE DADDY

You fucking better! That's what I'm talking about, Sis!!

LO

Wait a minute. The secret admirer?

So, you DO know what he looks like. 👀

I'm so excited about this!!!

He's fine as hell and OMG! He's made my body do things I didn't know it could do.

SKYE DADDY

I knew he was fine! That's that book boyfriend dick. 🤣 I love this for you!

LO

Yesss! I can't wait for the details.

Girl, You needed this!

38 / beep beep

Deirdre

6:27 p.m. | 50 minutes before 'the ninth incident'

I admire myself in the mirror as I clasp the gold necklace around my neck to complete my look. My hair turned out perfect, and this green corset dress Alora designed is *everything*. I spritz my cherry fragrance over my shelf and grab my evening bag before stepping out of the room.

"Happy birthday, César," I say as I come down the stairs to greet him.

"Wow. Happy birthday, indeed," he murmurs, taking my hand to turn me around. "You sure we gotta leave the house? Because I'm already thinking about bringing you back here to lay you out."

"Hmm. Hold that thought," I respond, holding my finger up before heading back upstairs.

I squat to retrieve the "toy box" from underneath my bed and search for a remote that looks like a key fob, tucking it in my palm. I find the matching toy, disappear inside the en suite to insert it, and return downstairs. With a smirk, I place the "key" in César's hand.

"What is this?" he asks with a raised brow.

"A key," I answer sarcastically.

"Key for what exactly?"

"Press button and see," I challenge with a wink.

césar

7:10 p.m. | 'the ninth incident'

I press the button and hear a faint buzzing, and Deirdre jumps a little.

"That kind of remote control. Alright. I like the way you think, Doe," I praise.

"I figured you would," she says with a smile, leaning in to kiss me on the cheek.

I toy with her a bit on the drive there just to see her squirm and am looking forward to an eventful night, thanks to her.

We pull up to this fancy new restaurant in town called Tastebud. I wanted to bring her here because it's apparently a favorite of hers back home. Her face lights up when she spots the sign, and I know that I've made the right choice.

I park and hand the keys over to the valet, excited for a real date with her on my arm. I know it's a risk for us both, but what's one night?

The hostess greets us and leads us to a table tucked away from the rest of the crowd, and I am glad I requested that considering the toy currently resting in Deirdre's pussy that's begging for my attention. I rest my hand in my pocket carefully to avoid pressing the remote.

Not now, Doe. Be a good girl and wait.

I scan the menu, but Deirdre is already excited to order her usual once again. I'm hoping on a night like tonight, she feels a little less homesick. The waiter takes our drink orders, and Deirdre starts making faces from her seat.

"Are you okay?" I ask with wrinkled brows.

"Of course," she assures with a playful smile.

I scan the menu as we make conversation. As she shares her favorite dishes, she lights up while talking about the roasted chicken, and it's so cute. She mentions the dessert menu and assures that we're going to have a good time tonight.

We most definitely will.

When she starts talking about work, I listen attentively, reminding myself not to accidentally share anything specific about *my* job. Then she stops mid-sentence and resumes talking, I glance up to find her eyeing me curiously.

What is going on with her?

"Doe, what's wrong?"

"Nothing. This chair is a bit uncomfortable."

"I'll flag down the waiter and get you a different chair, *mi beba*."

"No. I'll be fine," she states through gritted teeth, leaving no room for argument, and excuses herself to the bathroom.

The waiter approaches the table while she's gone, so I order for us. Steak for me and roasted chicken for her. I mention the chair to him before he leaves, and he swaps it out before she returns.

My hands rest in my lap as we talk more about our interests, treating this like the first date we should've had.

She flinches a few times more, and I stare incredulously, but she waves me off again.

I straighten my spine and give her a look, and keep my voice low. "Do you we need to go home? I can get our order to go," I assure.

She avoids my question and blurts nervously, "Do you want to go to the Divin anniversary party with me? It's the location's tenth anniversary, and it's a big deal for me. I'd like you to come as my date, if you're free. My family doesn't usually do anything with this branch, so we should be free of them for the night. Just us," she reassures me and shifts in her seat.

"Of course, I will," I say, reaching across the table to take her hands in mine.

Her eyes widen, and before I can even ask, we're interrupted by a young man who approaches our table to introduce himself as one of the valets.

"Is everything alright?" I ask.

He scratches his head as he explains that for some reason, he believes my key fob is dead since he hasn't been able to unlock my car door to move it.

What the fuck?

That's strange, and I'm not sure what I can do to remedy this. He is walking me through his experience and pressing the button in demonstration when I spot Deirdre out the corner of my eye fidgeting and taking deep breaths as she readjusts in her seat, then it clicks for me. That facial expression tells me all I need to know.

I know that face, she's about to come.

The valet continues unsuspectingly pressing the button with his back to her. At least he doesn't know what's happening. But the thought of another man making her come, even by accident, sends jealousy raging through me.

"Oh my goodness. I just remembered. That's the key fob for my wife's car. I'm so sorry about this mix-up. They look so similar," I say as I look into my pocket for the actual car keys. I place them in his hand and snatch the other keys. Deirdre sighs in relief of them being in their rightful place.

"Thank you so much, young man," I say, grabbing my wallet to tip him a hundred-dollar bill for the trouble he's unknowingly caused. He thanks me profusely for the tip, tucking it in his pocket quickly as if he's scared I'm going to change my mind.

Deirdre sits across from me stifling laughter and looks as if she is going to explode from holding it in. This tests my resolve as I do my best to maintain a straight face in front of this kid who has no idea what is going on behind him.

"I hope you and your wife have a wonderful night. Thanks again," he says softly to us both and exits the restaurant to *actually* park my truck.

My wife, huh?

When he's out of earshot, we erupt with laughter, and when we settle down, our food comes.

"I know it's your birthday, but can you do something for me?"

"Anything."

"Wear the mask tonight. I read it in a book once," she says in a low voice and takes a bite of food while she awaits my response.

I love when she asks for what she wants.

She's earned a break for the rest of dinner after that little mishap, but after we leave, it's on. I tease her with the toy randomly throughout the drive home, because if she wants to be played with, who am I to deny her?

We barely make it inside the house before she drops to her knees as soon as I lock the door behind us. Pawing at my pants and licking her lips as she removes my belt.

"Mask, please?" she asks, removing it from my pocket and holding it up.

She pulls out my dick and proceeds to rub the precum over her lips before sucking gently on the tip.

Dios mio.

I slip the balaclava over my face and thrust into her pretty mouth. She grips the back of my legs and peers up at me with desire in those watery eyes. I try to relieve her, but she pulls me in to take even more of me down that throat.

Fuckkk.

She gets whatever she wants. Even on my birthday, because she made it special.

I nearly come and have to stop her, because she needs to fall apart first. So, I pull my pants up and usher her upstairs where she undresses to reveal another crotchless lingerie set. Similar to one she's wore before, except this one is purple.

Coincidence? I think not.

She then kneels before me, awaiting my command. I slip into my role, the lion preying on the deer. So sweet, so innocent, so beautiful.

"Are you afraid, Doe?"

Her throat bobs with a swallow. "The opposite."

"*Déjame ver.* Spread those legs and show me how brave you are."

She obeys, climbing on the bed to splay herself in front of me, rubbing her glistening pussy while she holds my gaze.

"Such a good little doe," I praise as she performs for me. I am craving her, but I still want to play before I indulge.

I compare the first time I laid eyes on her to now, and it's just as thrilling. She could be my demise, and I'd welcome her with open arms. My only ask is that she makes it quick and painless.

"Do you want to be a little slut tonight? Just for me?"

She nods eagerly in response.

I approach slowly, enraptured in her facial expression as she makes herself come with her fingers.

I dip my head to slip a nipple into my mouth and suck, maintaining eye contact as she hums, maintaining the rhythm on that gorgeous clit. I rub and flick her nipples, and the sexy moans she makes have me dying to be inside her.

"Can I touch what's mine?" I ask, and she nods in response.

I kneel behind her on the bed, pressing my hard dick into her back as I wrap one hand around her neck, using the other to caress her sensitive clit. She arches into me and sobs in pleasure.

She comes alive at the touch of my hand, and I use that power wisely. I nip and lick her neck as she grinds her pussy to chase this high.

"Come on my fingers if you want me to fuck you, *mi beba,*" I order, tightening my grip on her neck.

"César," she cries, grinding faster until she unravels, uttering and weeping as she comes down.

Deirdre turns to me, and we lie back for a moment as she nuzzles into my chest. I indulge in that sweet cherry scent while I hold her in my arms.

"You tired, baby?"

"Not at all," she quips, running her hands along my erection.

"Show me, then," I challenge, and she wastes no time, reaching for her bedside table and retrieving a condom.

Take whatever you want, Doe. I'm yours.

She tugs down my pants and makes quick work of slipping the condom on and straddles my lap, like she can read my mind.

"Ride me, Doe. Use me like a toy to make yourself come."

Her breath hitches, and she moans as she rubs my dick over her clit before sliding down on it. She takes it slow as her pussy stretches around me, grinding slow and steady.

I spank her ass, and she moans in my ear, riding me harder.

"Fuck. You're so pretty, baby."

She beams under my praise, and I take turns giving attention to her full breasts, begging to be sucked.

She guides herself on me, picking up her speed, and I am amazed by her.

"That's right. Bounce that ass up and down on my dick. *Buena.*"

She moans as she grazes her clit and shuts her eyes.

That just won't do. I need to see her.

I tilt her chin toward me and place a kiss on her lips.

"*Mìrame,*" I demand in a low voice, and she nods and locks eyes with me. Her nails dig into my back as her pleasure builds.

"César, fuck. Please don't stop," she pleads.

"Come, baby. *Ahora mismo.*"

I feel her squeezing around me, and as she spasms on my dick,.I suck harder on her *tetas* as she rides out her pleasure on me.

"*Coño*. You took me so well," I compliment, and she bites her lip in response. "You want more?" I ask with a smirk,

"I didn't want you to stop," she challenges.

An idea comes to mind, and since it's my birthday, I hope she's on board with it.

"I need to fuck you in your office," I demand, leading her off the bed and outside the bedroom.

"Why my office?" she asks curiously.

"Because I want to bend you over that desk," I admit, holding her hand as we travel down the stairs.

"Well, that's reason enough." She chuckles and opens the door.

I reward her with a spank so loud, my dick twitches in my pants. Without argument, she does as she's told, bending over her desk and arching her back toward me. The heart shape of her plump ass drives me wild, and I can't help but to spread her cheeks and tongue-fuck that pretty puckered hole.

She gasps in surprise and whimpers as I snake my hand around to toy with her swollen clit, and she arches into me.

"Fuck, yes baby. You taste so fucking good," I praise as I rub the soft globes of her ass. I return to my height, standing behind her. "Can I fill *both* your needy holes?"

"Oh my god," she sobs, arching her back higher. "Yes, Sir. Please?"

"Tell me what you're begging for. *Cuéntame*," I urge, running my hands over her back.

"I need to be filled, Sir. Please?" she whines.

"Good girl, asking for what you want."

I tease her as I part her pussy lips with my dick and slap it against her until she begs. She's so eager that her walls clench around me as soon as I enter.

"Your pussy is so fucking greedy, baby. You need to be fucked so bad."

"Mmhm," she hums as I bottom out, sliding my thumb into her ass.

I thrust into her at a punishing pace, and she takes it, moaning and screaming as her pussy grips me.

"You need to come? Come with me. Come, *mi beba. Ahora,*" I order, smacking her ass as I spill into the condom and she unravels on *my* dick with none other than *my* name on her tongue.

Because she is *mine*.

If death looks this fucking beautiful, I may reconsider.

39 / don't bleed in front of the sharks

César

7:55 a.m. | 14 hours before 'the last incident'

Waking up with my Doe in my arms has been both a beautiful and painful reminder that I needed to make a decision yesterday. It's so easy to get enraptured in her and forget the task at hand, but I need to secure another client to make up for this loss with the Hales.

There's an anniversary party tonight at the Divin Distillery, and she invited me, despite the whole "let's be a secret" thing. I said yes, because I'd enjoy nothing more than to spend the evening with her in the place she's dedicated herself to. She guarantees her family won't be in attendance, and that puts me at ease.

While the Klarkes are intimidating, I'd expect them to be more cautious of whoever Deirdre dates moving forward.

She swears her father is the hardest to impress, but something tells me that Regina would be the biggest challenge and the one to worry about. Especially when it comes to finding out what led me to Deirdre.

I kiss her goodbye, and those beautiful brown eyes watch me as I get dressed and head out for the day. I have to be careful around her, because if I am not, I won't leave that bed.

I hop in my truck and pull out of her driveway to be on time for a debrief with one of my clients who's hired me to find out if there best friend and husband are sleeping together. This case should keep me busy today.

When's the right time to tell her?

Not tonight.

I'm thankful for the distraction when my Bluetooth announces a call.

"Incoming call from Dax Hale. Answer it?"

"Answer it," I say.

"Morning, Dax. Is everything all right?" I ask, nervous he's calling me so early in the day.

"Hey, mate. Would you mind dropping in today? There's a new development with the Klarke bid, and I'd like for us to have a plan," he informs me.

"Of course. I can stop by around noon. Does that work for you?

"See you then," he says before the line goes dead.

Noon rolls around quickly, and as always, I arrive early, running into a security guard standing outside of Dax's office door. Which is odd, considering I've never seen him before. He holds the door open and announces me when I approach.

"Thanks. Come in," Dax says. "Can you let Dara know I don't need her for this conversation?"

Why not?

I take in the room as I enter and train my facial expressions. He's sitting behind his desk eating a cookie, which seems harmless. But the energy in here is off. More than usual, anyway. I often feel uncomfortable around Dax, and Dara is so skittish that I assume she's afraid of me, but this is different.

"Have a seat, mate. Fancy a biscuit?" he asks, taking a bite of his, pointing to a box of sugar cookies on his desk.

"No, thank you. What's this new development you mentioned?" I ask, taking a seat in front of him.

"Hmph. All work and no play. We both know that isn't true, innit?"

What is this idiot on about?

He picks up a manilla folder and reaches inside to retrieve something. When he tosses a handful of photos down between us, I don't need to flip through them all to know exactly what they'll show. Me and Deirdre photographed every time we have been in public together.

Fuck.

"I found it odd when our *best* private investigator suddenly came up short. How could *you* not find *anything* incriminating on a family *full* of criminals? I didn't want to suspect anything, because Theo speaks highly of you, but there's a million dollars on the line. You must understand that I need to know I can trust my private eye." He takes a moment to chew his cookie before continuing. "I must admit that I hadn't expected to find you in such a *compromising* position with Deirdre Klarke."

Watch your fucking mouth.

"You will not disrespect her," I threaten through gritted teeth.

"Easy, mate. I don't fault you for shagging her. She is a looker. I like mine a bit leaner, but she has quite the arse," he adds with a wink.

Motherfucker.

I ball my fists in my lap and will myself not to lunge across this table right now. I know better, and that's the reason for the sudden need for security on standby. He wants me to be violent and overreact because that's how he sees us all.

It's not just Deirdre and Regina that he fears, it's me too.

"Now, now," he warns as he observes me, nonchalantly taking another bite of his cookie.

"Wrap it up, won't you? You don't have to answer. Obviously you'll end this and finish your assignment. That is, unless *she* is more important than your reputation. I can trust you'll make the right decision, mate," he says with a smug smile as he rounds his desk. "Consider this our debrief for the week, alright? I expect this to be handled by this time next week."

He places a hand on my shoulder, daring me to do otherwise.

It isn't until I get in my truck that I consider my options. There is no way out of this that ensures we can be together, and that realization makes my stomach turn.

I'm not a selfish person, and the one time I am, I'm reminded of why I put others' needs before my own. At least if I consider how my actions affect others, I don't do shit that'll blow up in my face.

I exhale, sending off a text to the only person that can find me a way out of the mess I've created.

I need your help.

EMILIANO

On it.

7:38 p.m. | 2 hours and 4 minutes before 'the last incident'

"Are you sure about this?" I ask as I shift the truck into park.

A stupid question to ask now that we're here, but I've been on autopilot since the meeting earlier with Dax. Deirdre deserves to hear the truth from me soon.

"I'm sure. My family doesn't usually attend these anniversary parties. It'll be fine. One night where we can be out in the open." She repeats her earlier reassurance with a smile that crushes me.

Our little secret isn't ours anymore. I stand to lose her either way, and that terrifies me. A few months ago, I wouldn't believe I'd be in a position like this, and I certainly didn't expect to be here when I took the case.

I was kidding myself when I kept saying it would be easy to walk away when the job was done, because I never wanted it to end. Now, it has to. I cannot allow myself to let my family suffer, even if it means *I* do for the rest of my life.

She can't be with someone that she doesn't trust, and neither can I. It's unfair after all she's been through to give her hope, and I will never forgive myself for this.

Deirdre reeled me into her orbit when she didn't even know I existed. Staying away was impossible, and it made me reckless. If I had stayed in the background, I would have been better off. She would've been better off never knowing who I was.

She may not let me live after this, and I wouldn't blame her. Because what life could I possibly have without seeing her smile again? Not one I care to think about.

"César? What's wrong?" she asks, waving her hand in front of me.

I clear my throat. "Oh, nothing. I think I may be getting sick."

She frowns. "Why didn't you tell me? I wouldn't have made you come."

"What's important to you is important to me. *¿Tú me entiendes?*" I ask, wrapping an arm around her to press a kiss to the top of her head.

She stiffens when a woman calls out in the distance, "My baby."

I glance up to find her mom, Dorothea Klarke, rushing toward us with open arms, her gaze locked on my Doe.

She resembles her daughter so much. Her rich brown skin glows in a shimmering gold floor-length gown. Her dark curls are full and defined, framing her beautiful face. Deirdre looks just like her mother.

So, that's where those eyes come from, I think. I'd seen them in pictures, but pictures don't do either of these women justice.

She approaches us and engulfs her in a squeezing hug. "Dee, I've missed you so much."

"What are you doing here?" she squeaks.

"You wouldn't come to us, so we came to you," her mother beams, her smile taking over her whole face.

When they pull apart, Deirdre returns to my side, and her mother eyes me curiously. "You hadn't told me you were seeing someone," she sings, swatting her arm. "And who might you be, handsome?"

I chuckle nervously. "César," I say, reaching out to shake her manicured hand.

She hums, "César, huh?" And looks at Deirdre. "When were you going to mention him?"

She glances over to me, hoping for a save, anxious and blindsided.

I've got her. I've always got her.

"We've only recently started dating, and felt it would be best that we spent more time together before telling our families," I quip, eager to rescue Doe.

"I see. Did she ever mention that she is arranged to be married to someone?"

What?

"Mom please," she begs, all but stamping her foot. "Don't lie. All you do is scare people away from me," she grumbles.

"What? We invited a few down here to meet you. Your father wanted to revisit the conversation, given how things ended with Law—"

"I don't want to talk about this. Not now. Not ever," she declares, cutting her off.

"You will not speak to me like that, Deirdre," her mother warns with a scowl, the mood now shifted into one even I can't save.

"If you'll excuse us," Deirdre says firmly, folding her arm in mine and ushering us away.

She trains her expressions into a forced smile, reapplying the mask she needs for survival. As hard as I've worked for her to feel comfortable taking it off, it pains me that she will shrink herself to feel safe. She needs someone to protect her, and I want that to be me, but how?

She leads the way through the halls of the distillery, seemingly to find a spot to be alone. I wonder if she has hiding places here to slip into whenever she grows weary.

"I'm sorry, César. I didn't know they'd show. My father doesn't enjoy traveling here. That's one reason I chose Austin," she explains, avoiding eye contact.

"And here I thought you came in hopes of finding me," I joke, attempting to comfort her.

She snorts. "How could I have known you were here waiting for me? I want you to know that I haven't agreed to marry anyone. After my ex, I figured they'd drop the marriage and grandkids talk. I've poured myself into this company in hopes to avoid our marriage traditions. It's worked for Darius so far. They —" She pauses. "I'm sorry. You're not feeling well. This is the last you need to be dealing with."

"Hey," I say, grabbing her attention. "Let me see your face. Please?" I ask.

I'm rewarded when she turns toward me, offering a soft smile.

There she is.

"It's okay. I'm here for you, and this is your night, remember? Don't let anybody ruin it for you. And if they try, they've gotta get through me."

"I appreciate that, but my family doesn't really back down. I usually just walk away, but I won't let them fuck with you. Look at my mom, we weren't even here for ten minutes, and she already tried to run you off."

"*Mírame,* I'm not going anywhere, unless you ask me to," I reassure her, tilting her chin up to meet me in a kiss. "This is to celebrate your hard work, Divin, and your staff. We're going to enjoy ourselves regardless of who is in attendance. And when you are ready to go home, we will. No questions asked, okay?"

"Okay," she whispers, staring adoringly as she leans in to kiss me sweetly. "I'm glad I'm here," I murmur against her lips.

"Me too. I'm sure you've met Regina, but in case you haven't met the others, I'll introduce you, and then we can get the hell out of here, if you want.

If you want to stay, it helps that you make good arm candy and you look like you know how to fight," she teases.

"Luckily, I do." I chuckle, holding my arm out for her to take, and we reenter the party.

I recognize Regina and Angelo Jr. speaking off to the side, and when they spot us, they begin to make their way over. I swallow and do my best to seem cool.

Deirdre pipes up, "These are my cousins. Regina and Angie."

"I was told you brought a man. I had to see it to believe it," she adds, looking me up and down. "Brave."

"Nice to meet you, I'm Junior. They call me Angie, but *you* don't call me Angie," he orders, his tone lacking amusement.

Are they all this serious?

"Fair enough. It's nice to meet you, *Junior*," I say, putting emphasis on his name.

"Thanks, man. See how easy that was," he says, looking at his sister and Deirdre.

Regina cackles. "Just because something is easy, doesn't mean *I'm* going to do it. It's been this way since we were kids. Stupid nicknames last forever. You're Angie, I'm Gene"—she points to herself—"and Roxanne is Rocky," she says, searching the room for her.

Deirdre asks her, "Where is my favorite cousin, Rocky?"

"Favorite?" She gasps dramatically. "She's around here somewhere on auntie duty."

Deirdre smiles to herself. "I'm glad you brought Audre and Andrea. I miss them."

Regina's dark-black hair flows down her back in loose waves, and she's wearing a floor-length backless gown. Her eyes shift to me, and she steps forward. "I'm Regina Delvecchio, but I'm sure my reputation precedes me," she says, reaching her hand out to shake mine. "I can smell the fear on you, kid. Don't let the other sharks get a whiff," she whispers, leaning in close. "It's a pleasure to meet you, César," she tells me when she pulls back with a smile.

"The pleasure is all mine."

She's more intense than I expected.

40 / her choice or mine?

Deirdre

9:28 p.m. | 14 minutes before 'the last incident'

The party has dwindled down, and I'm thinking it's time we go home, too.

That thought is interrupted when I feel a warm palm on my shoulder, and I turn around to find Angie wearing a look of concern.

"Hey, can we talk for a moment alone?" he asks.

"Of course. Let's go to my office."

I lead the way and punch in the keypad into the door. We step inside, and he shuts the door behind him.

"So, what's up?" I ask, crossing my arms as I lean against my desk.

He sighs, grabbing a seat on the sofa. "How well do you know your date? I knew I recognized him from somewhere."

My brows knit. "César? What about him?" I ask, maintaining a calm tone while my stomach drops to my feet.

"He ever tell you what he does for a living?"

"Yeah, he called himself a finder. Said it's his job to know things," I answer, my voice quivering with uncertainty.

"The fuck does that mean? That was good enough for you?"

"Get to the fucking point, Angie," I grit.

"You ever see a job application for a fucking *finder*? The guy is a private investigator," he says, rubbing the back of his neck.

"Why is that a problem?"

"He's a fucking PI who does occasional work for the Cartel, but he's not *in* it," he snaps, as if the reason for his anger is obvious.

"Okay? A PI isn't a fucking Fed," I say flatly.

"Not a fucking Fed, but he works for the Hales and has for a long time," he blurts, his eyes on the ceiling as if he can't witness my reaction.

I shake my head in confusion, unable to stop my heart from pounding. "For how long?" My question comes out in a whisper.

"Eight years. After Theo opened up shop down here. He's supposed to blackmail you into conceding the bid. When he couldn't find shit on *you*, he started looking into Regina." He finally meets my watery gaze once more.

"How do you know this?

"Not too long after you called me talking about some mystery guy, someone accessed surveillance footage of the distillery and our on-site computers. This raised suspicion, causing me to look further into it. I found it odd that the *only* computer they wanted access to in the entire company was yours," he informs me, pinning me with his stare that makes me stiffen. "But you already know about that," he adds, goading me. "I left it alone because you didn't ask for help, but when you called Regina talking about the bid, she asked me to look into it, and I found shit about César working for them. Imagine my surprise when you arrived on his fucking arm," he spits out, shaking his head once he's through.

"I'm such a fucking idiot," I mutter, swallowing the rising bile in my throat, my eyes to the floor as I will away the impending tears.

"You promised you wouldn't do anything stupid, Dee. How much have you told him?"

I want to scream.

"Is this really true, Angie? You're not fucking with me?"

"You know I wouldn't do that," he says with a shake of his head. "If I mentioned it to Gi or Uncle El, he'd be dead right now. There's obviously something going on, so talk to the guy. The ball's in your court, though, okay?"

"Okay," I breathe.

"I'm sorry, Dee, but I can't let you look like a fucking fool," he mutters, sincerity in his stare.

I sniffle. "It's fine. I needed to know. Thanks for telling me."

"You can't catch a fucking break, kid. I'm sorry," he adds, making his way to the door.

"So…what happens to him? Is it up to me or *her*?" I ask, stopping him in his tracks.

He turns to me with a calm expression. "The choice is yours."

"As long as she doesn't find out, right?" I ask with an unamused laugh.

He confirms with a nod. "I'm going to make sure the twins are packed up to fly back home tonight. I love you, cousin," he says, shutting the door behind him.

I need to hear this from César, but I cannot trust myself not to lose it if I leave this room. The last thing I need is to be seen crying over a man when my family is here. César wouldn't make it out of here alive.

He doesn't deserve to walk into a burning building that he won't exit. My earlier words replay on a loop in my mind.

Hey. Can you meet me in my office?

CÉSAR

Of course, baby. Be right there.

The lion wins, leaving me to choose his fate. And I can't bring myself to decide.

41 /
i'd rather go blind

César

9:42 p.m. | 'the last incident'

When I reach for the doorknob, I hear sobs on the other side of the door. I turn the knob quickly and find her staring back at me with fire in her eyes, unlike I have ever seen.

"Close the door behind you," she says, far more calmly than what her expression conveys.

"What hap—"

"Close the door. Please," she interjects, her tone heavy with irritation.

"Okay," I resign, shutting the door, waiting for the click to sound before this conversation continues. "Who upset you? I swear."

"What do you swear, *Scar*?" she prods.

I jerk my head back in confusion "*¿Què?* We're back to 'Scar' now?" I ask.

"Mmhm. 'Cause you're a fucking liar," she hisses.

"Where is this coming from?"

"You're a PI for the Hales? I need to hear you say it. You either are or you're not."

This is exactly what I feared.

"I am a private investigator, and they're one of my many clients."

"And?" she bites back, staring expectantly for me to hurry up.

"They hired me a few months ago to surveil you," I finally admit.

She laughs, but there's no humor in it. "Wrong number, my ass. How long did you watch me before sending that text?"

"Two weeks," I say in a hushed tone.

She scoffs. "I was *that* easy. Took the bait from a fucking album. I feel so stupid. Is *César* even your real name?"

Why would she believe anything I've said now?

"Yes. Cèsar is my real name, and it wasn't like that. I sent that message because I wanted to know *you*. Deirdre, you have to believe me." I take a deep breath. "Everything I told you about myself is true, except my job. I never intended to hurt you, I promise."

"What you intended to do doesn't matter to my family. I think you know that too. Regina *will* kill you because I won't. You need to leave. Now," she says, her tone leaving no room for argument.

Red-rimmed eyes and unshed tears stare holes through me. *I did that to her. Fuck.*

My stomach sinks at her words. How could I promise to protect her when she wasn't even safe from me? At this point, it's not death that I'm afraid of, it's losing her.

"I'm trying not to raise my voice to alarm them. I know this is just a job for you, but it was *real* for me," she mumbles under the weight of her tears.

"It isn't *just* a job." I sigh, wishing I could explain why I took the case, but that won't make this any better.

It stopped being about the job a long time ago.

"That night I let you stay over. You told them, didn't you? I hope you had a good laugh and whatever they're paying is worth it," she grinds out, finding her righteous anger again.

Say something.

"I didn't betray you, I protected you from them," I say weakly.

I would rather give all the money back than spend another day without her, and that terrifies me.

"Tell them you did your job. 'Cause I don't want that fucking property if this is what they'd stoop to for it. I'll call my agent tomorrow to concede. Those motherfuckers can have whatever they want as long they leave me *and* Divin alone. We were here first and will remain, regardless of the games they play."

As I study her heels pacing the hardwood, I war with myself the need to hold her. To reassure her. Touch won't suffice and words won't heal the pain I've caused.

"Have they ever told you they don't want that property? They just don't want *me* to have it. You know why that is? Hmm?" She pauses, leaning against her desk waiting for a response I don't have.

"Do you know why *I* need that property? So I can make sure my kids can have a choice between being in in the fucking mob or not. That good enough for you?"

They've never said they don't want the property in front of me, but didn't have to tell me. Their concerns with Deirdre and Regina are because they're successful Black women—that's painfully obvious.

"I am a Klarke. My family prides themselves on not being seen as 'the *good* Black folks,' because there's no such thing," she says, putting emphasis on her words. "They fear us all, but *we* give them something to be afraid of. People like you and I are expendable to people like *them*. It doesn't matter how much harder *we* work, they still feel we're undeserving.

"At least Theo Hale appeared to be a decent guy from what I hear, who *actually* knew the business. Dax is going to get himself killed, so I suggest you find a new employer."

She isn't wrong.

She continues, "I'm not letting white people piss on my dreams. Never have, never will. I've made it this far, and I'll be damned if I walk away. Whatever they've got planned is no match for me. I *will* honor my ancestors by behaving *exactly* how a Klarke should. That's what I want you to tell them. You can leave now."

I will, but I don't say that.

I drink her in for what may be the last time, committing her to memory. She deserves to feel seen, and I saw her. I can't say that I wasn't warned about Deirdre Klarke. Loving her is dangerous, there was bloodshed, and I may as well be dead because I stole her light.

"I'm sorry, Doe. You have to know that I am so sorry," I choke out over my own unshed tears.

"Just go. Please," she croaks.

I said I wouldn't go anywhere unless she asked me to, and I've gotta respect her wishes.

"And Scar?"

"Yeah?"

"I was falling for you," she sobs, making it ever harder to walk away.

My heart contorts at her admission. It serves as a painful reminder, reassurance, and the final nail in my coffin. If I say it back, I'd be telling the truth, but she won't believe me, so I nod.

Me too, mi beba. *Me too.*

I exit the party with my head held high, and it isn't until I get to my truck that a tear falls. Then another and another. On the ride home, I pass Regina on the road, she honks her horn and smiles, waving with a lit cigarette tucked between her fingers.

For a second, I lock eyes with undoubtedly the scariest woman alive and return the wave.

"Dax is going to get himself killed, so you should find a new employer" rings in my mind the entire ride home. That's why I contacted Emiliano for help. If anybody can save my ass, it's him.

42 / teddies & prayers

Deirdre

10:19 p.m. | 51 minutes after 'the last incident'

A knock on my office door startles me. Assuming it's César, I sink further to the floor. "Please leave me alone," I beg.

The knocks continue, followed by Regina cursing under her breath.

"If you don't open this goddamn door," she demands, jiggling the knob.

I stand, swiping at my tears as I unlock the door to let her in. "Sorry, I thought you were someone else," I mutter.

She stares incredulously and pushes past me to enter the room, scanning the space as if she is looking for something. I follow her, asking questions, but she remains silent.

After she's covered every corner of the room, she speaks.

"Rocky said Andrea can't find his teddy bear that Cidro gave him. He had it with him at the party. We can't fly home without it. I can't give my baby any more bad news," she says tearfully.

"We're going to find it."

"Okay," she sniffles. "Thanks."

"He was playing video games with Darius and Angie in

Dad's office, so it's probably there," I suggest, trotting up the stairs with her on my heels.

I enter the room where we had our loved ones stash their belongings, and sure enough, when I kneel to peek under the desk, that teddy bear is staring right at me. I sigh in relief that Andrea's memento is found, hoping it brings Regina some ease.

"I found it," I say, retrieving the stuffed animal.

"I miss him so much," she croaks.

I sit up on my heels to see Regina seated on the couch hunched over, and when I stand, a wracked sob escapes her lips.

Oh shit.

"Hey, it's okay. See?" I ask, holding up the stuffed bear as I rush to her side.

She cradles her face in her hands, and I awkwardly sit beside her, opting to rub her back while she gets this out.

"You know everybody thinks I killed him," she chokes.

"Cidro? No, they don't," I lie.

Yes, they do.

"People think that I killed the love of my life. My best friend. My fucking partner."

"I don't think that," I reassure her, telling the truth.

I have a lot of opinions about my cousin, but I know she wouldn't have harmed a hair on his head. She loved him far too much and is suffering more than she lets on.

"Why would I do that to him? My kids? Myself? Help me make sense of it," she sobs, reaching for the bear and clutching it as if it's a lifeline.

"Well, I know what it's like for people to say things like that about me," I add begrudgingly.

Lawrence wasn't the love of my life, but I fear César could have been.

Yet another thing this family has ruined for me.

She ignores my comment, willing herself to settle down. "It's so easy for people to judge and paint me as a monster. Cici always said she didn't mind the rumors and fear, but I have a hard time believing that. I bet she'd lock herself in her room at night and crumble like I do. No woman is strong enough to bear all this weight and show up for their children without fail. You're bound to fuck something up."

My stomach sinks at her confession. I'm guilty of looking at her the same way; as a monster. Meanwhile she's trying to survive and raise a family like Cici did.These same concerns are why I am unsure I'd be the parent my kids deserve while living under the Klarke shadow.

"I can't just take everybody out that doesn't like me. I don't have the support to survive a war, and I have to be mindful because my babies need me. No one understands the pressure I'm under. So yeah, my son losing his teddy was enough for me to crack," she admits, peering over at me.

"It's okay. We found it, so no bad news for Andrea. As for everything else, I don't know what to say, Gi. I wish Cici and Ace were still here to give us advice. Though, I think we both know what they'd say. They had a low tolerance for insubordination."

She nods in agreement, distracted by a chime on her phone, and I stand to gather my things. We found what she needed, and I want to be left alone, but I don't want to kick her out. Especially when it seems like the both of us are in need of a little company.

Low taps sound from her keyboard as she texts back a response, glancing up at me as if she just thought of something.

Whatever it is, no.

"Come for a drive with me."

"No thanks, I'm about to head home," I grumble, defeated, grabbing my clutch.

"I wasn't asking. C'mon," she orders, motioning to the door.

Never mind then.

"Fine," I resign, punching in the code to lock up as I follow her into the hall.

She trails me through the distillery, our clacking heels echoing on the concrete as we exit.

I settle into the luxury sedan, buckle my seatbelt, and sulk in my seat.

Not at all how I imagined my night to go.

She taps the push to start before backing out of the reserved parking space, an uncomfortable silence accompanying us on the drive.

I have no idea where she's dragging me to, but I can guarantee that we're both overdressed.

"We need to air everything out between us," she finally says.

No we don't.

"There's nothing to discuss, Gi. What's done is done," I huff as I look out the window.

"I disagree, but since you want to act like that. I got something for you. Bet."

She unlocks her phone, tapping that damn keyboard again and it halts.

Suddenly, Aretha Franklin's "I Say A Little Prayer For You" fills the space, and I roll my eyes.

"Turn it off, Gina," I beg, blinking away tears.

"Nope, I'm waving my white flag, Dee. You know the rules. What did Ace always say?"

Cici used to turn this song on every time we fought as kids. It was a tradition she held with Ace. When they had their first fight as boyfriend and girlfriend, he walked off to start the record player and this was his surrender song.

"Ace said that nobody can be angry when Aretha sings," I sigh.

"The only man who's been right, ever."

She taps her hands on the steering wheel singing the lyrics animatedly, holding her free hand out to me like a microphone for me to join.

We sing along out loud as we ride through the dimly lit city streets, and I realize that I haven't had this much fun with her in years.

The song fades, and she says, "I'm sorry, Dee. I should've talked to you about it first."

I scoff out my response. "You would've done it anyway, regardless of what I said."

"I won't lie to you. I would've done it anyway, but I am sorry that I hurt you in the process."

At least she's being honest.

"Once I learned that he wasn't only stealing from Divin, but the casinos, too, he became my problem, and I had to be the one to handle it. If I let shit slide, my credibility would've been questioned. I couldn't let a fucking thief who mistreated you live another day. Nobody crosses a Klarke and lives to tell the tale. Word is bond."

"I know."

"Cidro not being here leaves us vulnerable, and any wrong move puts my family in danger, even something as minuscule as letting Lawrence live. I don't regret what I did or expect you to forgive me, but you deserved an apology a long time ago. I'm sorry, Dee."

"I get that now, and I acknowledge I've been selfish. Not even considering the position he put you in," I acquiesce.

"Your feelings are valid, and it's not selfish to be angry with me. You shouldn't have been in that cell, I don't care if it wasn't for long. I told myself making it go away quickly would be best for you, but it only slapped a Band-Aid over a deep wound," she says, the car growing silent as I process this conversation.

My mind flits to César, and frustration boils in my gut. This always happens to me, and now I am convinced I'm not meant to date. Since there's always someone trying to use me to get to my family. Regina asks a question, releasing me from these thoughts.

"Do you miss him?"

"Hell no."

"You've been pissed at me over a man you don't even miss. Do you hear yourself?"

She's got a point. But I remain silent.

"Fair enough, but the world is better off without that sorry motherfucker. We don't have to speak kindly about the dead. Especially when there's nothing nice to say. Death doesn't absolve us of our sins, only prevents us from committing more," she states calmly while keeping her focus on the road.

"My god. You really are *just* like Cici," I gasp.

A smug smile stretches across her face. "Spitting fucking image, and it pisses you off, doesn't it?"

"Only when you strut through metal detectors fully armed." I pause to think of another reason. "Hmm. And when you set your gun on the table at work and at restaurants."

"I told you, it digs into my side," she scoffs.

I break out into a fit of laughter, and she eventually joins me.

"We're so damn stupid," I snicker to myself.

"I haven't laughed like that since my last night with Cidro," she admits. "Thanks for riding with me."

"No problem. I wasn't doing shit anyway. Where are we going?" I ask, peering out of the window.

"Church," she says flatly.

She's gotta be fucking with me.

"The devil can't set foot in a church," I tease, glancing at her in time to see her smirk.

"Says who? I'll have you know that I attend confessional *weekly*. Hmph."

"Fuck outta here." I chuckle at her ridiculousness.

"I'm deadass. I bring a bottle of Divin as an offering for the troubles I bring and go on my way."

Only Regina.

"That is unfortunate for the priest."

"I disagree. It comes with the job, and they get top-shelf liquor for free, just for sitting in a box and listening," she informs, pulling over to parallel park behind a black Mercedes in front of a cathedral.

"You coming?" she asks.

"Absolutely not. I'll wait here," I say, shaking my head before I look out of the windshield to admire the stained glass.

"Suit yourself. I won't be long."

She pops the trunk before entering the building, and I roll the window down to get her attention.

"Gi, wait."

"Hmm?" Her eyebrows shoot up as she approaches the passenger door.

"There isn't a mark in there, right? Please tell me you're not doing a hit tonight with me waiting outside," I whisper-shout, glancing around to make sure no one can hear us.

She side-eyes me with a scoff. "I'm not. That's all you think I'm good for, huh?" she asks, her tone riddled with annoyance. "Fifteen minutes, tops," she says before disappearing into the building.

10:58 p.m. | 1 hour and 41 minutes after 'the last incident'

Regina exits the building, eyeing me suspiciously until she gets in the driver's seat.

That doesn't make me nervous at all.

Two large men exit the building afterward, getting in the car in front of us. I notice one of the men is the lawyer that got me released.

Piñeros.

"What's the lawyer doing here?" I ask, my brows pinched.

She ignores my question to present me with one of her own. "Since we're being honest tonight, the fact that you *think* I don't know about your little boyfriend being a PI is laughable, because I do," she says with a smirk. "You know that motherfucker has been looking into me too? Were you ever going to tell me?" she urges.

"I didn't know before tonight, Angie told me before the party ended. Then I confronted him and told him to run because I don't want him to meet the same fate as Lawrence."

"Girl. There's a stark difference between César and Lawrence. I don't have to tell you that," she admonishes.

"Are you going to kill him?" I ask defeatedly as I blink away tears.

"I wasn't planning on it. Do I need to?"

"I don't think so, but he works for—"

She cuts me off, finishing my sentence. "The Hales. He's their in-house PI. They want to win that bid so badly, they fucked with the wrong family over it. They'll learn."

"Are you going after *them*?" I ask, worried because nothing causes a commotion quite like dead white people.

"Probably, but not before you win that bid," she says nonchalantly.

My brows knit as I ask, "What do you mean *I'm* going to win?"

"Oh, I forgot to tell you, they're terrified of me. So I'm getting in on this bid.

That motherfucker Dax might get angry, and I hope he does," she says with a deep chuckle as she pulls off into the street. "There isn't a war when the competition disappears."

"I don't understand. Why?"

"I'll put up all the bread you need to invest in your dream, *but* only if you feel comfortable," she tosses out like it's nothing.

"You're serious? You want to help make things legit?"

"Yes. While my money isn't cleaner than Uncle El's, I'd still like to invest in *you*. *If* you'll let me. You're right that our kids should be able to have a choice unlike we did. What do you say?"

Holy shit.

"Uh—thank you? I have a lot of questions, but I am interested." In partnership and in rebuilding our relationship.

"Good. We'll talk shop in the morning. And I don't know what's going on with you two, but you need to fix it. I met with my lawyer in there," she informs, tilting her head toward the church. "He assured me that his *friend* César is a good man. If Emiliano vouches for him, that's enough for me."

"But he lied, Gi," I remind her.

"Men lie, and water is wet. Don't act like you're any better. Did *you* tell him why your ex-boyfriend is dead?" she asks with a sideways glance before looking back at the road.

"No," I admit.

"See? You kept secrets to protect your family. and so did he. Gotta respect it," she advises as she presses her foot on the gas to enter the on ramp.

I suppose she's right.

"I plan to hire him to help me find out what happened to Cidro, but him being in love with you is a conflict of interest. And before you argue, watch this," she adds with a devious grin.

Aretha's "Think" blasts through the car, and she shares a knowing look before speeding up and changing lanes until she's in the fast one.

Touché, Regina. Tou-fucking-ché.

43 / left on read

César

12:05 a.m.| 2 hours and 37 minutes after 'the last incident'

I never meant to hurt you.

I didn't know how to tell you, but that isn't an excuse.

I am so sorry, mi beba.

Deirdre?

I miss you and I am so sorry.

I'm not giving up on you.

44 / prométeme

César

8:48 p.m. | 6 days after 'the last incident'

Everything has been a blur since we flew to San Juan the other night. As much as I've kept this in the back of my mind, the time has come.

I've kept myself busy around the house, staying out of the way as the rest of my family arrived. She woke up today wanting to talk more than usual and has been requesting alone time with everyone. She's asked for me a few times already, but I've been encouraging others to go instead.

The day winds down and almost everyone is asleep, but my racing mind is up washing dishes. *Abuela* is in her room speaking to my cousin Elías.

It isn't until he enters the kitchen with his head hung low that I know it's my turn to see her. I grab a towel and dry my hands, turning to face him.

"She sent me for you. Said I can use force." He chuckles weakly. "You gotta quit dodging her, *primo*. C'mon, man."

"*Coño,*" I breathe.

"I know," he assures, spreading his arms for a hug.

When I hug him back, he sobs quietly, and my heart lurches. I do my best to remain strong, but he's like the brother I never had.

Of all my cousins, Elí is unfortunately the most familiar with death. His mom passed away when we were kids and *Abuela* raised him. A few years back, he became a widow when his wife died in a car crash, and he walked away from his boxing career to raise their daughter, Solena.

Abuela's passing will be another heavy blow, but we've got each other.

"César, *ven aca,*" she cries out, her voice weak.

We pull apart, and he pats my back. "I'm going to check on Sol. Take your time, bro."

I nod, take a deep breath, and force my feet down the hall to her bedroom.

She smiles when she sees me, patting the bed beside her for me to join. *"Siéntate."*

I walk over hesitantly. *"Bendición,"* I say with a kiss on her cheek.

The bed dips beneath my weight as I sit. I've been dreading this conversation.

As soon as I turn to her, my guard falters and my eyes well up with tears. I expel a shaky breath and take the hand she's holding open for me.

Her dark irises assess me. "What's wrong, Chuki?"

My lips part to speak, but words struggle to come out. I squeeze her hand and try anyway.

What do I even say? I'm being selfish and she's in pain.

"What am I supposed to do without you?" I manage.

"You're going to live your life, *niño,* and stop hiding behind me," she says confidently.

She's right. I do hide behind caring for her, using family and work as an excuse to avoid dating and taking risks in my career.

I've grown so accustomed to the way things are that a change of plans derails me, like Deirdre. I resist change instead of embracing it, though I tried with her, until it blew up in my face.

"Is this about the woman you watch when you think I'm sleeping?

"*¿Què?*" I ask, pretending I don't know what she's referring to.

"*Cuentame*" she urges with pleading eyes. "I need stories to take with me."

I sigh. "I think I'm falling in love with her, but my job got in the way and I don't know how to make it right," I admit. "I don't think she'll ever speak to me again."

Abuela watches me intently, rubbing her free hand over mine for encouragement. "She will. Riveras don't give up easily," she adds with a knowing smile. "If your *abuelo* gave up on me, *you* wouldn't be here."

"I miss him," I sniffle.

"Me too." She nods. "But I'm going to see him soon. I'll tell him you said hello. *Prométeme* when I'm gone, no more excuses. Make room for love and tell my grandchildren about me. *¿Prométeme?*"

"I promise I will," I say tearfully.

"*Ora conmigo,*" she insists, pointing to the rosary on her bedside table.

I retrieve it, and we recite the final prayer before we fall into a comfortable silence.

"I love you, César," she says, staring up at me.

I lean over and wrap my arms around her, careful not to squeeze her hard, and she holds on to me for a while.

I never want to let go, and I wish I didn't have to.

"I love you so much," I choke, pressing my lips to her forehead. "It's been a long day, and I'll let you rest. I know you're tired."

"*Buenas noches,* Chuki. I love you," she says once more.

"*Buenas noches,* I love you, too." I take her in, knowing this may be the last time I see her alive, before shutting the door behind me.

I lie in bed, relishing the *coquís* as they sing, and replay every time I whistled for Deirdre. Every scowl, smirk, and laugh she'd make when she heard me nearby, I'll cherish forever. I open the bedroom window to record a voice message of the *coquís* for her.

She hasn't responded to any of my calls or texts, and I didn't mention leaving for Puerto Rico. Still, I don't miss a beat by telling her goodnight and good morning so she knows I'm thinking of her. *Abuela* thinks she'll speak to me again, and I hope that's true.

Goodnight, Doe.

I send the voice message and wait for sleep to take me, hoping their song brings her as much comfort as it brings me.

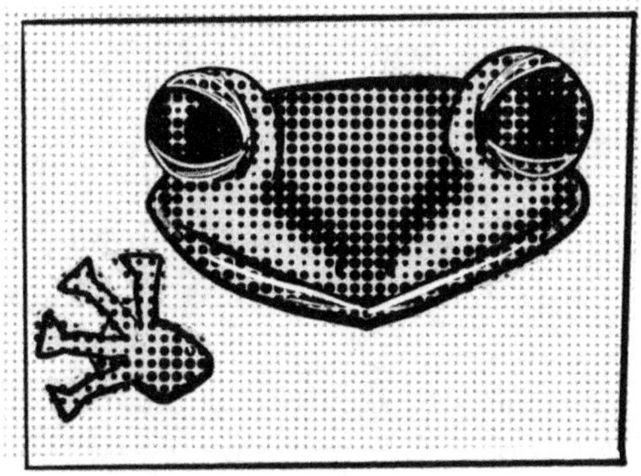

8:14 p.m. | 9 days after 'the last incident'

Abuela passed comfortably in her sleep after our talk that night, exactly how she wanted. As difficult as this all has been, I am grateful we were able to honor her wish.

Elías and I have been the glue for everyone as we've navigated the funeral arrangements and laid her to rest. Today was incredibly rough, but we celebrated her in the way she appreciated. A party, music, and good *pitorro*.

I remember having parties as a kid and *mis abuelos* danced all night long. She would demand he carry her off the dance floor when her feet started to hurt, and he would every single time. I imagine they danced with us today as they watched on. Celebrating never having to be apart again.

The day is done, and we've cleaned up, put away all the leftovers, and I could use some fresh air. I step onto the porch, greeted by the night sky and singing *coquís*.

Elías later joins me outside, emerging with a box of cigars that belonged to our *abuelo*. "We earned these. I'm gonna grab a drink. You want one?"

"I could use one," I admit.

"Alright then. Be right back," he says, disappearing into the house.

I know I have cases waiting for me, but I am not ready to return to Austin. I'm not looking forward to going back to the way things were before Deirdre.

I scroll through our text thread back to that first night. There was a mutual pull toward each other, and despite what she accused, I was genuinely interested in knowing more about her.

It was unprofessional regardless of my intentions, and I should've spoken up when I felt a need to engage with her, beyond being a subject. I know I fucked up, but when I get back I'm going to tell the Hales I'd like to dissolve our contract and move on.

I've spoken with Emiliano who offered his condolences. While he didn't have a definitive answer yet, I have faith in him. It may not smooth things with Deirdre, but I could acquire a client to do meaningful work for, instead of the bullshit I've been doing for Dax and Dara Hale.

I know I promised *Abuela* that I would make room for love, but I don't plan on it if I can't work things out with Deirdre. I'll be an insufferable *viejo* if I have to, missing her for the rest of my days, because she isn't someone you just move on from.

Elí exits the house with a bottle of Divin whiskey and two shot glasses in hand.

"Divin? Really?" I ask with an exasperated sigh.

The universe has gotta be playing with me right now.

He eyes me curiously, setting the glasses on the patio table and grabbing two white patio chairs for us.

"What did Divin do to you? I *love* this shit," he says, taking a seat across from me.

"Plenty," I say with a humorous laugh, joining him at the table. "I can't get her off my mind, and she won't even talk to me."

"*¿Qué?* Who? And what do they have to do with my favorite whiskey?" he asks, pouring a finger of brown liquid into both glasses.

"She's an owner of the company," I admit.

His eyebrows shoot up, and he starts fishing in his pocket, pulling out his phone with a smirk.

"Do *not* look her up, Elí," I warn.

"*Cállate,*" he says, waving me off. "Let the lonely widow google the woman that's got you ready to cry over a bottle of whiskey."

"*No me jodas,*" I beg, sinking into the patio chair.

His thumbs tap the screen, and his brows raise.

"Goddamn," he exclaims. "*She* wants *you*?" he asks with amusement in his tone, eyes flitting back and forth from the phone screen to me. "What'd you do? Hold her hostage?"

Something like that, I think.

"*Deja la jodienda,*" I huff.

"Since you fucked up, you think I have a chance?" he teases. "'Cause I know how to fight and would *love* some free Divin."

"Fuck you." I chuckle, taking a sip from the tumbler.

"Love you, too, man. You'd never beat me in a fight, though," he quips.

"I can hold my own and would fight for her. It wouldn't be the most ridiculous thing I've done."

His eyes are saying, " *try me*."

I hold up a finger, taking another sip before I drag him into this story.

"I may have pretended to mug someone she was on a date with to scare him away and…I was armed."

His eyes widen before he bursts into laughter, patting his chest and I join him, because it is wild and very unlike me.

"*¿En serio?* I thought I'd *never* see the day you'd turn into a *lovesick* idiot. You're down bad, man."

I confirm with a nod, saying, "More like a *lovefool*, but it doesn't matter now.

"Riveras don't give up, and you considered armed robbery to get a man away from her," he reminds me.

"I didn't take his watch. I held it before I gave it back," I muse, taking another sip.

He throws his head back and barks another laugh. "You're gonna have to start from the beginning if I'm gonna help you devise a plan to win her back. I'll tell you something about women. My wife loved *groveling*. Not that I fucked up often because I'm an angel, but she loved reading about it in her romance books," he says with a smile. "So, whatever we come up with needs a groveling moment," he adds with a knowing look.

"I don't disagree with that. I'd do anything at this point."

"One more thing, give me your phone," he instructs.

"Why?" I ask with knitted brows.

"You will *not* be texting her while we're getting fucked up and trying to fix this mess. If there's anything you need to say to her, do it now."

"That's a good idea."

I pick up my phone and send a nightly text to her, followed by a brief voice message of the *coquís*.

Buenas noches, Deirdre.

I miss you.

"Alright," I say, placing my phone in his hand for the evening. "Now, what I'm about to tell you *never* leaves this table," I tell him in a hushed tone, and we shake on it.

"It all started when she shot me," I say, lifting up my shirt sleeve to show the grazed wound, and he stares, stunned. "*But* let me explain why it was *Abuela's* fault," I joke, struggling to keep a straight face.

"I gotta hear this," he says, shaking his head in disbelief.

45 / sometimes you gotta pop the trunk

Deirdre

8:52 a.m. | 12 days after 'the last incident'

"You're in a good mood today," I say, as my cousin enters the boardroom.

"It's a special occasion. You might order your first hit today. I feel like a proud mother," she responds, smiling as she shrugs.

Regina stuns in a black pantsuit with a lace bralette peeking from her cleavage and gold hoops. Her dark curly hair is straightened in a side part and secured in a polished low ponytail cascading down her back. Her signature red lipstick sets off the look with a pop of color.

"For a woman who slays, you slay," I admit.

"Ahh. A double entendre. Okay, *Hov*," she says with a bright smile. "Thanks."

She doesn't look like she came in today to premeditate a potential murder, but neither do I.

My eyes catch on her wine stiletto nails as her handgun clunks on the mahogany conference table. She pulls out her chair and dives straight in.

"Now, let's talk shop. It's up to you if Dax Hale dies or goes to prison. Both are viable options, but the latter won't be much fun for *me*," she says, raising a brow with a smirk. "I want you to give this some thought, because either choice will require a lot of fucking hands to clean the mess after me."

Her phone trills, buzzing on the table, and she glances at it.

"Ah, hold on, Audrey is calling. She's watching the kids. I'll be right back," she informs me, standing to tuck her gun back in her waistband.

I don't think she needs the gun for a phone call when her bodyguard is here, but I can't say I don't understand.

"Tell her I said hi!" I call after her.

"I will," she says over her shoulder as she exits the room, dashing past Mr. Price who is on her heels. I guess he's not happy about her breaking away from her security detail.

Maybe I should've told her about the stalking, could've learned some pointers.

My thoughts are interrupted when a few texts fly in from the group chat. It couldn't have come at a better time. I miss my girls so much, and it's weird not being able to tell them *everything* that's going on.

SKYE DADDY

How are things with the new chiropractor?

LO

OMG yes! You haven't given us any details!

I know we've all been busy, but I have to know.

SKYE DADDY

Exactly!

We gotta live vicariously through someone's dick appointments.

I will share an update on the chiropractor soon. Hold me to it!

Regina's in town and we're in a meeting.

SKYE DADDY

Don't think we're gonna forget either.

I actually will forget.

LO

Reporting for duty! 🫡 I'm setting a daily reminder now and sharing it with you both.

I just got the reminder. 🫶 I'll check in soon! I love you!

SKYE DADDY

Love yall!

LO

Love you, babe!

That went over better than I'd expected it to. I need more time to figure things out. I shouldn't have mentioned him so early, just in case shit didn't pan out the way we hoped.

Except it felt so genuine with him and no one had ever touched me like that, and I *had* to tell my friends. That was a night to remember and one I still think of whenever I have a hard time sleeping without him.

Regina said she may hire him, and I'd see him more often if he came into the fold. I don't hate the thought of seeing him around, but I am not giving into him.

Though I have come close over the past few days. It's those good night texts and the *coquí* frog voice messages. They're so damn cute, and it's not fair. What is he even doing in Puerto Rico anyway? I hope he didn't run off because of Regina, even though I told him to.

Does he even know she's thinking about giving him a job?

She swings the door open and strolls back in with a calm expression. "The kids are fine. She had some questions."

"How is she?" I ask, straightening my spine in my seat as I thumb through the articles Angie sent over last night on Dax and Dara Hale.

"Good. Her and Rome's worrisome ass are babysitting Audre & Andrea. He wanted to cook for them, but was freaking about possible food allergies. They don't have any that I know of, and it's a valid concern, but he still annoys me," she says with a shrug as she returns her gun to its rightful spot on the table and sits opposite me.

"Why is Rome worrisome?"

"He thinks *I'm* a fucking criminal. The gall of that fucking guy. Thinks he's too good to represent the mob in court. That goddamn high horse he's always on," she shares with a deep sigh. "I don't know what Aud sees in him. He's got a stick up his fucking ass. Just like her brother, Andrew," she adds, rolling her eyes.

I chuckle. "Cidro wasn't a *normal* guy for you."

"That's because I didn't seek him out. He chose me, and I'm glad he did," she says with a smile. "Now, back to the trust fund babies. I must share that I don't *love* eradicating other women, so I need confirmation that Dax acts alone or if Dara is the brains of the operation before I walk in and start spraying."

Spraying? Oh my God.

"Gi, you wouldn't do that," I gasp.

"Uh—yes the hell I would. Within reason, of course. I'd also like for your peacekeeping ass to know that a rich motherfucker like him will live *good* in prison. Won't be much different from his life now, so if you ask me, hell would be more accommodating. The ball is in your court, though, I support whatever," she concludes, leaning back in her chair as she stares at me expectantly.

"I'd like it to go on record that this is the first time you've *ever* said anything about violence that I've agreed with."

She scoffs. "What about Alfie? Surely, you agreed with that."

I think back to the trunk phone conversation and remember it vividly.

"You're right. I did agree with how you handled Alfie. How is he by the way?"

"Keeping his fucking spit in his mouth. Struggles holding a hand of cards now, but other than that he's been a good old boy. Eradication works. Sometimes you've gotta pop the trunk to solve a problem," she adds.

46 / sleepy steamroller

Deirdre

6:36 a.m. | 16 hours before 'the last, last incident'

My alarm blares and yanks me out of my sleep. The ringtone is excessively loud and makes me want to scream. I'm lying in a puddle of sweat, and I'm in excruciating pain. My body feels as if a steamroller ran over me, and I can feel the impending headache as too much sunlight shines into my bedroom window.

Somehow I manage to get out of the bed, and thankfully I've been wearing period underwear so I wouldn't have another repeat since César invaded my life. There's no way I'm going into work, so I text Brian to inform him then Darius.

My brother being overjoyed that I am taking a few days off even if I am not feeling well proves that I work entirely too damn much. There is nothing more for me to do besides read and go back to sleep. Sleep it is.

47 / stranger danger

César

2:36 p.m. | 8 hours before 'the last, last incident'

Dara Hale has been calling me non-stop today, and I have no idea why, but I've had enough. I swipe the screen to answer.

"What is it?"

Um—hi, César? It's Dara. Why haven't you been answering? Are you all right?" she asks, her tone laced with worry.

"I'm all right, but I am out of office. Mi *abuela* passed away, and I've been in Puerto Rico with loved ones for the past week," I tell her with added bite in my tone. Her brother is a *pendejo*, after all.

"Oh heavens, I am so sorry for your loss. I don't mean to be a bother, but this is important and I have to warn you. It's not about work *per se*," she adds in a hushed tone.

"Okay, so what is it?" I urge, hoping she gets to the point soon enough.

"You have to believe me. Dax has been off his fucking rocker, and I've been trying to prove that to my father, but I fear it's too late. He had a meeting yesterday, hired some shady fucker, wired a large sum of money this morning and won't say what it's for. He wants to win this bid so badly, he's willing to harm her for it. If you're not *here,* then Deirdre is unsafe."

I have to get to her.

I swallow the rising bile in my throat. I am hours away from home and need to find a flight immediately.

"I am sorry to spring this upon you at such a bad time, but you had to know. She doesn't fancy me, but I will try to get a hold of her in the meantime."

"I gotta go, Dara. Thank you for telling me," I state calmly, despite the rage boiling within.

"Of course," she says, disconnecting the call.

Deirdre? Please call me. It's important.

Wake up, Deirdre. Get out of the house.

Deirdre. Fuck. Answer the phone.

I manage to find a nonstop flight to Austin and book it immediately, but I have to be at the airport in the next hour and a half *if* I stand to make it.

I scan my room and shove everything I brought with me in my luggage, but it isn't neatly folded so it's not zipping up.

Not now. I don't have time for this shit now.

Please?

It's not safe there and you need to leave.

Call me back?

I call and text profusely until I board the plane. Even leaving voicemails, but I find no luck. She doesn't respond to any of them. Thankfully, she hasn't blocked me, but she hasn't read any of my messages today. But she did last night.

Read: 10:04 p.m.

Of course, my flight doesn't have Wi-Fi and my phone is on 6%. I swore I had everything packed, but I left my fucking charger. I'll be using it to call and text to warn her until I get back.

Deirdre? Please wake up and get out of that house.

You need to leave the house.

Fine. I hate to bother you, but it's not safe at home.

Dax has sent someone to follow us and he may come to find you.

Call me? Please, Doe. Please?

I'm boarding a plane and won't be able to call for a bit.

Baby, please wake up. Fuck.

Please respond to me.

48 / goddammit, césar

Deirdre

10:59 p.m. | 'the last, last incident'

Pollo guisado is simmering on the stove, but I'm not even hungry. I stupidly want to feel close to him and I slept all fucking day. My kitchen smells incredible, and I suppose it's good that I'm cooking again, but I ran out of prepped meals from César so I have to.

It's been almost two weeks since I learned the truth about him, and I've missed him every single day. I hate being in this situation because I wanted to believe him, but I can't. Giving in and only seeing the good in people has burned me far too many times now.

People have always taken advantage of my kindness, but to learn everything about me and emulate the exact man I need? That's evil, and I've seen evil. I don't know that César's intentions were always ill, my gut tells me otherwise. That the man he showed me he was, he *is*.

But I cannot overlook him working for the Hales. Not because it's a job, but because he was violating my privacy to give them leverage to take something that's important to me.

I wonder if wherever he is, he's still watching me. A part of me wanted to take the cameras down and remove that access to me, but another part hopes he is still there. Not the private investigator Scar, but the man who removed his mask that night and bared himself to me. César.

He's been consistent with texting me; sending photos from Puerto Rico of his family and the scenery. He's sent voice messages so I can hear him and the *coquí* frogs, even sent me pictures he'd taken of them. I do appreciate him for including me.

In spite of my anger, César is still thoughtful and kind. He always has been no matter what I dished out. That's what makes it so much harder for me to accept that he betrayed me.

I wish things were different, and it's like this realization unleashed something in me, because I don't feel embarrassed to be a Klarke, knowing exactly what we're up against.

As if the universe answered my question or he can read my mind, I hear a door open, and my heart skips a beat. I know I should've, but I didn't change the locks yet.

The fact that Regina even wants to hire him is telling for his character.

I am still hurt, but am willing to hear him out now, if he wants to talk about it. I miss him so much, I'd gladly sit in silence.

"You're just in time for dinner," I say excitedly and am met with silence aside from creaking footsteps through the home.

I'll do three coquí whistles so you'll know it's me.

My stomach drops at the possibility of it not being him, and my eyes scour the kitchen for anything that can be used as weapons. Of course, I used my good knives to prepare dinner, so they're in the running dishwasher.

Fuck.

I have a gun down here, but it's in my office by the door they just entered from. Another in my car, and there's the collection locked in my bedroom. Once I felt safe with him, I stopped walking around the house strapped.

Fuck you for lowering my guard.

Goddammit, César. If I die, I will haunt you.

The steps grow closer, and I find a man dressed in black—who is not my César—staring back at me with dead eyes visible through the holes in his mask. I take off running out of the kitchen, and he's on my fucking heels. He grabs at me, but I don't relent. I *have* to get upstairs and fast.

49 / fight or flight of stairs

Deirdre

10:59 p.m. | 'the last, last incident'

Adrenaline flows through my veins as I dash up the stairs. He grabs ahold of my leg to stop me, and I hold on to the banister as I kick, but he's too strong.

I am not weak. I may not be a killer, but I am not against a good fight.

He tightens his grip around my leg and drags me down the steps, my kicks are wild and useless, but I don't stop trying.

On the way down, my eyes scan everything in hopes of finding anything I can use to subdue him.

I need to get upstairs.

We're about to pass an end table of small plants, some have concrete pots. I swipe my arms out to get one in my grasp. My hands are sweaty, but I manage to maintain my grip on one.

His attention stays forward as he drags me through the kitchen, seemingly taking me through the garage door.

I can do this, I tell myself. *You are not dying today.*

I chuck the concrete planter at him, and when it makes contact with his head, he screams in agony. His hands rush to assess the blow, and he releases his hold on my leg.

I don't waste a minute charging back where I came, and he

roars after me, his steps quick, but not as fast as before. I hike my knees up these long fucking stairs that I had to have for aesthetic purposes, and he unfortunately catches up, only a few steps behind me as I beeline for the top.

My bedroom door is in my line of sight when I feel his grip around my waist pulling me back down the stairs. His hold is awkward and provides enough room for me to shove my elbow into him, and I do. He groans, but it's not enough.

I cannot let him pull me away from these stairs again. I rear a hook, and the punch lands against his temple. My knuckles crunch, but I keep flailing and punching until he finally drops me.

"Crazy fucking bitch," he wails, rushing to cradle his head in his hands.

I dart up the stairs with no regard for him when I touch the doorknob handle, rip it open, and lock it behind me.

I stop in front of the safe and carefully remove the family photo covering it to lean it against the wall. My hands tremble as I punch in the code.

Three, nine, nine, one, zero, three, five, zero.

The hiss of the door releasing washes over me as my guns stare back at me, lined up and ready to be chosen. I take a deep breath, retrieve two handguns, and press the door shut, listening for the lock to click before I hide in my en suite.

I lost my phone amidst the fighting downstairs, but luckily my iPad is on the counter from watching a beauty tutorial earlier.

Being a girly girl might save my life.

I swipe to unlock and call César, but he doesn't answer. I try again, but I get nothing. So, I send a message to Regina, and wait.

> Someone broke into my house and I am locked in the bathroom.

I don't need help, and you better not call my fucking dad or Darius.

I have a gun and I will be fine.

Then I send another to César this time, in case I don't make it. I open our thread to find countless messages he sent earlier to warn me about this person.

My attacker is outside the bedroom door throwing himself into it to bust it down, and I need to be ready for him when that happens.

If I die tonight, I want you to know that you're an idiot and I love you.

In case something happens to me, delete that fucking video I made so Regina doesn't kill you.

I love you, César/Scar.

I hate that you lied.

I switch off the safety and wait for him. My back is pressed against the cold bathtub, and the wood is weakening from his body repeatedly slamming into the door. I train my breathing and will myself to focus. Cici's voice in my head rings once again. *"Klarke's don't hide from danger, they incite it."*

I stand and remember César's shooting pointers, aiming directly in front of me just as he gets the door open. The wood slams to the ground, and he charges through my room. My sweaty finger trembles on the trigger, but I hold it there.

"Come out, princess. Come on, now. I've had enough of your games. Come on out," he urges on the other side of the door.

Blood is rushing through my ears as he jiggles the doorknob. This door is far weaker than the bedroom door, and it won't take long for him to knock it down.

I slow my breathing and listen for him as he stands at the door jiggling the knob. I may have a direct shot.

Take the shot. Now.

I fire, the shot echoing in the confined bathroom. I hear the sloshing of the bullet piercing his chest, pained screams follow, but I can't stop. Moving closer, I fire again through the hole that now provides a view of him on the other side. Still standing, so I go again until I hear the thud of his body dropping to the floor. He's still alive and moaning in pain, but I twist that knob to find him bloody and aim for the head.

That blow is instant, I see the exact moment he dies and it is nothing like I imagined it would be. I fire again into his skull and again in his chest for good measure. Opting to unload the clip because why not? It may be overkill, but I have anxiety.

I stand over his lifeless body with a lot of emotions, one being fear, because who even this and did Dax fucking send him here?

I don't feel ashamed; I feel pride for a moment before my stomach churns. Nausea rises in my gut, but I need to handle the problem.

"Eradication is my ministry," I hear Regina say, and I grab my iPad to call her on speaker.

She picks up on the second ring.

"The fuck is going on? I read my kids a bedtime story, and now I'm seeing this fucking message from you. Babe? Dee?"

I don't know what to say.

I stammer, "Gi, I—I need a clean-up crew. Now."

A lighter flicks on the other end of the line, and she takes a drag.

Her and those goddamn cigarettes.

"And why would you need that? Tell me," she says.

"Someone broke in my fucking house and attacked me," I exclaim, eyeing the body as if it's going wake up and charge me.

"Say it, Dee. I need to hear you say it," she challenges, and I roll my eyes.

"I don't have time for your games, Gi. I don't know what you want me to say. I took care of it…Oh," I sigh. "The debt is paid."

"You check for a pulse?" she asks flatly and takes another drag.

"No, there's no need for that, is there?"

"Check for a pulse, Dee," she says, annoyance in her tone.

"I don't want to touch him," I grit, pacing the floor.

"Touch the fucking body and check for a pulse. Now," she bites out firmly.

"Fine," I resign, huffing as I wearily approach the body. Blood is pooled around him, and his eyes are still open.

Gross, and all over my favorite fucking rug.

How am I going to get brain matter out of it?

My hands tremble as I press two fingers into his bloodied wrist and wait for a sign of life.

Nothing.

"No pulse. Now will you fucking help me?" I ask, rushing to the bathroom to wash the blood from my hands, fighting the strong urge to gag. "Shit."

"We have a crew in Austin, and I'm texting them now. They're fifteen minutes away. Are you alone?"

"Yeah, well no. If you count this dead motherfucker at my feet."

"Where's César? Did you two make up, or is he…" she trails off.

"No, it wasn't him. He didn't answer the phone so I don't know where he is."

"Fuck. I know that feeling. I'm gonna stay on the line with you. Okay?"

"Thank you," I whisper, taking a seat on the other side of the room.

"I'm going to text you a contact. Name's Renata or Renny. Call her in the morning. And I know you keep looking at that fucking body. Stop it," she snaps in her mom voice. "You need to talk to someone. Like I was saying, Renny. Call her."

I tilt my head in confusion. "Who's she? And how do you know I'm staring at him?" I ask nervously.

"She's my therapist. Believe it or not."

I remain silent as I try to process what she said. Regina goes to therapy?

"Yes, I go to therapy," she responds as if she can hear my thoughts. "And because I know my cousin. They, uh, shit and piss themselves after. Did you know that?"

"Oh my God, gross. He's gonna shit on my fucking rug? Giii," I whine. "How do you get brain matter out of a carpet? You know a guy for that?"

She bursts into laughter. "I do actually. He's with the crew that's coming down, but they're thorough, so you won't need to ask."

"And what exactly do you tell her? You lie?" I ask, genuinely curious.

"Everything. Shit, she's in the mob too. Her pops is the Don of the Zippiati Family."

A mob therapist that you can tell incriminating things to. Interesting.

We take on a comfortable silence as I attempt to hear myself think. I get up and pace again, even checking for a response from César, and there isn't one.

What if he killed César before he came here for me?

My nausea fights its way up at the thought, but I swallow it down. I hear her taking drags and blowing smoke on the other end. She breaks the silence in a way only she can.

"So, you popped your cherry. Thirty-two years. Took you long enough to get your first blood. Did you throw up already?" she asks, amusement in her tone.

I take a deep breath to will the urge away. "No, but I want to. Did you?"

"Yeah, I did. My first shot was Cidro, and obviously I didn't take him out. He turned out okay," she reminisces with a sigh.

"César was my first shot," I admit. "What is wrong with us?"

"We're Klarkes, baby. It's the generational trauma and the need to laugh instead of cry."

"Woooow. You really do go to therapy," I gasp dramatically. "If you don't mind me asking, who was your first blood?" I inquire, hoping to keep my mind off the uncertainty about César.

She sighs. "Mine was a break in, too. Happened a few days after Ro didn't come home. I hoped it was him, but I was wrong. I did what I had to do to protect my kids and I haven't stopped because I will always choose my family."

"I under— "

We're interrupted when I hear three *coquí* whistles, and I freeze. I remain silent until I hear them again, closer this time.

"Doe? Where are you?"

It's him. He came back for me.

"César? I'm upstairs. In my room," I cry.

His heavy and familiar footsteps dash up the stairs, and he stands in the doorway assessing the scene before his eyes land on me.

Bloody, sweaty, disheveled, on the phone with Regina talking about murder from my fucking iPad. Not the reunion for the books, but I'm just thankful he's safe. Thankful that *we're* safe.

50 / no more secrets

César

11:42 p.m. | 43 minutes after 'the last, last incident'

"Well, looks like you've got company. Cleanup is in the neighborhood. Let them in through the garage. I love you."

"I love you, too, Gi. Thanks for having my back," Deirdre says.

"Always. Can your boy hear me?

"Yes, I can. Hello, Mrs. Delvec—"

"Regina is fine. Listen, kid, you're about to be unemployed because your boss is about to turn up dead. You hear me?" she states.

"Yes, I hear you," I confirm, not sure what's going on, my brows pinched in confusion.

"You any good at skip tracing?" she asks.

"Yes. Good enough to find out what happened to your husband," I say. Deirdre winces, and the silence is deafening. I said the wrong thing. *Fuck.* "I apologize. I didn't mean to offend."

"You didn't. I was just rolling a joint. When can you start? Say, two weeks from now?"

"Yes, absolutely," I answer eagerly, nodding when I notice Doe's weak smile.

"Bet. And whatever the fuckass Hales were paying you, I'll double it. Anything I should know?"

"Um, Dara Hale warned me about Dax. He sent this guy here to hurt Dee. I was on a flight to get to her. Dara is a bit timid, but she's not like him."

She sighs. "Alright. She can live, but she better stay the fuck out of our way. You got the job, kid. Dee will bring you to meet me."

I nod, even though she can't see me. "Yes. I'll be there. Thank you for the opportunity."

"And Dee? Tell that man you love him," she says before hanging up.

I stare incredulously at Deirdre as I await her response to that. "You love me?" I ask.

"Let's get away from the dead body for this conversation?" she asks with a smirk.

"You got a point," I agree as her guys enter the room with supplies. I don't want to know what they're about to do, so I follow her lead to a guest room.

She shuts the door behind us and leans against it with wrinkled brows. I sit on the bed to give her some distance because I know *that* look.

She's about to let me have it. That's better than her silence.

"I'm still pissed," she says, crossing her arms. "So, the mushy shit is going to have to wait."

"That's understandable. I would be upset, too."

"I'm willing to hear you out, but you need to talk. Now," she orders.

"Okay. I am a PI, and I took on a blackmail case, but I think I knew pretty early that I didn't stand to see this case through. Because you are everything I have been missing. I didn't expect to be so drawn to you, but you consumed me. Long before you even know I existed," I admit and swallow as she assesses me.

"I want you to know I never shared anything that you told me in confidence, and even when I wanted off the case, I didn't feel comfortable with someone else trailing you, so I didn't quit.

"I've done work for the Hales—*do* because I haven't terminated my contract, but I am. This is my career and how I provide for my family, so I needed a backup plan, and I tried to get one before you learned the truth about me.

"I needed to know if I chose myself, they wouldn't suffer. I pay my sister's tuition, help my parents, and *mi abuela—m*," I pause, taking a moment to find the right words.

"*Mi abuela* has been in hospice care and wanted to be home in Puerto Rico when she passed. I had to fly her down there after our fight and be there for my family. I'm sorry I didn't tell you."

Her face softens, and she eyes me with unshed tears. "I'm S —" she starts.

I cut her off, "There's nothing for you to be sorry about. I was there with family until I got a call from Dara to warn me about Dax hiring some guy to hurt the both of us. I kept trying you, but no response. I tried to tell you to get out of here before my phone died."

"Well I didn't see your messages until it was too late. I slept all day and couldn't find my phone when I woke up," she defends.

"César, I'm sorry for your loss, and I want to strangle you for being so fucking secretive. You were texting me *every day* and you didn't mention this at all," she says defeatedly as I rush across the room to wrap my arms around her. I press a kiss to her head and hold her for a moment. "I love you and I tried to tell you, but you didn't text back and I thought you'd been hurt," she cries.

She got me there.

"My phone died on the plane, and I didn't have a charger. I'm sorry. I'm very protective over my family and didn't want you to feel manipulated into speaking to me. And I missed *you* so much. I told her about you, and I'm grateful I was able to," I say with a smile. "No more secrets. None. I don't care how unsavory they are. We need to know things about each other, especially because I love you too."

She looks up at me with those big brown eyes and says, "No more secrets. I need to know things about you and vice versa. For example, I just killed someone. Right there," she says, pointing her thumb over her shoulder.

"Since we're being honest, I'm proud of you. You made him your couch," I joke, struggling to hold in my laughter, and she swats at my chest.

Curiosity may have dire consequences, but it led me to her. Deirdre Klarke may be deadly, but she makes me feel alive.

51 / a new beginning

Deirdre

2 months later

The bar may be in hell, but César raised it drastically. I admire him in a fitted suit from across the room, where he's having a conversation with Regina, Emiliano, Emiliano's fiancé Taina, Darius, and my dad at the bar.

Mr. Price is hanging close by, but letting Gi enjoy some time to herself. I'm sure she can appreciate that. My dad lets out a hearty laugh that I can hear faintly over the music, and it's a rare sight.

César has really hit it off with my family, and I couldn't be more grateful for it. Though, I got nervous when he beat my dad at a game of dominos last week, but he shrugged it off and said he was proud he could hold his own around the Klarke men.

Regina hasn't complained about him yet, so he must be doing well as her in-house PI or I'd be hearing about it. He has managed to find more breadcrumbs than the police did on Cidro's disappearance, which has given her some hope, and made her more pleasant than usual.

Dax Hale backed out of the bid, and it took some force, but we ended up getting the property, thanks to Regina. After some much-needed renovations, we are expected to open our new Divin location in Spicewood next summer.

I join César, who wraps his free hand around my waist, pulling me closer, and I notice Darius's lips tick into a soft smile as he studies us. His eyes drop to me, and the look of approval he shares makes my heart squeeze in my chest.

They're happy for me. We're celebrating getting one step closer to my dream, and this incredible man stands beside me cheering me on. He's embraced me as I am, and that's all I ever wanted.

I'm distracted when Regina erupts in a boisterous laugh, and I relish in this sight. Though she has been unusually happy this evening and I should get to the bottom of that.

"You're smiling a lot tonight. What's up with you?" I ask with a quirked brow.

She leans in to whisper in my ear, "The Hale debt is paid."

I clear my throat and touch her arm. "I see that we need to talk. Now."

She gives a knowing look.

"Babe, I'm going to talk to Gi in my office. We won't be long," I turn to murmur to him, already stepping slightly out of his hold.

"Okay, Doe," he says, pressing a kiss to the top of my head. "I love you."

"I love you, too, baby," I tell him, kissing him on the cheek, and he takes my empty tumbler from my hand to sit on the bar.

"Let me know when Vanessa Morelli gets here," Regina says to César, her voice low and one brow lifted.

"You got it, Gi."

We break away from the party, and she leads the way to my office, tucking her clutch bag under her arm while Mr. Price follows close behind. Our heels clack in a rhythm against the concrete floors until we stop outside my door. I tap in the keypad and let her into the dark room first, flipping on the light switch before closing the door behind us and her bodyguard waits outside.

She grabs a seat in front of my desk, placing her shiny clutch onto her lap, and I notice the thigh holster when she crosses her leg over the other.

Always strapped.

"So, I have got some questions. How'd you do it?" I ask, sitting in my leather office chair.

"You don't want to know, Dee. It was a good time though. To everyone else it looks like he just fucked off and took a vacation. Angie even posted some beachside photos on his Picturegram."

"And it's not going to come back on us?"

"Nah. The clean-up crew scrubbed everything down and he won't be found," she assures in a cool tone.

"How do you know? Sorry, I'm asking so many questions."

"Two words. Poured concrete," she says emphasizing each word.

"Oh my God," I gasp.

"I know. Ro taught me that one." She snickers.

"Speaking of Ro, how are you liking César working for you?"

"He's not bad. I'm a little disappointed that he doesn't laugh at my jokes."

"Are your jokes about 'eradication?'"

"Duh."

We're distracted by a knock at the door.

"Come in," I say.

The knob turns, and César enters the room with a smile. "Sorry to interrupt, but Vanessa and Nate just arrived."

"Perfect. We've got a deal to discuss. I'll find you later," she says over her shoulder as she exits down the hall with Mr. Price in tow.

César shuts the door and leans against it with a devious grin on his face.

His hungry eyes explore me, and I crook my finger to beckon him. He obeys, picking me up and setting me on the desk.

"So, you and I haven't had a moment to ourselves tonight."

"I know," I say with a pout. "We could do something about that," I add, biting my lip.

"I'd like to show you how good you look tonight," he whispers, tilting my chin and leaning in to entice me.

"And how are you planning to do that?" I ask against his lips.

He nips and gently tugs on my lower lip. "You think you can be quiet for me?"

Oh shit.

"Yes, Sir."

"Stand against the window and take off your panties," he orders in a gruff voice.

I rush over to the floor-length window, tug the lace thong down my legs, and step out of them before pressing my hands against the obscure glass. My breath condenses as I anxiously wait for his next command.

The sound of his belt buckle loosening followed by his soft footsteps approaching fill me with anticipation. He grinds his erection into my back and lifts the hem of my dress to place a hand on my pussy.

"Were you going to tell me you were this wet or wait until we got home?" he asks in my ear as his tongue trails down my neck.

"You've been having fun with my family. I wasn't going to interrupt."

"Your needs come first, Doe. Now tell me, what do you need?"

"I need you to fuck me raw against this window then we'll go back out there like nothing ever happened."

A dark chuckle escapes him that sends shivers down my spine. "Raw? You sure, baby?"

"Yes, I have my IUD, and I need to feel you dripping out of me."

A hushed "fuck" escapes his lips. "I can do that, baby," he

says as he dusts his hand over my clit. "Spread your legs and hold your dress."

He slaps his dick against my core until I grow impatient, and he's taking pleasure in this game. I poke my ass out, and he spreads my lips before slipping inside. The sounds of my wetness fill the room as he thrusts into me, while rubbing circles around my clit.

"Fuck," I groan.

"You feel so fucking good, Doe. Clenching around me. You don't want me to ever pull out of this needy pussy, do you?"

"N—no," I breathe.

"Shit. I might not," he utters softly, his free hand digging into my hip with a bruising hold.

I meet his thrusts, bouncing my ass into him, and he stills.

"Don't do that, Doe," he warns. "You're supposed to keep quiet. You wouldn't want anybody finding out that you like to be my little slut? So needy that you want me to fill you when anyone could just walk in."

I stifle my moans as my pussy tightens around him, rocking back and forth on his hard dick when he grips my throat to stop me.

"Or is that what you want? To get caught? You love this dick so much you want someone to see how good I fuck you?"

Oh my God.

"Tell me, baby," he orders, tightening his grip as he presses his face against mine.

"Yes, I wouldn't mind anyone seeing how good you fuck me."

"*Coño*, that's my little slut. Maybe when we're not in your office, huh?" he asks, releasing his grip as he pulls out and thrusts back into me.

"*Dios mio*, I'm going to wear you out when we get back home. Make this pussy squirt all over the fucking house. Would you like that?" he asks, with a slap to my wet pussy.

"Yes, fuck," I whimper, "Do that again, please?"

He responds with another slap before pinching my clit, and I resist the urge to scream as he drills into me. "You're gonna make me come," he growls.

"César," I pant.

"You're going to come with me, baby?" he asks, maintaining his pace as my climax builds.

"Mmhm," I moan and spasm around him, biting my lip so hard I draw blood.

He bites my back as he spills into me, fucking it deeper as he doesn't relent. I take his offering as my breath fogs the glass.

Soft kisses trail up my neck to my ear. "You took me so well," he pants, turning my head to pull me in a passionate kiss before drawing back to assess me.

"Now, clean me up," he demands, his tone leaving no room for argument and I won't argue with that.

Yes, Sir.

I drop to my knees and eagerly taste our arousal, wrapping my hand around his thick shaft as I flatten my tongue against him. My tongue twirls around his tip, and I greedily swallow every drop of us, moaning softly as he fills my mouth and maintains eye contact.

"Such a good girl," he praises, holding his hand out to help me off the floor.

"Stay right there," he orders, disappearing into the en suite. He returns with a warm washcloth to clean me up, and I can't take my eyes off of him.

We're fully clothed and ready to return to the party when a knock on the door startles us.

Regina's voice travels through the door. "Uncle El wants to make a toast. César, get off of my cousin. Boss's orders," she says with a cackle, and I swear I hear a laugh come from Mr. Price, too.

We meet them in the hallway and return to the party where Regina and I are whisked away by my father. I don't miss the knowing smirk César wears as I pretend everything is normal, when I'm dying to take him back home.

Then we'll go back out there like nothing ever happened.

We have dirty little secrets we don't mind keeping. Secrets kept in good taste.

Damn good taste.

the End

epilogue

César

the first meeting with 'the devil'

12:42 p.m. | 14 days after 'the last, last incident'

"I don't know why you're so nervous," Deirdre says, adjusting my tie.

I stare incredulously at her. "It's Regina Delvecchio. She's terrifying. Don't act like you don't know her."

She chuckles. "Well, she doesn't like being referred to as terrifying, so I'd start there. But when you get to know her she's cute like a puppy."

Bullshit.

"So, she's intense. Her bodyguard is scarier, if you ask me," she says with a shrug.

"What if she doesn't like me? Does she fire people? Or?"

"*Or*? I don't think Regina would kill another one of my boyfriends unless you stopped being good to me," she says, booping me on the nose.

"I guess I can breathe, because I'll never stop taking care of you," I quip, distracting her with a peck on the lips. "I *want* to get the job done and help this family find closure."

She steps back and sits at the foot of the bed with knotted brows. "Have you ever thought about what would happen if you found him alive? She insists that he is. Says she can *'feel'* it. Everyone thinks she's lost her mind," she adds, staring at her feet.

"What do you think?" I ask, eyeing her curiously through the mirror.

She meets my gaze and sighs. "I think Regina and Cidro are like Cici and Ace. Our grandparents had this connection that only *they* could understand. So, if Gi *feels* like Ro is alive, he could be," she finishes with a shrug.

Something tells me that there's more at play with Cidro's case, and I plan to get to the bottom of it.

"How do I look?" I ask, turning toward her, adjusting my cuff links.

Deirdre studies me and says, "I'd get on my knees and show you how good you look, *if* it wouldn't make you late for your first day of work."

I respond with an eye roll and huff. "Fine. I should get going. I don't want to make a bad impression."

"You won't. She's going to love you. Relax."

Famous last words.

* * *

HER DARK HAIR frames her face in loose curls and her signature red paints her lips. My eyes catch on her iced coffee, condensation dripping onto the coaster beneath it.

She seems to be working on something as I notice a pencil tucked behind her ear. It appears to be a crossword puzzle, from the newspaper.

I clear my throat to gain her attention. "Good morning, Mrs. Delvecchio," I greet her, and she glances up at me with a head tilt before standing.

"Good morning *Mr*. Nadal," she says, putting extra emphasis on my name as she reaches her hand over the desk to shake mine, those long red nails staring at me like daggers. "Are we formal now?" she asks with a playful smile.

"You tell me," I quip, attempting to match her energy, and grab a seat across from her.

"Regina is fine," she states, sitting back down and folding up the newspaper. "So, about Cidro. I asked Angie to put together a file on him that should help you get started," she says, placing the thick manila envelope between us.

"The last night I saw my husband was April 28, 2023. We'd renewed our vows that night, like we always did on our anniversary. He said he'd marry me a hundred times if he could and meant it." She pauses, taking a sip of coffee.

"He—uh got a call, and it was supposedly urgent and he needed to leave right then, but I could tell he didn't want to. Something felt off, even to him. Still, he told our driver to take me home after he dropped him off and kept me distracted for the entire ride. He was good about that, sensing my nerves and putting me at ease."

She swallows and takes a deep breath, avoiding eye contact. "He kissed me goodbye like he knew he might not come home and…" She sighs. "I need your help, César. I've been told you're the best."

She finally glances up at me, and I can tell she hasn't had to repeat this story for a long time, if not ever.

She's suffering.

"I'm sorry about this, Regina. I can assure you that I will do everything in my power to find him."

Now, what the fuck happened to Cidro Delvecchio?

afterword

Thank you for reading! If you don't want to sit through these rolling credits, flip to the next page and accept my parting gift. I love you!

My second book is complete. I did it. I made it to the fucking end, baby! It was looking bleak, but here we go! I have "Note To Self" blasting on a loop in my spot right now because it's a moment to be remembered and we have turned this book over in the eleventh hour.

You've rolled with me through this whole book and I thank you for it. This is nothing like what y'all are used to from me, but I appreciate you for giving me a shot.

Shadowed Obsession* is my Mike Jones era. *"Who? Mike Jones!" This was a project that needed to grow on people because it's not what I'm known for, but if you've made it this far, thanks for taking a chance on me.

The first fictional characters I ever wrote were Regina Delvecchio and her MIA husband, Cidro. They began as a screenplay because as an organized crime enthusiast, I wanted to try my hand at writing gangster flicks, but life happened and led me down many other paths.

Thankfully, they waited patiently (and sometimes impatiently) for their story to be told. I can say I'm finally home.

Regina & Cidro walked through my mind for fifteen years so that Greyson, Selah, Deirdre, César and the entire HIL could run.

I scrapped this manuscript four times only to go back to the original outline. I always learn valuable lessons when drafting a novel, and the lesson to learn this go around was to ***always*** trust my gut. I know myself, my readers and my heart. I will ***always*** write what I believe in and am drawn to and share work that I am proud of.

In case you didn't know, **Shadowed Obsession** is one of many stories within a shared universe I created with my best friends who are fellow authors: Giuliana Victoria, Cynthia A. Rodriguez and Kath Richards.

read from our shared universe:

- *Check out Giuliana Victoria's Philia Players series and her upcoming releases from the Secret Trials & Rosa Ranch series'.*
- *Cynthia A. Rodriguez's Folie à Deux series.*
- *Kath Richards' The Morelli Family series.*
- *Evelyn Leigh's Hapless In Love series.*

organized crime reading order:

- *A Love Most Fatal by Kath Richards*
- *Lovesick by Cynthia A. Rodriguez*
- *Lovefool by Cynthia A. Rodriguez*
- *Shadowed Obsession by Evelyn Leigh*
- *A Love Most Brutal by Kath Richards*

what's next?

For those of who read this book and asked 'what about Regina & Cidro Delvecchio?' **You're in luck.**
Expect more from Regina & Cidro in 2026!
Follow my Newsletter + Patreon for updates!

acknowledgments

This story would've always had some flavor because *I* wrote it, but it needed *sazón* to thrive. I am forever grateful for my sensitivity readers for their hard work, kindness and help on this project.

Amanda, Carla, Ycelsa, Z, Anya, Sofi, Ari, Janiah, and Mailene. Thank you!

Mama, Gram, and Bub, please don't read this book. If you do, let's not talk about it. Ever. The same goes for the rest of my loved ones. Don't ask, cuz I ain't telling you. "I'm an artist, and I'm sensitive about my shit!"

GiuGiu, Kath, Cass, Amanda, Court, Ken, BreAnna, Ashley, Hercules, Amira, Whitney, Kat, Tati, Olive, Ess and Kendra. I love you and thanks for riding with me though it all.

Cynthia A. Rodriguez, you are an angel on earth, and I love you more than you know. Thank you for sitting with me for countless hours to get through the water so I could make wine. Thank you for saving my ass every single time. It's all gonna be worth it, and I am so grateful we found each other. I love you and can't wait to change the fucking world with you.

Kylie, my sweet baby. It is such a pleasure working with you and you are amazing. I love you and cannot thank you enough for coming through clutch for me every time. I got through this season thanks to you.

Amanda, wifey and the love of my life. I find ways to weave my loved ones in every piece of art I create, and this story was no different. Thank you for sharing your culture and experiences with me. I truly hope I have made you proud.

Kyra, I love you so much and cannot thank you enough for holding on with me. It was such a blessing to meet you, and I am so grateful to call you one of my best friends. Feels like forever, but it's only been a few years. Thank you for always holding a safe space for me to be myself.

Tanya, you came in clutch, and I cannot thank you enough for your work on this project. I look forward to creating even more magic together in the future!

Lilith, my sweet angel baby. I absolutely adore you and am so happy our paths crossed. You understand my creative mind in a way no one has, and I am truly so grateful for that. This cover is everything I dreamed of and more. We have so much more magic in the works that the world isn't ready for. Thank you for being a part of this journey and the next! Love you!

Emma, thank you for bringing my characters to life with your gift. I think a lot about how they sparked something in you creatively and am so honored they did that for you. Your work on them shaped a lot of what this story came to be and inspired me more than you know.

Valeria, you are such a gem and a wondrous talent. I am in awe of your gift and so thankful for every gorgeous piece you've illustrated to bring my characters to life.

Thank you to every one of you who showed me even a lick of kindness this year. It's been a rough one, but you made it a little easier.

A special thank you to my amazing Patreon subscribers, who read this novel as I wrote it. Thank you to Havoc, Amanda B., Andrea, Emma B., Valeria, Tanya, Shaye, Lindsey, Jess, Brittany, Maya, Alexa, Gisel, Aurelia, Emily, Emma D, Enola, Amanda A, The Last Chapter Chicago team, and The New Romantics team!

Last, but not least, thank you to my incredible readers. I am so honored to share stories with you. You've made my impossible dreams possible, and I love you all!

also by evelyn leigh

hapless in love

Elevator Pitch

Daya + Silas' story is coming Fall 2025

standalones

Shadowed Obsession

Regina & Cidro's Story 2026

about the author

Evelyn Leigh is an indie contemporary and dark romance author based in the Midwest. A multifaceted Gemini who's lived a thousand lives both in and out of books. Writing worlds for you to escape to using the imagination she never quite outgrew. Evelyn loves creating underrepresented characters that are relatable for you to live vicariously through. She likes sharing fast paced stories sure to make you laugh, cry, swoon and blush. After reading countless happily ever afters, she wrote her own. **Here's to her next chapter.**

She is represented by Sade Rena at Beck Literary Agency

www.ingramcontent.com/pod-product-compliance
Lightning Source LLC
LaVergne TN
LVHW012130170926
848365LV00036B/1088